Body Heat

Body Heat

Book 2 in the Jocasta Hughes Mysteries

by

Candy Denman

BODY HEAT © Candy Denman
ISBN 978-0-9933815-9-1
eISBN 978-1-912563-00-5

Published in 2018 by Crime Scene Books

Cover design by blacksheep-uk.com
Printed and bound in Great Britain by Marston Book Services Ltd, Oxfordshire

For Bob, as always.

Acknowledgements

A big thank you is owed to the real Chris Butterworth for allowing me to use his name and for being one of my trusted readers: giving me feedback on early drafts, telling me when a character has made tea but drinks coffee and spotting unnecessary extra spaces. He is an absolute demon at spotting those extra spaces!

And thank you to my sister Alex for also being a trusted reader and for picking out all the places I managed to repeat myself, and there were quite a few of those.

I would also like to thank the team at Crime Scene Books, especially Sarah Williams for having faith and for her suggestions along the way, Kelly Mundt-Czerkawska for her legendary organisational skills and Hari Teah for her very thorough copy editing along with proofreader Maria Waite.

And finally, thank you to my family for allowing me hours of happiness writing peacefully in my garden shed, but no thanks to Dennis, the puppy, who was a constant source of distraction. I have found that it is very hard to write with a puppy on your knee, particularly when he is resting a paw on the keyboard, or chewing the mouse.

Prologue

He was driving carefully, making sure he didn't attract attention, although he hardly saw another car once he had left the town. He had driven this route several times in preparation, knew all the bends and dips, the houses and driveways, every potential threat. What he hadn't accounted for was the excitement and tension of doing it for real and the effect of all that extra adrenalin. He thought he was driving exactly as he had in the practice runs, but in fact he was driving considerably faster, a little too fast for a corner that came up sooner than he had expected. He braked hard, and panicked as the rear wheels drifted and hit the grass verge. He overcorrected and the car lurched onto the wrong side of the road, throwing his passenger from side to side as he struggled to straighten up and regain control. He was lucky the road ahead was empty. He pulled over to the side of the road and rested his head against the steering wheel, waiting for his heart rate to come down to something near normal. He couldn't afford to have an accident. Not now. He took a deep breath to calm himself and then turned to check that she was all right. He had taken care to strap her in with the seat belt when he put her in the car, even though she wouldn't sit up straight to help him. Couldn't. She looked fine, slumped in her seat, her head lolling to one side, seemingly asleep. She mumbled something incoherent, but he felt her tone was critical. Bitch.

'Sorry,' he said as he looked at her with disgust. She gave a little smile that could have been a grimace, or wind, and mumbled again. He thought it might have been:

'S'okay.'

That was better, he thought, more respectful. She looked as if she might be sick. He hoped not. He hated the smell of vomit, and he didn't want her to spoil the moment. If she only knew what he had planned for her. He smiled to himself, feeling instantly better as he thought about what lay ahead, excitement building in his gut again. He started to drive, but more carefully this time. Slow and steady.

At last he pulled into a deserted parking area. It was ideal, remote and surrounded by trees. He had chosen well, he thought with satisfaction. He opened his window and the fresh air seemed to rouse her a little. She blinked, trying to work out where she was, and then noticed her skirt had ridden up slightly leaving her lacy panties on show. She giggled at the sight. The whore.

'Just getting a rug out of the boot,' he explained as he got out of the car. 'Don't want you getting cold.' He smiled to himself at the irony, then quickly checked she hadn't noticed. But she was too busy pulling her skirt down, trying to make herself look respectable again, to worry about what he was doing.

He hurried to get everything out of the boot. The folding bike was awkward to handle. It caught on the lip of the boot and he had to wrench it clear. He stopped, listening in case she realised what was going on, and he heard her try and open her door. He needn't have worried. In her befuddled state it took her a while to realise that she couldn't. She didn't seem to understand why it wouldn't open and kept trying. He smiled. He had plenty of time. He carried the bike to the edge of the trees and returned for the rest of his equipment.

She stopped banging the door against the post as she saw him return to the driver's window.

'Can't get out,' she said, voice slurred with drink and drugs. 'Don't feel well.' She started to climb towards the driver's side, but her tight skirt made movement difficult and it took her a moment to understand what she had seen in his hand. A petrol can. She looked up at him, puzzled, just as he started to splash the liquid inside the car, and over her.

'What the fuck?' she shouted, trying to shield herself from the petrol with her hands, suddenly sober. But it was a futile attempt to stop the inevitable, and he didn't bother to answer her, just emptied the can and threw it behind him, towards the trees where he had left the bike. He took out a book of matches, tearing one off, lighting it and then using this match to light the rest of them. He threw the flaming matchbook into the car quickly, before it burnt his hand, grabbing the petrol can as he scurried back. Fast. He didn't want to get caught out by being too close, but he didn't want to move too far either, he wanted to see. He wanted to see her burn. He wanted to see her punished for her sins.

It took a moment for her to realise what had happened. What was happening. The first flames danced, prettily, and she tried to pat them, put them out with her petrol soaked hands. He almost laughed out loud as she waved her burning hands in the air, hoping the wind would douse the flames. Panicking now, she tried her door again and then started to climb across to the driver's side, through the flames. She was shouting something, but he couldn't hear her over the roar in his ears. Was it the roar of the fire taking hold or excitement? He thought she might have been shouting for help, but he couldn't be sure.

Her hair was on fire now, her carefully styled and coloured hair was crackling and burning, leaving nothing but a blackened, blistered scalp, and she hadn't even got across to the driver's side yet. There was a sudden whoosh as the back windows blew out. Despite moving away from the car fast, he felt the rush of hot air on his face, not enough to burn or scald him, but a warning that he was too close. He would remember that in future. When he did this again. It was a shame, but he needed to keep his distance. He wouldn't want to have to explain away any injuries later.

As he backed away from the car, dragging the bike and picking up the discarded petrol can, he watched as her attempts to escape grew less. He unfolded the bike and put the can in a plastic bag, stowing it safely in the back pannier. Her hands, already like claws, were still moving in a futile attempt to put the flames out, a scream frozen on her open mouth, her skin charring before her vaporising eyeballs. And then she stopped. There was a pause as the fire really took hold, followed by an explosion as the petrol tank blew. Not as dramatic as in the films, but satisfying all the same. Was she dead before the petrol tank exploded? He would never know, but he hoped not. He took one last look, to make sure he had left nothing behind before pedalling away, burning leaves floating down around him, as he smiled at a job well done.

7

1

It was early on a Sunday morning and Jo was wishing it would rain, and rain heavily at that. What she wanted was a deep, cleansing downpour, to wash away the terrible, overpowering smell of burnt flesh, despite knowing that it would also destroy any evidence. The awful odour emanating from the car in front of her was making her heave, even with the liberal dose of vapour rub she had applied just inside and under her nose, and she knew the smell would remain with her for hours if not days, as particulates would be lodged in her fine nasal hairs. She looked around; the car park was little more than a clearing in the woods at the end of a muddy track. The trees, which were showing signs of new spring growth with pale green leaves just appearing, had been scorched by the flames and hot gases, but had not fully caught alight and the fire had burnt itself out without needing help from the fire brigade. No need for hoses meant that the ground wasn't a quagmire, but it also meant that nothing was keeping down the smell, either. Already dressed in the obligatory gloves and paper suit, Jo slipped on a mask to further protect her from the foul odour and moved to take a closer look at what was left of the body in the burnt shell of a car. The remains were badly disfigured, the blackened skin cracked in places to reveal waxy, white, avascular flesh below, the intense heat having coagulated the blood and cauterised the blood vessels. Nothing much seemed to remain of any clothing, although they might find something in the debris or under the body, and there looked to be some lumps of melted plastic on the floor that might have been a handbag and possibly the remains of a stiletto. Hopefully, there would be enough left to help identify the victim, but for now, Jo wasn't even sure if the stiletto belonged to a woman or a man.

Jo had read somewhere that those who had survived being engulfed by flames said that it was surprisingly pain-free and even induced an ecstasy-like state, but she didn't believe it for one moment. It seemed more likely that the brain blocked out the memory and was helped in this by all the painkillers given to burns victims after the event.

As she looked at the open-mouthed grimace of the corpse in the car, even knowing that the expression was called a rictus and was caused by the contraction of muscles and tendons in the intense heat, the body seemed to be shrieking in fear and pain, and she found it hard to imagine this person died in ecstasy. Very hard indeed. She closed her eyes and shuddered. What a horrible way to die.

After her moment of weakness, Jo opened her eyes and got back to work. The size of the body was hard to estimate because the arms and legs had been pulled up as the tendons contracted in the flames, pulling the body into the position sometimes described as foetal, other times as a boxer's crouch, hands in front of the face, or rather, where the face had been, balled into pugilistic fists and with knees drawn up to the body, except that in this case one leg seemed to be straighter, stretched out behind the body, but she couldn't quite see why.

A shout broke her concentration.

'No, not that one, it's too close, use that tree over there.'

Jo turned to see Colin Brewer, the short, muscular crime scene manager, doing what he did best: organising. He was supervising the uniformed officers who were taping off the area, and clearly hadn't approved of their choice of trees to use as anchors. He looked at his watch impatiently, willing the rest of his team to arrive soon so that they could start collecting evidence and then, with a small sigh, he carried on doing what he could. He designated one officer to guard the way in and keep the sign-in sheet, telling the others to keep back and not trample on any evidence. They scuttled back to the designated perimeter, happy to keep their distance. The smell of charred meat was hanging in the air, and the grotesque remains in the car were the stuff of nightmares. Working a death by burning case was never easy to forget.

Jo looked around the small car parking area. It had been a well-known haunt for lovers and doggers alike until a recent raid by the police had scared them off, and anyway, she didn't think they usually torched the car afterwards, but what did she know? She shook her head, now was not the time to think about her disastrous love life, and she resumed her examination of what was left of the car. While the driver's door was fully open, the passenger door was about an inch ajar. The body was leaning towards the driver's side, lying half across the skeletal remains of the passenger seat and with one foot in the driver's well. The leg that hadn't contracted into the crouch position was still in the passenger side of the car. She changed her position to see better and saw that the foot had caught under the frame of the passenger seat, and had been partially protected by its position. She walked round to the passenger side where she could see that the car was parked up against a row of wooden posts that delineated the car park boundary, making it impossible to open the passenger door enough for an adult to escape. This seemed to explain why the victim had been trying to get across to the driver's side.

Jo crouched down, and gently pulled the door open the two or three inches that it could go before hitting the post, and looked into the car. The foot trapped under the passenger seat appeared to be small, with the remains of a high-heeled strappy sandal attached, indicating to Jo that the victim had probably been female. It looked as if she was trying to escape through the driver's door, but fumes and flames had overcome her before she had managed to climb across, let alone get out. The poor woman must have been terrified. Jo could only imagine her last moments as she realised she was trapped, on fire, and in terrible pain, but still the instinct to survive had pushed her on to try and escape. To try to live. Jo paused, and then pushed the door back to its original position in order to look more closely at the blackened post. It was difficult to see if the victim had pushed the door hard enough to mark either the door or the post, such was the damage from the flames.

'Mmmhmm, I love the smell of crispy bacon in the morning.'

Jo stood up quickly. There was only one person she knew who would say something quite so gross and insensitive.

'What're we doing here, Col?' the voice continued. 'One of the stupid twockers hurt himself?'

A man in his fifties, with thinning hair and a thickening waistline, was walking from the road towards the car park entrance, swearing under his breath as he struggled to put on his purple nitrile gloves. Detective Sergeant Bob Jeffries. His body shape was not enhanced by the white coveralls he was wearing over his clothes. Jo knew that the police referred to joyriders as twockers because they were usually charged with the offence of 'Taking Without Consent' or 'TWoC', but she hated the derisory way it was used, particularly by DS Jeffries.

'Bit more than hurt,' her cool voice admonished him. 'Perhaps you'd like to show a little respect?'

'What's up, Doc?' Jeffries grinned as he signed the log and pulled on his mask.

Jo was distracted as a second man approached from the road and she felt her stomach lurch. Where DS Jeffries went, Detective Inspector Steve Miller was likely to follow. Or vice versa. Younger and taller than the man who had been speaking so ill of the dead, he was a dark, good-looking and solidly built man in his late thirties, with the slightly bent nose of a rugby player.

'Dr Hughes,' Miller said with a nod to Jo, as he also signed the log before entering the scene. 'I take it you've pronounced?' he continued, pulling up his facemask and settling it comfortably over his nose as he walked towards the wreckage that had once been a car. And a woman.

'Yes, Detective Inspector, I have pronounced life extinct,' she told him. 'Although you probably didn't need a doctor to tell you that.'

He barely broke stride as he responded.

'No, I think we can all see that this man is dead.' He was standing on the opposite side of the car to her now, peering in through the driver's door.

'As a dodo,' Jeffries added as he came round the car to the passenger side.

'Woman. This woman,' Jo corrected them, 'if I am not mistaken.' She had hoped to see a reaction from Miller, but was disappointed. 'And it's clearly not from natural causes.' She was finding it hard to hide her irritation at Miller's cool and offhand manner towards the scene, and her.

'Quite.' Miller looked at her expectantly. 'Anything else, Doctor?'

'The passenger door can't open because it's blocked by a post, and the victim seems to have been trying to climb across from the passenger seat to get out, which would suggest it wasn't suicide.'

'Unless it was a last minute change of heart. She could have parked deliberately against the post to stop that exact eventuality, couldn't she?' He looked directly at her for the first time since he had arrived.

His hazel eyes had a hint of amber and Jo struggled to concentrate as they locked on hers.

'Of course, but…' Jo stopped because Miller had already turned away and was talking to Colin.

'We'll need to alert the pathologist to organise the PM and get the fire investigators out, too.'

'Fire Investigator's on his way, Guv. The fire crew alerted them.'

'Fire crew?'

'They left as soon we got here, Guv,' Colin explained.

'The fire was already out and they were needed elsewhere.' A voice came from behind them, and they all turned to see who was speaking. It was hard to tell anything much about the man who was approaching them from the perimeter as he was fully covered in a crime scene suit, but the Fire Investigation van parked in the lane was a clue.

'Chris Butterworth,' the newcomer held out his gloved hand as he introduced himself, and Miller shook it. 'Fire Investigation Unit,' he continued. 'I can give you all their details so that you can interview them later, but there was a bit of a rush on. Warehouse fire over in Bexhill.'

'No problem,' Miller nodded his acceptance of the situation. 'As you say, we can take statements later.'

Butterworth stopped and looked around at the scorched trees before continuing towards the burnt-out shell of the car. Both policemen followed behind him. Miller seemed surprised that Jo was still there.

'Have you finished here, Doctor?'

'Yes,' she couldn't believe he was dismissing her like this. 'All finished,' she almost spat at him, and was finally rewarded with a surprised look from Miller, and she thought she saw something else, a look in his eyes that could possibly have been hurt, before he quickly turned away and returned his attention to the fire investigator.

Jo walked slowly back towards the perimeter, wondering about that look in his eyes. Wondering what he was feeling underneath the crime scene clothing. When she got to the way out, a constable held out the log of everyone who entered and exited, and every exhibit that was removed. Once signed out, she paused to remove the crime scene clothing and dispose of it in the bin bag attached to a nearby tree, all the while watching and listening to what was happening by the car.

She could see that Butterworth was walking carefully round the outside of the car, taking a look at the damage, peering into the open boot and through the blown out windows before he crouched down beside the driver's door and took a look at the body.

'I'll take samples to confirm, but I'm pretty sure an accelerant has been used,' he said as he looked carefully round the site.

'From the fuel tank exploding?' Miller queried.

Butterworth pointed to some scorched grass and some faint marks still visible across the rear floor of the car.

'I'll need to have a more detailed look, but, for what it's worth, my initial impression is that it's not from the fuel tank exploding. See those lines there?' he pointed at some marks in the scorched grass. 'They're called pour patterns, and are from when the accelerant was splashed about.'

'But the victim could've doused the car before getting in and setting it alight, right?' Jeffries asked.

Butterworth gave Jeffries a pitying look and called across to Colin Brewer.

'Have your guys turned up a container yet?'

Brewer shook his head.

'No,' Brewer paused, before adding with a look at Miller, 'and we've completed the preliminary search of the area.'

Butterworth turned to Miller.

'Can't see the remains of anything that could have been used to hold the accelerant in the car, so unless it's been thrown quite a distance or someone's nicked it...'

'It's not suicide,' Miller finished for him and looked across at Jo, who tried not to look triumphant to have had her view confirmed.

'He was being a completely arrogant...' Jo struggled for the right word.

'Sod,' Kate happily supplied it for her furious friend, knowing her dislike of using even the mildest of swear words. 'Prick. Bastard. Wanker. Take your pick, so to speak.'

It was ten o'clock on Sunday morning and Jo was recovering from her early morning call to the scene of the burnt-out car by having coffee with her best friend Kate. They were in Kate's sitting room, a room of rich jewel colours and luxurious textures. Deep red velvet curtains contrasted with the purple throw flung across the burgundy sofa. It was too early for Kate to be up and dressed after her usual Saturday night social life, so she was wrapped in a soft and comfortable robe, patterned with swirls of pink and purple. Not something that Jo was ever likely to wear. The two friends' taste was as different as their characters. If Kate was an overflowing glass of Merlot, warm, dark and full-bodied, then Jo was a precise measure of Pinot Grigio in a champagne flute, cool, light and crisp. Jo's minimalist apartment, overlooking the old town where Kate lived, was decorated in neutral tones, light wood, and stainless steel.

'There we were, at the crime scene, and he treats me like I'm something he trod in. Didn't acknowledge me or what happened at all.' Jo brushed a speck of dust from her immaculate jeans. The clothes she had been wearing at the crime scene had gone straight in the washing machine as soon as she got home, and she had spent a long time in the shower, washing herself and her hair in a mix of shampoo and lemon juice in an attempt to get rid of the smell before coming to see Kate.

'Perhaps he was waiting for you to say something. After all, he did save your life a few short months ago,' Kate quite reasonably countered.

'I would have, but he made sure I didn't get a chance,' Jo was still seething. 'He hasn't been in touch since the case was closed and when we do meet, over this poor woman's body, he completely ignores me.'

'I think the relevant point there is "over this poor woman's body". He was probably just keeping it professional.'

Jo wasn't about to be pacified that easily.

'And as for Jeffries describing her as crispy bacon, well that's hardly professional is it? In fact, it's just plain disrespectful.'

'You know what he's like. Policemen's black humour, it keeps them sane. Or comparatively sane, anyway.' Kate was a solicitor specialising in criminal work, and so had more than a passing knowledge of the policemen at the local station in Hastings where they both worked and lived. The majority of her clients, like Jo's, were low-level cases of drink driving, drug possession and drunken assaults. As a forensic physician, or police doctor as she was sometimes called, for the area where she was also a part-time GP, Jo would take their blood samples, assess any injuries and declare them fit for interview or not, and Kate would represent them legally during those interviews. Kate's practice, Harriman Sydenham and Partners, actually consisted of just her and her long-dead partner, Neville Sydenham; no one could quite remember who Harriman had been or if he had ever existed at all. She had kept the firm's name after Neville's death from cirrhosis of the liver because she couldn't be bothered to change it and because getting all their stationery reprinted would have cost an arm and a leg. Now there was just Kate and a succession of temps to answer the phone, and she longed for the day when she would have enough work to afford a legal clerk to send to the police station and support clients in the middle of the night, rather than having to go there herself. Kate and Jo often moaned that people really needed to learn to get into trouble during the day rather than the middle of the night, but they both recognised that this wasn't going to happen anytime soon.

'Anyway,' Kate continued, 'you are acting like you want more than a professional relationship with the handsome inspector, so perhaps I should remind you that he is married?'

Jo closed her eyes. Detective Inspector Steve Miller. Did she want more than a professional relationship with him? When she had first met him, she had disliked him intensely, thinking that he was arrogant and a bully, but then, as she got to know him better, her opinion of him had changed. She had decided that he was complex, strong, and dependable. He liked to be right, yes, but he was prepared to listen to arguments and change his mind where necessary. Oh, he was still irritating and occasionally patronising, but, as she worked with him, Jo had found herself more and more attracted to him. It was just a shame that he was married, and therefore out of bounds as far as Jo was concerned. More than that, though, he loved his wife. Despite knowing that he was attracted to her there was no way Jo would break up a living marriage, no way at all. Besides which, perhaps she should change her opinion of him again after the way he had behaved this morning.

'I don't want a relationship with him at all, but if I have to see him I just want some sort of acknowledgement that we, that we, oh I don't know, that we are more than just vaguely acquainted colleagues, I suppose.' Jo didn't sound convincing even to herself and Kate's raised eyebrow and knowing expression told her she hadn't convinced her friend either.

'So what do you think happened? How did that poor girl die?' Kate moved the discussion away from the obviously difficult topic of how her friend felt about Steve Miller.

Jo sighed and took a sip of her coffee.

'Well, it looks like she was still in the car when it was torched, and that they didn't wait for her to get out.'

'What an awful, awful accident and a terrible way to go.' They sipped in silence as they thought about the victim's last few moments of life.

'I just can't help thinking that it wasn't accidental,' Jo said at last.

'Why's that?'

'Because the car was parked up against a wooden post, so the passenger door couldn't open, and they must have known she was still inside.'

'That's terrible. You don't even want to think about what must have been going through her mind when she realised.'

'No,' Jo responded thoughtfully. 'You don't.'

Jo blew her nose, hoping to clear the last of the smell that was probably now only inside her head.

'Do you think she was a specific target or just random?'

'There's really no way of knowing that yet.'

'I suppose not.' Kate thought for a moment. 'I sincerely hope she was the target, I'd hate to think there was someone out there doing it for kicks.'

'Yes,' Jo agreed. 'Because that would mean he might do it again.'

Kate gave a shudder and quickly changed the subject.

'How's your dad?' she asked, reaching for another biscuit. Jo was thankful for the chance to discuss something other than the horrible death.

'As well as can be expected, considering he lives with my mother,' she answered, holding up her hand as Kate began to interject, even though her mouth was full of chocolate Hobnob. 'And we are not going to talk about my mother or her attempts to marry me off, mainly because since I let her down so dreadfully with the Great Consultant Gynaecologist Disaster, we've barely spoken.'

Kate smiled, pleased that her friend could now joke about her most recent bad choice on the boyfriend front, but then looked serious again.

'I meant, how's your dad since whatsisname the pathologist died.'

'Dr Dunbar?'

'Yes, I mean I couldn't help but notice that he did not look well at the funeral, and you were worried about him even before that.'

Ian Dunbar had been the local pathologist, her father's oldest friend, and Jo's godfather. In fact, she believed he was to blame for her being named Jocasta. A name she had spent most of her life trying to forget once she realised who Jocasta was, or rather once her school-mates discovered the Oedipus connection and teased her mercilessly about it. Now that Ian Dunbar was dead, killed by the man who had so nearly killed Jo a few months before, Jocasta was only used by a dwindling number of people, to whit her parents and the senior part-ner at the practice where Jo was a GP, for which she was very thankful.

'I've seen Dad a few times since then and he's clearly a bit down, which is understandable, but I think there's something more going on. He never does anything. He forgets what day of the week it is, he doesn't even seem to be able to complete *The Times* crossword. He and Ian used to have competitions – who could finish it the fastest, but now he just doesn't bother.'

'Depression?' Kate queried.

'It might just be that,' Jo was hesitant to voice her worries, as if by doing so it might make them real, 'but the fact that it all started before Ian's death makes me wonder if he might have some sort of degenera-tive neurological disorder.'

'Have you spoken to his GP? Can't they do some sort of dementia test now?'

'Yes they can,' Jo nodded, 'and I suggested to Ma that she should speak to their doctor, but she just brushed me off and said that Dad just needed to pull himself together. Ridiculous woman.'

Kate smiled. Jo and her mother had never exactly seen eye to eye on anything, particularly boyfriends. Mrs Hughes had been delighted when she heard that Jo was going out with a consultant gynaecologist, and she practically had the wedding booked when, unfortunately, he turned out to be already married. A fact for which she seemed to think her daughter was entirely to blame.

'Has she fixed you up with any more potential husbands?'

'She's tried, but I've managed to avoid them all. Pressures of work.'

'That old excuse. It's a shame though, I always love hearing about them afterwards. The rich merchant banker who liked to be spanked or the academic who insisted that meal times should be silent so that his digestion wasn't disturbed.'

Jo smiled.

'At least that date was quite peaceful, but he really couldn't understand why I didn't want to see him again.' She sighed, 'So come on then, I know that look, it isn't my love life you want to talk about.'

Kate curled up on the over-stuffed sofa like the cat that got the cream.

'I thought you'd never ask. I've been dying to tell you,' she settled herself comfortably. 'I met him at the gym.'

'You went to the gym? Without me dragging you there?'

'Well, only to the café. It's such a great spot to ogle the talent. All those muscles. All that sweat.' Kate giggled and Jo gave another exaggerated sigh, but sat back to enjoy the story of Kate's latest conquest, happy to forget her troubles, her family, her own lack of a love life, the arrogance of Detective Inspector Miller, the insensitivity of Sergeant Jeffries, and the awfulness of the burnt corpse in the car. For the moment, at least.

2

Monday mornings are always the busiest time for a doctor's surgery. Patients prefer to wait all weekend in order to see their usual doctor, the one who knows them and their problems, rather than risk the lottery of the out-of-hours cover. Jo's practice was no different, and everyone was expected to pull their weight and see extra patients on a Monday. No sickness was allowed, amongst the staff that is, and Jo knew it was the one time of the week when Dr Hugh Grantham, the senior partner at the practice, would not tolerate her taking time off for her police work, so she had to fit it in during her breaks.

Jo wanted to find some time get to the mortuary, not only to find out what was happening with the woman who had died so horrifically in the car, but also to get the post mortem report on one of her patients who had recently died unexpectedly; this latter reason being the one she would use if questioned by Dr Grantham. She was speeding through her patients as quickly as she could, not even stopping for a coffee break, and was dismayed when she noticed that an extra had been added to her list, and even more dismayed to see that it was Mr Herring, her least favourite patient. A fussy little man, and a hypochondriac, he persistently refused to believe Jo's assertion that there was nothing seriously wrong with him, and it was her constant fear that one day, simply to spite her, he would be proved right.

Knowing that she had no alternative but to get it over with, she pressed the buzzer to call him in, and seconds later the door opened. He must have been standing on the other side of the door; ready to rush into her room the moment the buzzer went.

'Hello, Mr Herring, do take a seat. What can I do for you today?'

'I must congratulate you, Doctor. One minute early. First time that has ever happened. Perhaps we will be able to get through a few of my outstanding complaints.'

Jo tried not to show her dismay as Mr Herring reached into his pocket for a piece of note paper, with his small and precise script covering the whole of the page.

'Number one. Bowel actions. Now these have been less regular of late...'

Once she had finally persuaded Mr Herring to leave, with a completely unnecessary prescription clutched in his hand, Jo leant back in her chair with a sigh. She was now running late despite her good start, and she desperately needed a break, something to eat and a cup of coffee, but she knew there would be a mountain of paperwork waiting for her in the office upstairs, and if she ventured up to use the kitchen she wouldn't be allowed to leave it until later. Repeat prescriptions, test results, hospital letters, they all needed her attention, but if she could just slip off to do her visits without being seen, drop into the mortuary while she was out, and then get back in time to do the paperwork before evening surgery, Dr Grantham would have no cause for complaint.

Jo sighed, just thinking about how busy she was just made her feel tired. Running two part-time jobs, as a GP and a police doctor, was supposed to give her variety and flexibility, but more often than not it just meant that she worked long hours and satisfied nobody, including herself. She closed her eyes for a moment and leant back in her chair. If it came to choosing just one role, GP or forensic physician, which would she pick? Her mother would tell her that her reluctance to accept a full partnership and give up the police work was simply another way of avoiding commitment, like she usually did, particularly where men were concerned. Jo yawned delicately and closed her eyes.

She was startled by a knock on the door, and looked up at the clock as Linda Crompton, the practice manager, came in.

'Taking a nap, were we?' she asked.

'Just closing my eyes for a moment.' Jo was relieved to see that she really had only been asleep for a minute or two.

Linda put a cup of coffee on the desk and added a couple of chocolate digestives beside it.

'I thought you might be needing these after Mr Herring,' she said.

'Thank you, I do, even though I am deeply suspicious that you have an ulterior motive,' Jo gestured at the bundle of prescriptions Linda was holding.

'Always,' Linda agreed. 'Dr Brown feels he has done enough this morning and has left without doing these urgents. I thought if you could just check and sign them for him?' Linda hesitated slightly, because she knew it wasn't Jo's job, but equally she knew Jo wouldn't let patients go without urgently needed medication just because someone else didn't care.

'Oh for the luxury of being a locum and not feeling any sense of responsibility.'

'I don't think Dr Brown would feel any sense of responsibility even if he was substantive,' Linda harrumphed. 'The man's a royal pain in the you-know-what, and the fact that he's still here is simply a measure of how desperate we are. Last week he left a baby clinic dead on four when there were still two patients waiting.'

'So I heard,' Jo said as she started signing the forms. 'Gauri told me all about it. At length.' Dr Gauri Sinha was one of the full-time partners at the practice, and had been incensed when she had been called in to see the last two babies for the locum.

'There,' she said, handing the last of the prescriptions to Linda. 'Can you call down my visits and let me know if there's anything urgent I need to deal with now? I'll do the rest when I get back.'

She smiled at Linda, who knew full well what Jo was trying to do.

'You'll have to find time to do it all before evening surgery, because I don't want you leaving it until after so that we end up closing late again.'

Jo agreed, but they both knew she always ran late because she tried to cram too much into every working day, and there was no reason to expect that today would be an exception.

Jo was walking fast as she approached the mortuary, which had been built on the far side of Hastings General hospital and was some distance from any of the visitor car parks. A row of leylandii had been planted in an attempt to screen the building from public view, but they were so thin and spindly that the closed metal trolleys could clearly be seen as they came and went with their lifeless cargoes.

Jo ignored the main door marked 'Chapel of Rest', and instead entered by a small and anonymous side door. The corridor it led to was windowless, and the walls completely bare. Straight ahead were the plain steel double doors of the lifts. Once in the lift, there was only one direction to go: down.

As Jo stepped out of the lift into this subterranean world she was struck by the silence. Ian Dunbar had often played music as he worked, but now there was nothing. She shuddered slightly and wondered if she would ever be able to enter this place without remembering how she had found his body in the autopsy suite. She had been here since, of course, speaking with the stream of locum pathologists as the hospital struggled to replace Dr Dunbar. It was sad that they hadn't found anyone permanent, but it seemed that nobody wanted to take a post in a mortuary known for the horrific murder of its pathologist. She gave herself a mental shake, hurrying along the corridor to the main office, and saw with relief that the door was open and Lucy Cavendish, the current locum pathologist, was in there, speaking to Mike Parton, the coroner's officer.

'Hello, Mike,' Jo greeted him. He nodded, giving her a small, dignified smile and looking for all the world like a funeral director.

'Good morning, Dr Hughes.'

'Lucy, glad to see you are still here,' Jo continued.

Lucy scowled. She was a thin colourless woman in her thirties with a pointy face and a permanent look of discontent. She was completely swamped by her hospital scrubs and their dingy green colour did nothing for her pale and rather sallow complexion.

'Why?'

Jo had to admit it was a good question. Lucy was miserable and angry that she had ended up as a locum in a backwater like Hastings, when she considered she was worthy of a much better position. Unfortunately, a minor professional mishap in her past had left her with little choice.

'Well, it's nice to have a bit of continuity,' Jo managed to say, looking to Mike for support.

'Absolutely, yes,' he nodded, although Jo knew he missed Ian almost as much as she did.

Lucy pursed her lips and returned to her computer screen, ignoring them both.

'What's happening with the burns case from yesterday, Mike?' Jo asked as Lucy pounded on the keyboard, taking out her frustration on the inanimate object.

Mike cleared his throat and looked uncomfortable, and Lucy snorted with derision.

'The great Home Office Pathologist has decided to do the post in a better facility,' she said, despite the question having been directed to Mike. 'Apparently my humble workplace isn't good enough for him.'

'It was decided to transport the deceased to the Brighton and Sussex Mortuary, as it is better equipped to handle the more delicate requirements of a badly burnt corpse,' Mike responded tactfully, totally ignoring the pathologist's outburst.

Lucy finished typing, and the printer by her side whirred into action. She grabbed the sheet of paper as soon as it was spewed out by the machine and handed it to Mike.

'Thank you, Dr Cavendish. Much obliged.' He tucked the paper into his briefcase, gave Jo a solemn nod, and left.

Jo gave Lucy a nervous smile.

'Brighton again?' She was well aware that most of those working in Hastings felt that the money, and kudos, always went to Brighton, but the plain fact of the matter was that it was a bigger hospital, attached to a university and medical school, serving a larger population, so Jo had no doubt that it was reasonable for it to be better equipped. Lucy scowled at Jo again, managing to convey that, like the burnt corpse, she was better suited to the facilities provided in Brighton. Jo decided that discretion was the better part of valour and changed the subject.

'So, can you tell me about my patient Julie Smith? The unexpected death? Was it a heart attack?'

Lucy shook her head.

'Sub-arachnoid haemorrhage. Massive, absolutely no chance,' she fished around for the report and opened the file, thrusting it towards Jo. 'Look at the size of that aneurysm.'

Jo dutifully looked at the picture of the ruptured aneurysm. It was definitely big. Sad for the woman, but at least Jo knew there was very little that anyone could have done, as she hadn't complained of so much as a headache before the event.

Having got nothing further out of the pathologist, Jo stopped to have a word with the technician who was the direct opposite of the man he had replaced. She found him in the main autopsy suite. Small and thin, with more tattoos than teeth, he was, nonetheless, helpful when she needed information or results.

'How's it going, Jim?' she asked. 'Anything of interest happening?' Jo was openly fishing for news of the burns case and hoping Jim would be a better source of gossip than his boss.

'Did you go out to that burning case, Dr Hughes?' he asked in return, as interested in it as she was, it seemed.

'Yes, I understand the body was taken to Brighton?'

'Odd, that case,' Jim continued, with Jo's full attention now. 'I heard that preliminary findings were that she was old. Late twenties to early thirties.'

'Not a textbook joyrider, but hardly a pensioner,' Jo admonished him gently. After all, that was her age, and she wasn't old, was she?

'Mother too, well, at least there were signs she'd given birth at some point,' Jim continued, and Jo was impressed with the high standard of his information. She knew he was likely to know someone in the Brighton pathology department; after all, he'd worked there previously and had been brought in temporarily at first, to cover the unit after its troubles, and had decided to stay. She had thought that with Ian's death she would no longer be in the loop, but it was pleasing to find that Jim was happy to pass news on.

'Just what on earth was she doing in that car?' They both silently gave that some thought before Jim shook his head and started to prep the autopsy table, whistling tunelessly as he straightened the instruments, checking they were all there.

It started to spit with rain as Jo walked to her car. She broke into a run, holding her handbag over her head to protect her hair with one hand and cursing the fact that firstly, she had left her umbrella in the car; and secondly, she was wearing a white cotton blouse and it would undoubtedly go see-through when wet.

She reached her midnight blue Audi TT and threw herself inside just as the rain began in earnest and her mobile phone began to ring.

Pulling the phone out of her bag, Jo saw that the call was from the surgery and answered it, while checking her hair in the vanity mirror.

'Hello, Jo here.'

'Hi, Jo,' Linda Crompton replied, in a whisper. 'We've had a call from the police, can you pop in there on your way back? They've got a suspect they want you to look at and say if she's fit for detention.'

Jo thought for a moment. She hadn't been to see her last visit, an elderly, housebound lady who needed a medication review.

'Thanks Linda, I'll do that now. Can you reschedule Mrs Tomkins for a visit tomorrow?'

'You've rescheduled her twice already and you know how she looks forward to your visits.'

'I know, but if I go today I'll be rushed and won't have time for a cup of tea and a chat, which is why she really wants me to visit.'

Linda sighed.

'Oh alright, I'll say there's been an emergency, but you'd better go tomorrow. I'm not covering for you again.'

'I promise,' Jo smiled as she disconnected. They both knew that she could make a promise to be there, but there were many potential reasons why she might not be able to keep it.

3

Whenever she entered the large modern building that was the Hastings Police Headquarters, Jo felt a buzz of anticipation. She could never really know what she was about to face, and while most of her work for the police was mundane, there was always the possibility of something more interesting, something other than the seemingly endless parade of drunks, drug addicts, and the aftermath of petty violence.

She knew most of the uniformed sergeants and many of the constables by sight if not by name and, being a regular visitor, Jo was recognised by the civilian on the front desk and buzzed through the door into the body of the police station. She walked briskly along the corridor and down the stairs to stop at another locked door, ringing for attention and smiling up at the CCTV camera. The door lock clicked open and she passed through into the reception area of the custody suite, stopping at the desk to let them know she had arrived and was ready to see the patient, before heading to the treatment room to wait.

The custody suite treatment room was slightly smaller than her consulting room, but felt much more spacious as it had less clutter, as well as a somewhat different array of equipment reflecting the different role. The cupboards held syringes and tubes for taking blood samples from drunk drivers, and first aid equipment such as dressing packs, plasters and steristrips, to patch up both prisoners and policemen. There was a sink to wash her hands, complete with the obligatory notice reminding her to do so frequently. As if she needed reminding. Most of the patients she saw here hadn't bathed in recent memory and were sweating off an excess of alcohol. It always took a good soak in scented bathwater before she could get rid of the custody smell. As well as two chairs and a desk, the room also had a couch so that patients could lie down, if needed, but this was currently covered with several boxes of swabs for taking DNA samples. It was more like a nurse's room than a doctor's, and that was what the job was most of the time, which was why police doctors were a slowly disappearing breed.

Jo sat at the desk and read the custody notes for the prisoner she was about to see, quickly realising the information was superfluous. Marcy Draper was a long-time patient of Jo's, a prostitute and a drug addict, and she was a regular at both the surgery and the police station.

There was a knock at the door, and it was opened by the custody sergeant.

'Come on, Marcy, don't keep the doc waiting,' he said as a woman who looked about fifty, but who Jo knew to be only thirty-two, shuffled into the room.

'Sorry, Doctor,' Marcy said, misery oozing from every pore, 'I've messed up again.'

Jo sighed. Some things never change, and Marcy, it seemed, was one of them.

Once she had dealt with Marcy, giving her enough medication to keep withdrawal at bay and certifying her fit for detention while she waited to go up before the magistrates, Jo headed for the canteen. She needed to pick up a sandwich to eat on the way back to the surgery. She hated eating in her car because of the mess it inevitably left, but there was no time to stop and eat elsewhere if she was going to get her paperwork done before evening surgery.

The canteen was busy with a mix of people having a late lunch or an early tea break. Jo looked round, spotting Penny Davidson, a uniformed constable she had met before, sitting at a table with two other uniforms. It looked as if they were about to leave, so Jo grabbed a chicken salad sandwich and a bottle of water, and headed for the till.

'Hi, Penny, have you got a moment?' Jo asked, slightly out of breath as she caught up with her at the canteen door, thinking that she really ought to find more time to get to the gym, and not just to pick up buff men.

'Sure,' Penny replied and turned to her colleagues who had also stopped when Jo approached. 'I'll catch you guys later.' They left with a wave and Penny came back into the canteen, indicating to a table by the door.

'Have a seat. You look like you need one. What can I do for you?'

Jo almost didn't sit down out of sheer cussedness, but she decided to ignore being treated as if she was old and decrepit and sat with her back to the canteen door as Penny took the seat opposite.

'Nothing majorly important, it's just that I pronounced death for the body in the car and wondered if you knew anything about the case? I heard that it was a mature woman, not some teenage joyrider.'

Penny shifted in her seat and looked at something over Jo's shoulder. Too late, Jo realised that somebody had come into the canteen after them and was standing just behind her.

'Constable Davidson, I trust you're not being asked that because you are the station gossip,' a voice Jo knew all too well said, and she leapt to her feet and faced Detective Inspector Miller.

Away from the crime scene and out of the unflattering protective clothing, Miller was dressed in a smart blue suit and a crisp white shirt. Jo was standing uncomfortably close to him and could smell the faint scent of his sandalwood aftershave as well as an undertone of something soapy, as if he had just got out of the shower; a pleasant change from the stale odour of booze and fags exuded by the clientele of the custody suite, both detainees and policemen alike.

'Can't have you leaking information to members of the public, Constable,' Miller continued. The shower image disappeared in a puff of smoke and the look Jo gave Miller was blatantly hostile.

'I am hardly a member of the public, Inspector, after all I was involved in this case, so I am bound to have a professional interest in it.'

Miller hesitated briefly.

'Well, why don't you come up to the incident room and I'll give you an update, Dr Hughes? If it's just a professional interest,' he looked pointedly at Penny. 'Better than hanging around the canteen trying to pick up bits and pieces of inaccurate hearsay.'

Before Jo could explain that she was in a rush, DI Miller turned and left the canteen.

Jo made a quick decision and hurried after Miller, mouthing 'sorry' to Penny as she left. The constable waved her away with a smile and a gesture that suggested, all too eloquently, what she thought of her superior officer.

As Jo caught up with Miller, she attempted to defend the constable.

'Penny didn't say anything she shouldn't have.'

'I know,' he said with a little smile as he opened a door for her, 'she doesn't know anything.' He ushered Jo through the door and closed it before he continued. 'I am far more interested in how you heard that the victim was a mature woman.'

'Oh you know, I do have my sources elsewhere.' Jo was pleased to see the look of irritation cross his face as they walked along the corridor.

'I am sure you are aware of the need to keep information like that quiet, Dr Hughes. Jo. We haven't identified her yet and I wouldn't want this to get out to the press before we've had a chance to speak to her relatives.'

'Of course. I'm not stupid, Inspector, just curious. And you never know, I might even be able to help.' He might have decided to relent and use her first name, but she wasn't sure if she was ready to do the same just yet, given his frostiness at the crime scene.

As Miller ushered her into the incident room she could sense the atmosphere of excitement that was part and parcel of a major enquiry, at the start at least. As the investigation progressed, that excitement would become tinged with anxiety, particularly for the Senior Investigating Officer. Miller was the SIO on this case, and he was all too aware that it could make or break his career. Promotion would likely follow if he made a swift arrest, but he might find himself in charge of traffic or community policing if he failed to make a case, let alone get a conviction; the ultimate measure of success. There were eight desks in the room, and Jo was pleased to see a familiar face in Sergeant Nigel Nugent, whom she knew in his usual role as custody sergeant, realising that he must have been borrowed to set up and run the incident room. He was busy directing the people connecting up computers and phones, who were diligently and awkwardly crawling under desks trailing wires as they went. Nigel would be sticking the wires in place with hazard tape once they were finished, she was sure; he was that sort of person. Sometimes called Nerdy Nigel, even to his face, Sergeant Nugent had excellent IT skills and was methodical, thorough and pedantic, which didn't win him many friends but would make him an ideal person to be in charge of an incident room. He gave Jo a small wave of acknowledgement before a hapless constable dropped a box of equipment and Nigel hurried over to sort out the mess.

Miller was leading Jo towards his office, which was at the end of the room where a whiteboard with a few photographs of the scene was already in place, and two men were setting up a second board next to it. Jo paused by the whiteboard and looked at the photographs. Close-ups of the car were beside a handwritten note of the make, model, and registration details, including details of the owner. The car had been reported stolen at 10.30 pm, and was last seen in Ebenezer Road at approximately 8.30 pm.

The photos of the car in situ at the car park, or rather what was left of it, illustrated how closely it had been parked to the post, making it impossible for the passenger to escape. There were also some pictures of a match and what looked like a burnt-out matchbook.

'Is that what the killer used to start the fire?'

'Yes, the first match was used to light the rest and then discarded. We're hoping to get some forensics off it, but…'

Jo could imagine that it wouldn't be easy to get anything off a single match, particularly if the killer wore gloves. Miller waited patiently as Jo moved on to look at pictures of the corpse both in and out of the car. An arrow pointed to the photos with a question mark and the name Sarah Dunsmore.

Jo approached the board for a closer look.

'Is this who you think she is?' she turned and asked Miller.

'It's possible. She's the only misper who fits the profile from the post mortem,' Miller confirmed. Jo knew that he would have been checking reports for any missing person who had not been seen since Saturday in the hope of identifying the body as early as possible. With most victims being known by their murderers, if not actually related to them, knowing who they were could quickly lead to the culprit, or at least narrow down the list of suspects.

'The PM has been done already?'

'And I have the preliminary report,' he led her into his office, picked up a file from the cluttered desk and held it out to her. 'Strictly not for sharing.'

Jo glanced at her watch briefly and saw that it was gone three o'clock. Her evening surgery was due to start at four, and there were bound to be calls that needed answering before she started. Silently apologising to all the patients who would be seen late, Jo took the file and quickly opened it.

Cause of death was given as smoke inhalation; the superheated smoke had pretty much destroyed the lungs. That this had happened before the fire had managed to do anything more than superficial damage to the rest of the body was strangely comforting. At least the worst of the burns had happened after death.

Jo went on to read the more detailed report on the body. No gross abnormalities, the presence of erupted wisdom teeth, fusion of epiphyses, structure of the skull, condition of the pelvic bones, and more besides, had led the pathologist to conclude that it was the body of an adult Caucasian female, approximately twenty-six to thirty-five years old. The pathologist had added that further microscopic examination of the osteons, the minute tubes within bone that contain blood vessels, might enable a more accurate estimate of age. Jim the mortuary technician had also been right in that evidence of pelvic bone scoring suggested the woman had given birth at some point in the not-too-recent past.

Miller asked her to explain one or two things from the report, and she realised that he had asked her up there for a reason, rather than to satisfy her curiosity, and what's more, that she had been able to help him, in a small way at least. Not that he was likely to admit he had needed help or that she had been any use.

She explained that the report suggested the woman had been alive when the car was set alight, the burning gases searing her lungs, which then flooded with fluid, effectively causing her to drown. A horrible way to die. Jo could only begin to imagine the fear that must have passed through the victim's mind as she realised what was happening. She was being burnt alive, and her escape routes were either blocked or too difficult to reach in the short time she had left.

'What on earth was she doing in the car?'

'Looking for excitement, maybe?' Miller suggested.

A new voice broke in.

'Well, she got that didn't she? Only, I think it was probably more fucking thrilling than she expected. Nice to see you again, Doc. Come to look at our pretty pictures?'

Jo turned to glare disapprovingly at Jeffries, who was standing in the office doorway, unnoticed until he spoke, but it was like water off a duck's back. He was munching a biscuit and had a mug of tea in his hand. Jo saw Miller look at the newly set up refreshment station which Nigel had furnished with a kettle and mugs borrowed from the canteen, and a supply of tea, coffee and biscuits. It already looked as if it had been hit by a tornado, with the lid off the coffee jar, sugar spilled across the surface, and a solitary teaspoon left beside an almost empty packet of custard creams. No doubt the tin for people to contribute to the cost of supplies would be empty, as it was generally considered the SIO's responsibility to pay for it.

'There's that fireman downstairs, Boss, the investigator, insisting on speaking to you. Do you want him brought up?' Miller nodded and Jeffries turned to a young female constable.

'Tell 'em to bring him up then, Tracy love.'

What Tracy thought about being called love was hard to tell, but she did as she was asked all the same.

Jo handed the post mortem file back to Miller and turned to leave.

'Are you using dental records to identify her?' she asked, as he walked with her towards the incident room door.

'Initially, yes. We've got the contact details of Mrs Dunsmore's dentist, and he's emailing her records and recent X-rays to us and to the pathologist for comparison. Obviously we'll have DNA too, but that will take longer.'

They both looked up as the door opened and Chris Butterworth the fire investigator was shown in. Now that he wasn't wearing crime scene overalls, Jo could see that he was a lean and muscular man in his forties, with his dark hair cut very short. Completely ignoring the policewoman who had shown him in, Butterworth spotted Miller and quickly walked over to him.

'Good of you to bring the investigation report over in person,' Miller said, holding out his hand, whether to shake Butterworth's or to take the file from him was unclear, but either way the fireman ignored the outstretched hand.

'Inspector, I wanted to let you know as soon as possible that I think I know this arsonist. From his MO. I thought I recognised it this morning, but I wanted to check my files before saying anything, and I was right. He's a regular and always starts fires this way.' At this point he thrust his file at Miller who took it eagerly, as Jeffries tried to take a look at the name on the front. The three men retreated into Miller's office and Jo found herself left outside with the door firmly closed in her face.

Any thawing in her feelings towards Detective Inspector Miller vanished. He hadn't even bothered to thank her for the information she had given him about the cause of death. She glanced at her watch, forgot all her frustration at being ignored, and ran down the stairs. Being this late was going to need a lot of explanation and apology.

Evening surgery had been every bit as bad as Jo had expected it to be. Starting late meant that every patient came into her consulting room already cross and determined to be heard. Now she was in the office, doing all the paperwork she should have done before surgery began, trying to complete it before all the receptionists left and she ended up with the additional job of locking up the building when she finally finished. She didn't mind locking up; it was working alone in the building that worried her. Not because it was spooky or frightening, but because there were always people knocking at the door, wanting a doctor or a prescription and unable to understand that they needed to come back in the morning. They seemed to think that as she was there, she should deal with their problem right now, however petty or unimportant it was or however easily it could wait until morning. And then, of course, there were the ones who actually couldn't wait. Jo had once been stopped just as she was leaving to go home by a man wanting to see a doctor urgently. It was quickly clear that he did need to see a doctor urgently as he was having a heart attack, and Jo had to wait with him, praying he wouldn't go into cardiac arrest before the ambulance arrived. She knew her limitations and wanted him to get to the heart attack centre before he did anything dramatic, because they would be so much better equipped to help him, not to mention that they would be much more experienced at resuscitation than she was; she hadn't had to do CPR since she started as a GP. She regularly went on refresher courses, but that wasn't the same as actually doing it for real.

She was just getting to the last report and the receptionist hadn't even looked at her watch or started muttering about time to close up, when Gerry Brown, the locum, came over to her. She was surprised he was still there, given his reputation for leaving strictly on time.

'Hi, Jo, I had a patient of yours earlier, they only needed a repeat prescription and seeing as you were running late, Linda asked me to deal with it.'

'Thanks, Gerry, who was it?'

'Can't remember the name, needed thyroxine. Anyway, you know me, always happy to do you a favour.' He hurried on, seemingly oblivious to Jo's look of disbelief. 'I'm sure you'd do the same for me. Speaking of which, could you take a couple of patients for me tomorrow morning? I have to finish early for my half-day. I've sorted it on the lists for you. Cheers.'

He didn't wait for a reply, which he probably sensed wouldn't be polite, but grabbed his bag and hurried out of the office, leaving Jo irritated and wondering why he thought that doing one repeat prescription constituted such a big favour that he could dump a couple of patients on her tomorrow. She checked her list and saw that he had actually moved a total of five patients across to her list, meaning that he would finish at eleven and she would probably still be there at two. Silently seething, she had to admit it was probably karma for the many times she had got colleagues to see patients of hers whilst she rushed off to do police work. She just hoped whatever Gerry Brown was up to at lunchtime was worth it.

Jo looked round at the receptionist who nodded towards the doorway Dr Brown had just left through and mouthed the word 'tosser', before looking pointedly at the clock.

'Just finishing, won't be a moment,' Jo hurriedly said, hoping she wasn't about to be left on her own, and looked relieved when the receptionist replied,

'No problem, I'll just check the windows are all shut,' and set off to do a round of the building, making sure all was in order before locking up, leaving Jo to finish off her work and gather her things for home, where a frozen ready meal and some elderly salad leaves were waiting for her. As she drove back, she couldn't help but wonder what would be waiting for DI Miller when he finally managed to get home. It was only a few months ago that he had confided in her that his wife was bipolar and was having problems remaining off medication as she tried to conceive. She hoped for his sake that his wife was okay at the moment, because running a major investigation was hard enough. He really didn't need any added complications.

4

The following day, the Hastings Advertiser used a picture of Sarah Dunsmore in a strappy evening dress that revealed a large amount of décolletage, and the outline of her nipples underneath the thin fabric. She looked a lot more attractive in this photo than the charred corpse that Jo remembered all too well.

She took a sip of tea and read the accompanying text.

'The body found in a stolen car, early Sunday morning, has been named by police as being that of Sarah Dunsmore, 31, of Ashburton Close, Hastings. Forensic experts used dental records to identify Mrs Dunsmore. Her husband, Brian, a salesman, stated that he had no idea why she was in the vehicle, and that he had thought she was on a girls' night out. He then asked for his privacy to be respected at this difficult time, so that he and his two children, Molly, 5, and Alfie, 3, could grieve in peace.'

Jo wondered who 'the girls' were and if Miller had asked them why Sarah hadn't been out with them. Could it have been an innocent mistake? A school meeting? A reading group? A different friend? Jo thought not. Why would you tell your husband you were going on a girls' night out when you were really going to discuss a book you'd recently read. Perhaps the girls had been her alibi before when she had been meeting someone in secret? Jo imagined that someone to be a lover. The provision of alibis might have been a regular feature of the group, perhaps they arranged these nights out so that they could all cover for each other. Jo wondered how long it had taken Miller to get the truth out of them, for she was sure he would have succeeded by now. They wouldn't hold out long. They would be shocked by what had happened to their friend and anxious to help, but they might not know the whole story. Sarah might have kept the name of the person she was meeting a secret, even from the friends who were providing her cover. They may not have had any information that would help Miller, apart from the fact that she was probably cheating on her husband. Under those circumstances, it wouldn't take long for Miller to suspect the husband himself, those nearest and dearest to the victim always being the first to fall under suspicion, and with good reason. Even the Bible said that your worst enemies would be in your own family, although Jo couldn't remember precisely where it said that, one of the Gospels, she thought. Husbands in particular were suspects until proven otherwise, even more so if the marriage had cracks, as this one so clearly did. Brian Dunsmore said he had no idea why she was in the car, but was he telling the truth? Even if he had been, he probably had his suspicions by now. What a double blow to her husband to find out that not only was his wife dead, but that she was also having an affair. Unless he was the killer, of course.

Jo got up and looked out at the spectacular view from her living room window. She lived in the penthouse, which took up the whole top floor of a brick-built, Georgian manor house situated in a commanding position high up on the East Hill. At some point in the past twenty years it had been converted into flats, or apartments, as the estate agent had insisted on calling them when Jo came to view it. The house had surprised her with its tall windows and graceful lines. It stood out as being different from the Victorian villas more usual in this part of town. Although it consisted of just three rooms: a bedroom, a bathroom and a living room with a kitchen area along one wall, the conversion was elegant, the rooms were large and well-proportioned, and the period features had been left intact. But what had sold it to Jo the moment she walked into the living room was the views. Through the two large windows the coast was visible, from the funfair on the far left along almost to the new town, until the West Hill blocked a view that would otherwise have included St Leonards and Marine Court, the block of flats built to look like a majestic liner sailing towards the old town. Down and to the right of her the old town nestled in the valley, crowded and compact, and further across to the West Hill lay the castle ruins and the swathe of green parkland crested by a terrace of white houses. It was a view that never ceased to impress her, whether it was early morning with the rooftops floating on a sea mist, the castle back lit by a setting sun, or with the streetlights in the valley twinkling invitingly below. She had bought the flat for these views, paying more than she had planned in doing so, but it had been worth every penny.

As she thought about what might have happened to Sarah Dunsmore the night she died, Jo couldn't help being distracted by the persistent flashing of the answerphone on the coffee table. She knew she had a message, but did she want to hear it?

She had put off listening to her messages while she read the report of the murder in the local paper, but now she had run out of delaying tactics. Sitting back down, Jo took a deep breath before pressing play.

A synthesised voice announced that she had three new messages. The first, as usual, was her mother, asking her to call and probably fishing for news on the boyfriend front. Jo sighed and deleted the message before her mother had got fully into her stride. The second message was from Kate, suggesting they meet for an exercise class or, failing that, a calorie-laden meal out later in the week; tomorrow, maybe? Jo smiled and decided that a meal out sounded like a great idea, she'd let Kate know and suggest going to the seafood place by the Stade, the shingle beach used by the Hastings fishing fleet, as she had been wanting to try it for ages. The third message was her mother again, but this time Jo detected a hint of anxiety, as her mother suggested Jo drop in for coffee sometime soon. Jo's mother never suggested she drop in for coffee, or anything else, unless it was a dinner party and she had a blind date set up for her. Her mother's unusual behaviour combined with her own concerns about her father was faintly worrying. Something was definitely up. She looked at the carriage clock on the mantelpiece, an heirloom left to her by her paternal grandmother. Five o'clock on a Tuesday meant that her mother would be out playing bridge, so she could catch her father alone and find out what was going on.

She dialled and walked to the window again, watching the old town lights coming on as the sky began to darken, subconsciously counting the number of rings before the answerphone kicked in. She left a breezy message for both parents, saying she'd called for a chat and would try again another day, before disconnecting. She continued to stare out of the window, concern growing. Where was her father? He liked to stay in when her mother was out, glad of a bit of peace and quiet. So why wasn't he answering the phone? She began to fret that he was ill, but then she gave herself a stern talking to; he was probably in the bathroom or the garden. He was a grown man. He didn't need her to worry about him. But she made a mental note to try again tomorrow or perhaps even to call in, just to be sure, even if that meant she risked having to speak to her mother.

5

Jo had almost finished her marathon surgery, but was waiting for the final patient to produce a urine sample. He had been gone for about ten minutes already, so she was pretty sure he had a problem.

Whilst she was waiting she took a look at Dr Brown's list from the evening before. The only one of her patients who had been to see him didn't have a thyroid problem, so, curiosity piqued, she checked for any of her patients who had had a prescription for thyroxine yesterday. There was only one, Jillian Hollingsworth, but she hadn't attended surgery, she must have just telephoned or dropped in a medication request form. Gerry Brown hadn't even seen the woman, simply issued a repeat prescription, in return for which he had added all these extra patients to her list. Jo seethed with fury and stood up, ready to storm upstairs and tell Linda exactly what she thought, when there was a tentative knock on the door and her final patient, a frail and wizened ninety-year-old man, apologetically shuffled in holding out an empty sample bottle.

'I'm sorry, Doctor, but I can't seem to manage to get any for you, although I feel as though I need to go.'

Jo sat back down, and gave him a reassuring smile; her complaints about her colleague could wait. For now, her patient needed her full attention.

'Right, Mr Smith. Can you pop behind the screens and take your trousers and pants off for me? I need to examine you to see if your prostate is enlarged at all.' Jo was pretty sure it would be, she just hoped it had the smooth feel of a benign growth rather than the hard and knobbly feel of a malignant one. Either way, she was going to have to send him for blood tests and possibly even for an urgent intervention if the bladder was becoming obstructed or if he was in retention. Last patient of the morning, or rather afternoon now, and there was no way this was going to be a quick consultation.

'Are you ready for me, Mr Smith?' she asked, and hearing a quiet yes she slipped behind the screen.

'First of all I want to feel your tummy, to see if your bladder is full.'

'It's just not right, Hugh.' It was Wednesday lunchtime before Jo managed to get Dr Grantham on his own. 'He skives off at the drop of a hat, and even when he does do something helpful like a repeat prescription for one of my patients, he expects something in return.'

They were standing in the tiny kitchen, Jo effectively blocking Dr Grantham's escape by standing in the doorway.

'He's a locum, Jo, what do you expect?'

'I expect him to behave like a decent doctor,' Jo responded angrily. 'He brought up Jill Hollingsworth's records to print the prescription, so he would have seen that she was well overdue for a medication review. If it had been you or me we would have added a note to that effect, and printed out a blood test form for her as well, but no, just because he's only here temporarily we have to put up with a job half done.'

Hugh sighed.

'I agree, but you know how difficult it is to find anyone in the current climate. It took us three months to find Gerry.'

Jo knew he was right. Hugh looked pointedly at the corridor, clutching his mug of coffee and hoping she would let him get away.

'I'm just saying we need to keep on trying to find someone permanent to replace Neil.' Neil had been a partner at the practice for several years when his anxiety about everything, but mostly his own health, had finally led to a breakdown six months earlier. It wasn't looking likely that he was ever coming back.

'Well, we haven't given up hope that one of our part-time GPs will decide to give up her job on the side and join us as a full-time partner.' He gave her a meaningful look and slipped past her into the corridor and the office beyond.

Jo sighed. He had a point, just not one she wanted to consider at the moment. She had increased her hours after Neil went sick, not quite to full-time, but more than the three days a week she had been doing previously and, not having children, she covered more than her fair share of weekends on call. It had been a temporary arrangement when Neil left, but with the increasing workload and with Gerry not pulling his weight, it didn't look like she would be able to go back to three days for a while yet. They really did need another full-time partner, and soon.

She opened the biscuit tin; nothing but some broken rich tea fingers were left, but she took one anyway. When in need...

Benji the pug settled down next to Jo and refused to take any notice of her subtle efforts to show that he wasn't wanted. The more she delicately pushed him away, the more he lovingly leant up against her and slobbered, covering her with slime and hair. Her suit would have to go to the cleaners. Finally, deciding that a more direct approach was needed, she gave him a shove. He yelped as he landed on the floor.

'That's right dear, be firm with him,' Mrs Tomkins said as she hobbled back into the room, carrying a plate of biscuits. Jo was embarrassed that she had been caught, but Benji didn't seem to be worried. He was much more interested in the biscuits.

Do you want a biscuit then, my love?' For a second Jo thought the old lady was talking to her, but Mrs Tomkins picked Benji up, sat him next to her on the sofa and wriggled to make herself more comfortable, her short fat legs not quite reaching the floor. She had the biscuit plate between her and Benji as she selected three or four, while the dog sniffed and slobbered over most of the rest. Jo had a moment of disorientation as she realised how alike they looked. Flat round faces, noses so small they were almost non-existent, and slightly bulging eyes.

'Help yourself to a biscuit.' Having chosen theirs she held the plate out to Jo.

'No, no, I just ate lunch. Thank you.' There was no way Jo was going to eat a biscuit that had been anywhere near Benji. Mrs Tomkins put the plate down on the table.

'Please yourself,' she turned to the dog. 'All the more for us, eh Benji boy?' she cooed as she fed him a custard cream, which he swallowed pretty much whole.

'It's good of you to drop in, Doctor. I've been a bit more out of breath recently and wondered if I needed something a bit stronger.'

As she could hear both her patient and the pug wheezing from across the room, Jo knew she was right, although fewer biscuits and more walks for Benji might help them both more than another course of steroids. Realistically, Jo knew that Mrs Tomkins was coming up for ninety and Benji was pretty old for a pug, so perhaps it was a bit late to be putting them both on a diet and exercise regimen. She sat back and drank her tea, hoping that the dog hadn't been anywhere near it, and listened as the old lady listed her symptoms, the man next door's symptoms, and some long and involved story about an Aunty Mabel, long dead. It was clear she didn't really expect her doctor to do much, other than write a prescription before she left, so Jo sat and allowed her mind to wander. This was her final visit, and Wednesday being her half-day, her time was her own once she had finished. She would be able to do her shopping, have something to eat, and then drop in on her dad; after making quite sure her mother was out. It was the fourth Wednesday of the month, which was book club, she thought. Thank goodness her mother had an active social life. Jo was making a mental shopping list and Mrs Tomkins was recounting a story about a badly behaved poodle when her phone started buzzing. Once she had fished it out of her bag, Jo saw that it was Helen Austen, a local social worker and sort of friend. Jo couldn't think why Helen was calling, but it was possible that it was something urgent to do with one of her patients

'I'm awfully sorry, Mrs Tomkins, but I have to take this,' Jo apologised as she answered the phone, and stepped into the kitchen to speak to Helen.

'Hi, Helen, how can I help?'

'Oh Jo, thank goodness. The police picked up Mark Caxton this morning. They want to interview him about that awful car fire and he needs an appropriate adult. I'm pleased they realise he needs one, but angry that they didn't give me more notice.'

'Mark?' Jo knew the young man Helen was referring to, because both he and his mother were patients. Both had mental health problems. The mother was an alcoholic who had struggled with the stress of being a single mother after Mark's father had died of heart disease, and Mark himself had learning difficulties and had been in trouble on many occasions for arson. Jo closed her eyes. Of course, the fire investigator had recognised the method used to start the fire.

'I know. Completely mad to think Mark had anything to do with it, but the police are pushing for someone ASAP.'

'You don't think he's the person who did this, then?'

'No way! I mean, I know he sets fire to cars, but there's a big leap from that to killing someone, isn't there? And you know what he's like, liable to admit to anything if he thinks he'll get left alone.'

'What about his mother?'

'Not in a fit state, and before you ask, I can't go because I have a vulnerable child conference starting in five minutes. It seems they've even tried to get a volunteer in but no one is free, thankfully, because you know what Mark's like with strangers. He gets so frustrated that he can't articulate his needs and he sometimes comes across as aggressive.'

'Yes, but…'

Helen didn't give Jo a chance to think of an excuse.

'Look, you are his doctor and I know you have Wednesday afternoons off, so it couldn't have worked out better, could it?'

'Well, I'm not sure I'm the best person…'

'I understand your concerns, believe me I do, but to my mind you are the absolutely perfect person. You are Mark's doctor and he trusts you, plus you have experience of the way the police work.'

'It's because of my work for the police that I might not be the right person. What if there is a conflict in my role there and being Mark's appropriate adult?' Jo finally managed to get out.

'All you have to remember is that Mark is your patient and so he comes first. Simple.'

'I wish it was that simple, Helen. I mean, I am employed by the police…'

'For the care and welfare of their staff and those in their care. Like Mark.' Helen clearly wasn't prepared to listen; at least, she wasn't prepared to take no for an answer.

'I'd need to check that they were okay with it first.'

'For goodness' sake, Jo, you need to get off the fence and decide whether you are a doctor or a police officer. It's decision time.' Jo had to concede that Helen had a point.

'I'm sorry Mrs Tomkins, but I have to go now.' Jo held up her phone as she came back into the sitting room, in case her patient hadn't heard enough of the conversation to know that she had been called, reluctantly, away.

'That's alright dear,' the old lady told her, 'I know you're a very busy woman. Much too busy to spend time listening to my little problems.' Mrs Tomkins perfectly pitched her words to succeed in making Jo feel as guilty as possible.

Miller was sitting very still, outwardly calm, and waiting for an answer, while the good-looking lad on the other side of the table sullenly and silently glared at him. Jo had tried to explain her role to Mark, but she wasn't convinced he understood the subtlety of her position, and he kept looking to her, expecting her to answer for him. She was conscious that he seemed to be getting more and more irritated that she wouldn't.

Miller himself had been angry when he'd come down to the interview room to discover that Jo was there as Mark's appropriate adult. He was sure that it couldn't be right for a police doctor to be acting as an appropriate adult, and had rung through to his superior officer and even to the CPS advisor to check that it was in order. Under the Police and Criminal Evidence Act 1984, a child under 17 or any adult that could be considered vulnerable, such as someone with learning difficulties like Mark, had to have an appropriate adult with them when interviewed under caution. Miller didn't want any information he gained as a result of the interview to be thrown out because Jo's relationship with the police prevented her from being considered appropriate. Needless to say, this was not a situation that had much in the way of precedence, and the CPS advisor had taken ages to consider his answer before reluctantly telling Miller that he thought it was probably okay. Probably was hardly definitive, but with the alternative being having to delay the interview further while they waited for Helen to be free or for Mark's mother to sober up, Miller decided to press ahead. If the interview was thrown out he would blame Jo and the CPS advisor equally. Jo, meanwhile, had been getting more and more irate herself. What a colossal waste of time this would have turned out to be if she had spent her free afternoon cooling her heels in an interview room only to be sent home. An afternoon when she should have been doing something useful, like her shopping and laundry for the week. Finally, once it had been agreed that they could go ahead with Jo sitting in, Miller insisted on explaining her role, making sure she realised that she was not there to interfere with the interview, but simply to support Mark, as if she didn't already know that, but perhaps the re-iteration would help Mark to understand it. A legal executive from one of the local firms specialising in criminal law who had represented Mark before had already spoken to him and advised him to make no comment, as he knew that Mark was not competent to answer questions without the risk of incriminating himself. He intended to be present for the interview as well as Jo and, she felt, he was best placed to interfere if interference was needed, quite frankly.

And now the interview had been going on for almost an hour, going round and round in circles, with Mark constantly repeating 'No comment' to every question, apart from denying that he had anything to do with the car fire or the body.

'Why did you torch the car with the woman still inside it, Mark?' Jeffries asked bluntly.

'No comment.'

Jeffries leaned forward as far as he could, trying to intimidate the boy, while continuing with a barrage of questions.

'Did you enjoy it? Did you enjoy watching the woman burn? Get a kick out of it, did you? Get a hard on?'

'No I didn't!' Mark was horrified, but Jeffries was delighted to have finally got a rise out of him.

'Did you like it as she screamed? Or the smell as her flesh sizzled and burnt?'

'No! No! No! Stop it!'

Mark put his head down and covered his ears with his hands, anything to get away from this onslaught from Jeffries.

Jo put her hand on Mark's arm and turned to Miller for support.

'Inspector, I must protest. Mark's...'

Mark snatched his arm away from Jo's touch and raised it as if he might hit her. Miller jumped to his feet with a face like thunder and there was a tense silence for a moment before Mark lowered his arm and went back to staring at the table. Once he was convinced the threat was over, Miller sat down again.

'I'm sorry, Mark,' Jo tried to sound normal, although her heart was pounding. She had been convinced he was going to hit her. 'I didn't mean to alarm you. Just try and stay calm, okay?'

Miller glowered at Mark, but the legal executive was nodding, approving of Jo's intervention, although she was thinking that perhaps he should have stopped the interview earlier, and glared at him to get her point across.

'Perhaps you could move on. My client is clearly upset by the tone of your questioning,' he finally said.

'Not half as upset as his victim's husband or her children,' Jeffries said harshly, but the legal advisor heeded Jo's look and waded in.

'He has already told you several times that he knows nothing about the car that was set on fire at the weekend, Inspector.'

'Let him say it again then.' Miller watched as the boy looked at Jo. She was surprised that he seemed to be asking for her approval despite his anger at her a moment before. She nodded at him encouragingly, knowing that the interruption had done what was needed and given Mark time to recover a little.

'Go on then, Mark, once more for the tape.'

'I don't know nothing about the car. I was at home Saturday night from early. I didn't torch anything, honest. I don't know nothing. Can I go now?' He almost pleaded, looking out from under his long floppy fringe, all aggression gone. Jo was sure that one more push from Miller and he would confess, just as Helen had predicted, and she was sure that Miller and Jeffries knew it too. But Miller would also know that Mark would recant his confession as soon as he was out of the room, and that Jo would almost certainly stand up in court and tell the jurors he was pressurised into confessing. Jo felt there was a good chance she would be believed, because she was a professional who worked with the police and Mark had the sort of endearing looks that would make the jury want to mother him. The prosecution would have to have evidence to support a confession if there was to be any hope of a conviction. Jo could see all of this going through Miller's mind as he debated with himself whether to press on or not. Jeffries was chomping at the bit, wanting to make the final push. It was decision time, and Miller had made his call.

'Have you got a girlfriend?'

Jeffries looked disappointed by the question, knowing that Miller was backing off, but Jo was suspicious. Only Mark accepted it as just another question in a long and seemingly never-ending interview, and at least it wasn't about the dead woman.

'Course.'

The legal exec mouthed 'No comment' to Mark.

'Tell me about her.'

'Inspector…' the legal exec started to interrupt, but was silenced by a look from Miller.

'What's she called?'

Mark looked at Jo again, but she wasn't sure what to do, should she tell him to listen to his advisor?

'Mel,' Mark said as Jo hesitated.

'Is she pretty?'

'She's alright,' Mark thought for a moment. 'Have you got one?'

Jeffries tried to hide a smirk and Miller ignored the question.

'It's nice having a girlfriend, isn't it? Do you see her a lot?'

Mark nodded and looked at Jo again. It seemed a pretty harmless line of questioning, so Jo looked at the legal man; he was making notes and hadn't told Mark not to answer again, so she didn't interfere.

'For the tape, Mr Caxton nodded yes,' stated Jeffries. Miller was annoyed by the interruption, however much he knew it was important for when the tape was played back. He had been gaining Mark's trust, but now he was distracted again.

'So did you see her that night?' he asked. Jo looked at Mark's legal advisor, uncertain whether to remind Mark again that he should say no comment. It was clear that Miller was trying to find out if Mark had an alibi, which could work for or against him, depending on his answer. In the end, neither stopped Mark from answering.

'What night?' Mark was confused by the change in direction.

'Saturday night?'

'Erm…' Mark was trying to think back.

'That was three nights ago.'

Mark thought some more before answering.

'Dunno.'

Three nights ago was clearly a long time to Mark.

'Well, did you see her last night?'

'Yeah,' Mark smiled at the memory.

'And the night before?'

'No, she was at her Nan's, I think. We don't see each other when she's at her Nan's, 'cos it's too far to walk.'

'And the night before that? Was she at her Nan's then?'

'I don't remember.'

'So had it been a few days since you'd met up when you saw her last night?'

'I dunno. Might've been,' Mark struggled to think, then shook his head. 'I just see her when she's around, you know?'

Mark genuinely didn't seem able to remember.

'We'll need her full name, Mark,' Miller said with resignation. He would need to make absolutely sure that Mark was not with his girlfriend on Saturday night, or anywhere else he couldn't remember, because this was exactly the sort of uncertain story that enabled the defence to plant reasonable doubt into the minds of the jurors. He sighed and looked at Jeffries, who was clearly irritated. They both realised this wasn't going to be an easy conviction after all. They were going to have to do it the hard way, by collecting the evidence and building the case.

Much to Jo's relief, Miller ended the interview.

'I'm not sure this is right,' Jo told Miller. He had caught her just as she was about to leave. Mark was being released on bail while they checked his alibi and tried to find further evidence against him.

'I'm pretty sure it's wrong for you to be his appropriate adult, but you still did it.' Miller was still angry about that, it seemed.

'I know you have some circumstantial evidence linking Mark to the murder, but, I mean, look at the boy, why would a mature woman get in a car with a young lad like him?'

'I can think of a number of reasons, and it's more than just circum-stantial evidence. You saw what he was like, for goodness' sake, he almost hit you for just putting a hand on his arm, what would he have done if you'd put your hand on his knee or something?'

Jo had to concede he had a point. She had been shaken by his vio-lent reaction, just as much as Miller had been, and if the victim had come on to him? Touched him somewhere intimate? Perhaps that might have been enough to provoke him into killing her.

'The boy's a powder keg, so I don't want you to see him alone in surgery or anything like that. Get one of your colleagues to be his doctor, if needed.'

Jo looked at him in amazement.

'You have no right to tell me which patients I can or can't see, Detective Inspector.'

'I'm just trying to protect you…'

'I do not need your protection. I am not stupid and I will take suitable precautions, but I will see whoever I need to see and I certainly don't need your permission to do it.'

She turned on her heel and left.

6

As Jo brought her car to a gentle stop on the sweeping gravel driveway of her childhood home she could feel the tight ball of anxiety building, deep down in the pit of her stomach. She knew the dread she felt about going home was disproportionate, but it had been steadily building throughout the day, aided and abetted by her frustration with Gerry Brown, Miller and, unfairly, Mark Caxton. Together they had pretty much ruined her afternoon off.

Jo loved her parents dearly, but she was aware she was a disappointment, to her mother at least. A mother who, Jo reminded herself when she was feeling particularly unfairly victimised, had never had a career, had only managed to produce one child, and had few, if any, real friends. A mother who still managed to make her feel a failure because she was unmarried, had no children, and was a mere GP. Jo often wondered, if she suddenly became all the things Diana Hughes professed to have always wanted her to be, exactly what her mother would find to be disappointed about next.

She took a deep breath and stepped out onto the drive. The Old Vicarage was a beautiful house, symmetrical and graceful. Its dove grey stucco would be festooned with pale lilac-blue Wisteria blossoms later in the spring, but now just the twisted, woody stems, with a few buds visible amid the dead leaf sprays and velvety seed pods, clung to the walls around the front door and the ground floor windows.

Jo hesitated one last time, before opening the front door.

'Hello?' she called brightly. 'It's me. Anyone home?' She sincerely hoped that her mother didn't answer. There was a rustling noise from her father's study and he appeared, looking dishevelled and sleepy, half-moon glasses askew.

'Jocasta! How lovely to see you.' He gave her a hug.

'Diana?' he called to his wife, 'Jo's here.' He ushered her into the kitchen, looking round the empty room in bewilderment.

'It's Ma's night out.' Jo looked at her father closely, surprised that he seemed to have forgotten.

'Ah yes. Bridge.'

'Book club. Bridge is on Tuesday,' Jo corrected him.

'Of course,' he quickly recovered. 'That's the problem with being retired, I can never remember what day of the week it is anymore.'

He turned to pick up the kettle, giving Jo the distinct impression that he was buying himself time.

Charles Hughes had retired from his job as a consultant orthopaedic surgeon almost a year ago now, and Jo knew he had struggled with the loss of purpose to his life. He had always said that he looked forward to retirement; to pottering in the garden, playing more golf, visiting places he had never had time to see before, and he had even said he would take up watercolours again. But since actually stopping work he didn't seem to have done anything at all. When pressed, he told Jo that golf more than once a week quickly got boring, that Diana was better at the gardening and had a nice young man to help with the heavy bits, that he didn't want to waste time in the car, let alone on an aeroplane, and that he had lost his eye for painting. Excuses all, and Jo didn't know why he was making them. Why were the hobbies that he always complained he had no time to indulge suddenly so unattractive now that he had all the time in the world? Perhaps he was depressed. Or maybe no pastime was as interesting when you had all the time you could want to pursue it.

They took their coffee through to the sitting room, which was impeccably clean and tidy as always. The only room in the house where her mother tolerated any mess was her father's study, provided he kept the door shut when visitors came. Jo knew it was a constant source of irritation to her mother, whose need for perfect order was firmly in the obsessive/compulsive spectrum, but the cleaner was only allowed in the study by invitation, and under strict supervision. Charles hated anyone moving his books and journals, and complained for weeks after he'd let poor Edna in to clean that he couldn't find anything.

'Sorry to have woken you, Dad,' Jo said as she sat on the chintz sofa and carefully put her coffee on the occasional table to the side.

'Don't be silly, I wasn't aslee…' The word trailed off as Charles saw his daughter's look, and he smiled ruefully, 'All right, so I was having a snooze; a power nap they call them now, don't they?' He settled himself into the armchair next to the unlit log fire, and Jo took a closer look at him. He'd straightened his glasses now, but his hair was still messy. Other than that, he was still her old dad; smartly dressed in brown slacks, check shirt, tweed tie and cashmere cardigan.

'So what have you been up to,' she asked him, 'apart from getting under Ma's feet?' Jo began to relax as he chatted about walks and gardening, and she even began to believe that she was worrying unnecessarily; her father seemed the same as always. Why shouldn't he take naps and forget which day of the week it was now that it didn't matter? It really wasn't anything too abnormal, was it? Why did he need to know any of it anyway?

'So you can see I really lead a very, very boring life these days,' her father finished, with a smile. 'How about you? You must have far more interesting things to talk about?'

'Ha, I wish,' Jo laughed, 'although I did have to pronounce death on that poor woman who was burnt in the car. Very grisly.'

'Burns are never pleasant,' her father agreed. 'Was it an accident?'

'No, no, the case in the paper. It was murder.' Jo was surprised her father didn't know, she could see the local paper on the stool at his feet.

'Oh that. Nasty case,' he said, as though he just hadn't connected the two stories, and again Jo got the feeling that her father was covering up his forgetfulness, and the uneasy feeling that something was wrong began to creep back in.

Jo had always appreciated being able to talk about her difficult cases, both police and medical, with her father. His brusque common sense often helped her come to decisions about the best treatment for her patients or how to mentally deal with some of the horrors she encountered as a forensic physician. Of course, Ian Dunbar, who had been both the local pathologist and her godfather, had been particularly good for that as well.

'We haven't really had a chance to speak since Ian's funeral. How are you coping?'

'What do you mean, "How am I coping?" you sound like one of those dreadful counsellor people. I know he was my oldest friend, Jo, but that's the point. He was old. So am I. We old people have to get used to friends dying on us.'

Despite his robust dismissal of her concerns, Jo wasn't convinced.

'Of disease, yes, but it's rather different when someone is murdered. You can't get used to that.'

'Death is death, Jo. Sometimes it's expected, peaceful even, but it can also be abrupt, painful or brutal. It makes no difference in the end. We all wind up dead.'

It was unlike her father to be so bleak.

'You're still comparatively young, and you're in good health, Dad. It could be many years before you die. Or is that what you're afraid of?'

He fixed her with a beady eye.

'Please don't try and psychoanalyse me. I admit I might be a little low at the moment, but I am not depressed, merely realistic. There is currently very little point to my existence.'

'Then you need to find one.'

'I'm glad you didn't say that of course there was a point, I am a father and a husband, because both you and I know full well that neither you nor your mother need me anymore.' He held up a hand to stop her protestation at this. 'No, you would miss me, I am sure, but neither of you actually need me.'

He was right of course, and Jo was relieved that he had such a clear understanding of the situation. The simple fact of the matter was that after a lifetime of being needed it was hard to adjust to the change retirement brought. At least it didn't seem likely that he was developing dementia, as she had previously feared. He just needed to find a reason to live, which was a far more straightforward problem to solve.

'What you need is an interest…'

'Please don't tell me what I need, Jo. Your mother is endlessly telling me. She says I need a hobby. Why don't I join a club?' He snorted in derision. 'As if I'd ever want to join a club that would have me, to paraphrase Groucho. I don't want to hang around with boring old farts discussing the relative merits of one car or, God forbid, caravan over another. And nor do I want to play golf with them. A good walk spoiled and all that. I'd only end up arguing with them, if only to liven things up a bit.'

Jo knew he was right. Charles Hughes had a history of arguments and feuds with colleagues, mainly because he disagreed with their methods or conclusions and could never admit that there could be more than one right way of doing something or more than one right answer, let alone that he could ever be wrong. He would be a nightmare in a golf club, and joining the bridge club with his wife would soon lead to divorce.

'Yes,' she agreed. 'You do have history on your side.'

'I don't know what you mean, Jo,' Charles said, all innocence. 'I always get on with people, it's your mother who falls out with them.'

Jo couldn't really argue with that, but her father was definitely the worst offender. Her mother seemed to know how far she could go with friends, if not family, and stopped just short of causing a permanent rift. In truth, Jo was surprised they had any friends at all.

'Well okay then, not clubs. What about something, like, I don't know, learning Russian.'

'Hardly likely to be of any use to me, is it?'

'That's sort of the point, learning something for learning's sake. But if not that why not something practical like plumbing?'

'Plumbing is for cardiologists. We orthopods are more like mechanics. Don't worry, Jo, I will find something. I promise. I just don't want to rush into something and get bored five minutes later. It's got to be a real challenge. And I promise I'm not about to kill myself, so you can stop worrying about that as well.'

'I was more worried you were going to kill Ma, if I'm honest.'

Charles smiled, accepting her point.

Jo was pleased that just thinking about what he might do seemed to have brightened his mood.

'Alright then, I accept that you are fine and all is well. Just let me know if there's anything I need to worry about, okay?' She tried to feel reassured, although as they continued to talk he still seemed to have difficulty remembering things, words and names, even of diseases and complications he would have had at his fingertips a few months ago. They chatted a while longer before Jo made her excuses and left, well before her mother was due home, just in case she decided to come back early. Jo really couldn't face the Spanish Inquisition about her non-existent love life that would be inevitable if her mother came back and found her there.

With a final wave towards the house, Jo drove away, thinking about her relationship with her parents. Her disagreements with her father were about things that were not necessarily trivial, but they were always light-hearted and never personal, so they didn't leave her feeling unwilling to see him again. They included things like whether an Audi TT was a sensible car for a GP, or if being a GP was in itself a sensible career given the current crisis, whereas her mother's constant criticism of her marital status, or rather non-marital status, really hit a nerve and had led to Jo avoiding her mother. Her father always shrugged and told her that she would find the right person one day, she just needed to make time to find them. The question was not so much finding the time but the place. Where were all the single men? Kate found them at the gym, but beautiful bodies didn't necessarily mean beautiful minds, in Jo's experience. Where else? Work? Mixing work relationships with romance was not going to happen; pretty much every GP she knew was married or gay, and dating patients would get her struck off. Perhaps she'd find the man of her dreams in the supermarket, eyes meeting over the frozen meals for one. If she ever remembered to go shopping. Thinking of which, having spent her free afternoon at the police station, she was out of milk. Again. With a sigh she turned towards the old town, and wondered if Kate was free for a cup of coffee or if she would be busy with the gym bunny du jour. Time to find out.

Jo arrived for work bright and early on Thursday morning, determined to clear all the paperwork in her basket before starting her morning list. She planned to leave her car in one of the spaces reserved for the doctors in the surgery car park. With only two spaces provided for patients and three for doctors, they were on a strictly first come, first served basis; except for Hugh Grantham's. As senior partner, his parking space was sacrosanct. All the other staff knew they had to park elsewhere or walk to work. It was made clear when they first started their jobs that no parking was provided for them, but it wasn't a major consideration as most of the staff lived locally, so walking to work was relatively easy. Jo usually went home to pick up her car if she was doing visits or was called to the police station, but today she wanted to fit in a quick visit to the supermarket between surgeries, and she had a baby clinic as well, so she had driven.

Arriving at the car park, Jo was surprised to see that even this early both of the general doctor's spaces were full. She recognised one of the cars as Gauri's, but the other was unknown to her. Now she had a dilemma; Hugh's space was definitely out of bounds, but he was also adamant that the two patient spaces should be left free for those who needed them. Many of their patients were elderly or infirm and were unable to walk from the council car parks or from the seafront, even if they were able to get a space there. Carefully manoeuvring out of the tiny car park, Jo began scanning the surrounding streets for somewhere to park. It took her twenty minutes to find a free space, so far up the East Hill she was almost back home, and then she had to walk back down to work.

As she collected her basket of paperwork from the main office, Linda was sorting through the list of calls made to the out of hours service during the night.

'Good morning, Linda, anything interesting?' Jo asked her.

'No, not that I can see. The youngest Hennessy was breathless and had to be nebulised and started on steroids, old Mr Dryden at

Hillholme Care Home was in pain and the duty doc gave him Oromorph. A couple of worried parents and snuffly kids with temperatures. That's it.'

'A quiet night, then.'

'Yes, thank goodness.'

Jo started for the door, but turned and asked as an afterthought:

'Who else is in?'

'Just you and Dr Sinha.'

'So whose is the other car in the doctors' space?' Jo was indignant. There was a chain across the car park entrance overnight to stop locals from using it.

'Oh yes. That's Dr Brown's,' Linda looked embarrassed.

'But you said that only Gauri was in?'

'Yes. Dr Brown left his car here last night.' Linda was busying herself and not looking at Jo. 'He does that sometimes.'

'Why would he do that? He lives in Fairlight, he can hardly walk home from here, can he?'

'I wouldn't know,' Linda said tersely, and turned away before Jo could question her further.

Jo took her work basket through to the doctors' office, where Gauri was just finishing her own paperwork and packing everything away. She looked up and smiled as Jo entered the room.

'Good morning, Jo,' Gauri said brightly. 'You're in early!' It was just an observation, but Jo felt guilty that she didn't come in early more often.

'Hi, Gauri. Yes, I needed to catch up,' Jo indicated her overflowing work basket. 'Did you know that Gerry Brown left his car here sometimes?'

'Wednesday and Saturday nights,' Gauri answered her.

'Every Wednesday and Saturday?'

'Yes, indeed. Every Wednesday and Saturday night.'

Jo was having difficulty interpreting the look she was getting from Gauri.

'So what does he do on those days? And doesn't his wife mind him not going home?'

'I do not have the answers to your questions, Jo. Perhaps it is Dr Brown you should be asking?' And with that, Gauri left. Jo was bemused. Everyone seemed to know something about Gerry Brown that she didn't, and they seemed unusually tight-lipped about it, as if they disapproved. Looking at the pile of work in front of her, Jo decided she would have to think about it later, perhaps even ask Gerry himself, although she suspected he wouldn't tell her the truth if it was something shameful or embarrassing. Perhaps she should invest in some chocolate biscuits and tackle Linda again over a cup of coffee, see what she could prise out of her? That usually worked. With a shake of her head, Jo got on with her pile of test results and letters.

Jo's plan to pop over to the supermarket had been delayed by a call from Helen Austen, the social worker, letting Jo know that Mark Caxton's mum had called and told her that the police were searching their house. Helen was angry because Mark's mother was as vulnerable as he was, and as a result she was now in a terrible state. An agoraphobic alcoholic, it was extremely distressing for her to have the police invade the only space in which she felt she was safe. Helen believed the police were fishing and had no real evidence against Mark, but her reason for calling Jo was that she was worried the pressure was getting to him, and that he might do something stupid like confess, or go out and commit arson again. After all the hard work Helen and Adrian Lambourne, his psychologist, had put in to help Mark, and with such success, it would be a crying shame if the police pushed him into re-offending.

'So what do you want me to do?' Jo asked her, warily. Sensing that her two roles were about to collide, again, and much as she was angered by Miller's interference in her role with her patient, she had no wish to either obstruct his investigation or get beaten up by anyone.

'Can I bring him in to see you this afternoon? See what you think?' Helen asked.

'Erm,' Jo scrolled through her evening list, which was completely full, as usual. She knew that Helen was essentially covering her back. If Mark confessed or re-offended, a doctor's view that he had been put under undue pressure would be invaluable. It would also seriously irritate the police, if it were possible for her to irritate them more than she had by acting as Mark's appropriate adult in his interview.

'What about Adrian Lambourne? Wouldn't he be better placed to see Mark? His opinion would carry more weight, surely?'

'I tried him. He can't see Mark until next week and I'm worried that might be too late.'

Jo conceded defeat. Helen was right; her first duty was to her patient. 'Okay. Could you get him here before evening surgery?' she asked Helen. 'I'll fit him in first.' The supermarket would have to wait, better that than to see him at the end and risk being alone with him. She wasn't that stupid.

The baby clinic was just finishing, and the last screaming infant had been tucked up in a nice warm pushchair when Jo heard from Helen that Mark had been arrested. It seemed that the police had found a box containing old matchbooks similar to the ones used to start the fire, and Helen was on her way to the station to be Mark's appropriate adult alongside his solicitor. Jo immediately felt guilty about the wave of relief that washed over her. Now she would have time to nip to the supermarket and fill her car up with petrol before evening surgery, as she was generally excused visits on days when she had the baby clinic. She was also undeniably happy not to have to interfere with the police handling of the investigation. No matter how nice it would be to think about getting one up on Detective Inspector Miller and his sidekick, she knew that in reality she was the one who would come out the loser in the long run.

It wasn't until later, sitting in her consulting room, finishing off the last of her chicken salad roll, being careful to clean up every crumb so that none of her patients would know she sometimes ate at her desk, that the guilt overtook her, and, with a quick look at her watch to reassure herself that there was still time before she was due to see her first patient, Jo reached for the phone. She hoped that Detective Inspector Miller would have finished or, if he was being particularly obstructive, have left Mark and Helen kicking their heels, and not even started the interview. She would bet on the latter. Either way, she was put straight through to his office and he answered.

The conversation, in which Jo had hoped she could express her concerns for Mark's welfare, find out how the investigation was going, and offer her help and support to both the police and her patient, didn't quite go the way she had planned.

Miller seemed deeply suspicious of her motives in asking about Mark.

'Why do you need to know how he is?' he responded to her enquiry about Mark's mental state.

'Because I'm his doctor,' she replied, and was met with stony silence. 'Look, I know he over-reacted yesterday but...'

'Dr Hughes,' Miller interrupted her, 'your patient is fine and I have an investigation to conduct. While I appreciate your concern, he has an appropriate adult here, and quite possibly a more appropriate one than yourself.'

Jo silently smarted at that, even though she knew Miller was probably right.

'I am sure I don't need to remind you that you also have a role as a police employee. Have you been asked to come in to check his fitness for interview?' He continued.

'Er, no,' Jo was surprised to be asked. 'Why? Do you think he might not be fit for interview? Perhaps it might be a good idea if...'

'No,' Miller quickly interrupted her. 'You are not needed, he's fine, and perhaps it would be better if you admitted that you have a conflict of interest and remove yourself from any further involvement in this case.'

He hung up, leaving Jo seething with anger.

'Rude, arrogant, stupid...' Jo struggled for a word to describe Miller, 'man!' was the best she could do, before slamming the phone down and realising that Linda had come in after a perfunctory knock and was looking at her in surprise.

'I take it someone's upset you?' Linda asked.

'Was it that obvious?' Jo replied, embarrassed.

'Only to me and everyone in the waiting room.'

'Well, that's all right then,' Jo managed to smile despite her irritation.

'I just popped in to give you a couple of telephone messages,' Linda handed over two notes, closed the door firmly and sat down in the patient's chair, 'but I'm not leaving until you tell me exactly who that upsetting man was, and what he has done to you, and don't think you can keep any details back.'

'Much as I hate to disappoint you, he was a policeman and it was a work-related matter,' Jo responded stiffly. She was right; Linda was disappointed.

'Shame, I thought you had another war story about a blind date your mother set up. Oh well, I'll let you get on with your list, unless, of course, this policeman is handsome and single?'

'No,' Jo lied about Miller's looks because she didn't want to admit that she did actually find him quite good-looking, 'and anyway, he's married. You haven't added any visits, have you?'

Linda raised an eyebrow at the obvious change in subject.

'No, Gauri took them all in gratitude that you managed to do the whole baby clinic and not dump any screaming infants on her, which is just as well,' she indicated the messages and left.

Checking her messages, Jo saw that the first one was a patient wanting advice, but the second was from the police station. The custody sergeant wanted her to come and examine a prisoner who had minor injuries incurred during his arrest, and, despite Miller's insistence that Mark was fine, the way he had jumped in and told her so vehemently that her patient was okay, Jo had a pretty good idea who that prisoner would turn out to be. She checked her watch. Four o'clock. If she was quick, she would just have time to see him before evening surgery, and with a bit of luck, she would seriously irritate Detective Inspector Miller by doing so.

Mark's injuries were very minor; it looked as if he had taken a slight blow to his face, either from a policeman's fist or some other solid object. There was a small amount of bruising, but his lip and nose had long since stopped bleeding and she only had to clean him up a bit, making sure she explained what she was doing and getting permission from him before touching his face. She didn't want to prompt any kind of reaction. Her main concern, and the custody sergeant's as well, was his level of anxiety. She was seeing him in the treatment room, alone, but there was a panic button nearby if she needed help, and a police constable hovering just outside the door with orders to come in if he heard anything untoward.

'Can you tell me what happened, Mark?' she asked 'How did you get these injuries?'

'I tried to stop them taking my collection.'

'Collection?'

'My dad's matchbooks. They're mine now. He gave them to me. They have no right.'

'You're not allowed matches, Mark,' Jo explained gently. 'Not when...'

'I don't use them to light things anymore. They were my dad's.'

Jo could imagine Mark had tried to stop the police from taking away his precious mementos of his dead father, and his injuries seemed consistent with a struggle to get them back. She tried to get more detail from him, but he became barely coherent, one minute asking her if she could help him get his matches back, and the next worrying about his mum, then asking who would look after his cat. Worrying about everything and everyone except himself.

Jo considered prescribing him an anxiolytic but thought she would prefer to speak to his psychologist before doing that, because Mark was on a number of other drugs to help control his behavioural problems and she didn't want to make matters worse. Instead, she spent some time talking to him and trying to calm him. Unfortunately, it wasn't very long before the custody sergeant apologetically knocked on the door and asked if he was okay to interview, because the detectives were waiting. Jo would have liked longer but, knowing that Mark had Helen and a solicitor to support him, she confirmed that he was and allowed him to be taken to the interview room. She took her time writing up her notes before leaving the treatment room, in the hope that she wouldn't meet Miller on her way out, but just as she was leaving the custody suite he came flying down the stairs, almost knocking her over in his rush to grab the door before it shut behind her.

'Sorry,' he said reflexively, before fully taking in whom he was apologising to. 'Oh, um, I'm in a hurry,' he explained unnecessarily, and continued through the door, letting it slam behind him. Jo was too angry and too slow to give him a sarcastic response, but as she looked at his retreating back she was pleased to notice his neck slowly reddening as he approached the custody desk. He must have been told she had been called in to see Mark, despite his insistence that her patient was fine, and she hoped he was embarrassed about it. She would make sure she reminded him of it if he ever tried to interfere in her work again.

Back in her flat, and still furious with Miller, whom she now felt was not only arrogant and chauvinistic, but also could not be relied upon to protect the vulnerable, Jo poured herself a large glass of white wine. A very large one. She knew all the reasons why this was not a good idea. She had counselled patients on not drinking to relieve stress. She knew alcohol was empty calories and raised her risk of a variety of cancers. She knew precisely how many units of alcohol were in the glass and she knew it was more than her daily limit, according to the current government health guidance, but she was going to drink it all the same.

As she began to feel the relaxing effect of the wine, she thought about Mark. And Miller. She wondered if he was responsible for Mark's injuries, but, in the spirit of fairness, decided that it was more likely to have been Jeffries. She had to admit, even to herself, that the damage had been minor and didn't really need to have been examined by a doctor. She took another sip of wine. She didn't know if Mark was innocent or guilty, and that wasn't really her concern; her job was to make sure he was fit to be detained, and as his GP she also needed to consider his physical and mental wellbeing. With that in mind, she resolved to contact Adrian Lambourne again, to make sure he was made fully aware just how fragile Mark was at the moment, and this time she'd back up their conversation with a written summation, just in case he fobbed her off again.

Jo was nicely relaxed now, and flicked through the television channels while eating an omelette and salad, looking forward to a long, hot soak in the bath before an early night. She had to concede that a glass of wine could sometimes be the answer to a stressful day, but she was never going to admit that to her patients.

8

It had been a long and frustrating morning. It was technically Jo's administration time, when she had no patients booked but was expected to be in the office to catch up on all her paperwork and also do any studying needed to keep her up to date with her personal development plan, as required for revalidation. However, just because Jo was free to make phone calls didn't mean that everyone else was also available. She had started out by calling the custody suite to check if Mark was still being held. Under PACE he could be held for twenty-four hours, which could be extended to thirty-six by a senior officer's review. As he had only been arrested the previous afternoon, she thought it was likely he was still there, which he was. On hearing that he was still there and that he remained anxious and stressed, Jo decided to ring his psychologist straight away and get some advice on how to help her patient.

As she listened to the phone ring and waited for the answerphone to kick in, she made a note to visit Mark's mother and see how she was doing, and also decided to call Helen to try and find out how the interview had gone. She left a message asking Dr Lambourne to call her back as soon as he was free, mentioning that it was about Mark and that it was urgent. Then she tried unsuccessfully to reach Helen and left a message for her too. Next on her list was Jillian Hollingsworth. She left a message on her phone as well, asking her to collect a blood test form and to get one done before her next prescription was due, stressing the importance of monitoring her thyroid function regularly.

Half an hour and a dozen abortive phone calls later, Jo had had enough. She took a look at her revalidation folder, shoved it back in her 'to do' pile, grabbed her bag and went out.

The row of council houses where Mark Caxton lived with his mother was shabby and in need of repair. The render was cracked and could have done with a coat of paint, fences were broken and had been mended with old bits of wood and wire, and a variety of old cars, broken toys, and household implements decorated the front gardens. Jo looked carefully around before walking up the path to Mark's house and pushing the doorbell, thankful that the press didn't seem to have got hold of the story of Mark's arrest just yet, and noting that the yellowed net curtains next door twitched as a neighbour checked who was visiting. There was no answer, and realising that she hadn't heard any chimes from the bell, she knocked loudly.

Jo heard footsteps in the hallway, but still no one answered. She knocked again.

'Mrs Caxton? It's Dr Hughes,' she called through the letterbox. 'Please can I come in? I just want to see how you are.'

After a few more moments of foot shuffling the door was finally opened, emitting a blast of stale smoke, and Jo was allowed in. She followed Mark's mother into the kitchen, which was surprisingly clean and tidy. Only a dirty glass and a half empty bottle of vodka betrayed the fact that Mrs Caxton had been drinking, until Jo took a closer look at her. She was haggard and swaying slightly as she stood, using the counter to help her stop the room from spinning. She took a deep drag of her cigarette before crushing it out in a dirty ashtray. It was by no means her first of the day, by the look of things.

'Why don't we sit down?' Jo said gently, indicating the two chairs either side of a small breakfast table. Mrs Caxton gratefully lowered herself into one of the chairs and grabbed her packet of cigarettes. As she took out another cigarette and reached for her lighter, Jo tried not to let her distaste show on her face. She hated every aspect of smoking, but recognised her patient's need. She hoped it would help her to relax enough to talk about what had happened, and sure enough, it didn't take long for Mrs Caxton to open up and tell Jo about the police search of her house and how it had affected her. How terrifying it had been, how she felt violated. This was her space, her safe place, and they had come and trampled all over everything, messing things up. In fact, once she had started, it was hard to get her to stop for long enough for Jo to ask any questions. It seemed that, as she had thought, Mark had got hurt when he tried to stop the police from finding and taking his precious collection of matchbooks away as evidence.

'Stupid bloody matchbooks. Rubbish. That's all they were. Dennis used to bring them back from all these places he visited as a salesman, picked them up in the bars and hotels and that.'

'He was a travelling salesman?' Jo queried unnecessarily, just to keep the conversation going.

'Yeah. He sold cleaning services for factories and businesses, like, you know, all over the South East. Brought a new packet back for Mark every time he stayed away. Not much of a present, not really suitable for a kid, but Mark was always fascinated by them, thought his dad was staying in all these exotic places. Littlehampton, Ipswich and that, not so exotic really.'

Jo silently agreed.

'Course, not many places give away matches these days, what with the smoking ban.' Jo was grateful that Mrs Caxton blew the smoke out of the side of her mouth, rather than directly across the table, but it was a small mercy. A very small one. She was going to stink of smoke for the rest of the day, or at least until she was able to shower and wash her hair.

'Mark adored his dad. Became obsessed with those stupid match-books. The only thing he had left of him when he was gone.'

'How did he die?' she asked.

'Heart attack while he was driving home. He called and said he'd had some chest pains, and I told him to go to the hospital, but he wanted to get back for Mark's tenth birthday, stupid bugger.' She took another drag and ignored the ash that fell onto her lap.

'And Mark used these matchbooks when he set fires?'

'Yeah. It was all his dad's fault. Giving a kid matches. Asking for trouble. After Mark got done for arson the third time, they told me I had to get rid of them, so I threw them out, but Mark must have taken them out of the bin and hidden them.'

'And he carried on using them?'

'No, he used boxes of matches after. I didn't know he still had the ruddy books or I'd have got rid.'

'But he could have gone back to using the books?'

Mrs Caxton thought about that for so long that Jo thought she might not have heard her, but just as she was about to ask again, she answered.

'I suppose he must've.' There didn't seem to be much to add to this depressing acceptance that her son had killed a woman, and Jo decided to leave her to her cigarettes and vodka. A sad case, but there was little she could do for the woman except refer her to the drug and alcohol team, again.

As it was still technically her study morning and no one was returning her phone calls, Jo decided to go back to her flat and do a bit of research online about arson and arsonists, and shower and change to get rid of the smell of cigarette smoke that had lodged in her clothes and hair. Once online, she typed arson into a search engine and started working her way through the vast numbers of hits the search threw up. She was not surprised to find that most arsonists started their experimentation with fire when they were young, unless they were burning properties for reasons of fraud or personal gain. She read that in cases where the subject has difficulty relating to people in a one-to-one situation, fire could become their friend, mentor, and even their love. She knew that Mark's first conviction came when he was ten. Shortly after his father died he had set fire to a neighbour's garden shed. He continued with assorted rubbish bins, sheds and outhouses around the neighbourhood, which must have made Mark and his mother unpopular with the locals. By the time he was fourteen he had escalated to torching cars, because he liked the explosion when the fuel tank went up. Initially he had set fire to them where they were parked, but after an incident when the fire had got out of control and spread to a nearby house, he had changed to taking the cars away and setting them alight in remote locations. Jo wondered about the matchbooks. If he had stopped using them, why start again now? Jo could only think that it was because he had escalated to a more serious crime, which in itself posed another question: if Mark was indeed the arsonist, why had he started killing? And why a woman? Unfortunately, Jo had already thought of one scenario that might explain it. Perhaps something had happened in his relationship with his mother, and, unable to hurt her, he had found a substitute. It was even possible that she had sexually abused him, much as that was a repugnant thought, but that could be the cause of his dislike of being touched. Jo hoped she was wrong, but it did make a sort of sense, if burning a woman to death could ever be said to make sense. She shook her head in frustration. She couldn't honestly believe it. He was such a gentle lad and the murder had been truly brutal, but if it wasn't Mark, who else could it be?

She decided to concentrate on the matchbooks, as they were unusual and the one physical link to Mark. Jo knew that forensics might be able to identify the burnt remains of the matchbook, even when it seemed impossibly blackened and damaged, and if so, they might be able to show whether or not it could be one from Mark's collection, that is, an old one and from a place his father might have visited. If it was, that would show an almost direct connection to Mark, and the police would have enough to charge him with at least arson, and probably murder, as a result. The provenance of the matchbook was crucial, both to the likelihood of Mark being charged, but also to Jo's belief that he wouldn't have done it.

Bearing in mind what Mrs Caxton had said about hotels and pubs not giving away matchbooks since the smoking ban came in, Jo began thinking about where someone would get a matchbook these days. She googled matchbooks and discovered that they were remarkably easy to buy. Apparently phillumeny, the hobby of collecting match-related items, including boxes, labels, covers and books, was very popular. She could buy them branded to promote her business, or order personalised ones for her wedding, and if she wanted to buy a whole collection of old ones, eBay had them grouped together according to vintage or country. There were even collections with saucy covers being advertised for sale. Perhaps it wasn't going to be as easy to show a direct link to Mark as she had thought. Anyone could have got hold of them, and if that was all the evidence the police had then they would have to let him go.

Jo had just finished evening surgery when she heard from Helen that Mark had been released. She also told Jo that he was in such a state that he was having an anxiety attack and wouldn't leave the house. With a sigh, Jo agreed to visit him. She would have preferred not to do it so soon after he had been released, to give him more time to settle, but the weekend rota started at six and she wasn't on call, so she felt it would be better to go and see how bad he was rather than leave the initial assessment to a doctor who didn't know him. She could then leave a note with the out of hours service that Mark might need further help over the weekend.

Before leaving the surgery, she tried calling Adrian Lambourne again. Mark had seen a number of psychologists over the years, but Lambourne had made real progress with him, and she wanted to see if he could give her any pointers on the best way of helping their patient. She had already left several messages without getting any joy, and was surprised, given how late it was, when she managed to get through to him this time.

'Oh hello, Adrian, it's Jo Hughes, Mark Caxton's GP. I wondered if you could spare a moment to discuss his case with me?' she asked him.

'Ah yes, Dr Hughes. Yes, um, it's a bit difficult.'

Misunderstanding his reluctance to speak to her, Jo assumed it was because she was calling too late in the day.

'It won't take long, but if it's a bad time, just say when would be better.'

'No, no, it's not a bad time, as such, it's more that I have to consider client confidentiality.'

Jo was taken aback by this response.

'I'm Mark's doctor,' she clarified, 'so confidentiality isn't an issue.'

'It's more complicated than that, though, isn't it? Because of who you work for, I mean.'

'I'm not sure what you are referring to,' she countered, but she was beginning to get an idea. 'Do you mean because of my work as a police doctor?'

'Exactly,' he seemed relieved that she was the one who had actually broached the subject.

'Anything you say to me as Mark's doctor remains strictly confidential, and I would not disclose it to the police unless I had Mark's permission to do so.'

'I am sure you wouldn't, Dr Hughes, but I am anxious to avoid putting you in a difficult position.'

'I am quite used to difficult positions, Dr Lambourne,' Jo was beginning to get very irritated by his prissy attitude.

'Even so, there is always the danger of the police finding something out on their own, and suspicion falling on you as having revealed it in some way. I really wouldn't want you to be accused of breaching confidentiality.'

'I certainly won't breach any confidentiality, and I am sure the police would support me if there was any misunderstanding, so I don't see it as a problem, Dr Lambourne.'

'But it could very easily become a problem, Dr Hughes.'

'Is that a threat?' Jo was incredulous.

'No, no, of course not. However, I really think it would be in my client's best interests if I do not speak to you, and indeed, I shall be recommending that he change doctors. Goodbye.' And he hung up on her.

Jo took a deep breath. She knew that her joint roles could potentially put her in difficult situations, and that was without the added complication of her acting as Mark's appropriate adult, but it had never been a problem before, and Lambourne's assertion that he was doing this to protect her as much as Mark made her blood boil. The fact that Miller had made the same suggestion about a conflict of interest the day before only made it worse.

It was with a feeling of déjà vu that Jo parked her car in front of the terrace of council houses where Mark lived and knocked on the door. She heard footsteps in the hallway and could see someone standing there through the textured glass in the door. She knocked again.

'Mark?' she called through the letterbox. 'It's Doctor Hughes. Helen asked me to visit and said she'd let you know I was coming.'

There was no response, but she could hear some shuffling, and peering through the letterbox she could see a pair of feet covered in a pair of grubby, worn, sport socks. One big toe poked out from a hole.

'Mark, I know you are there, so open the door for a minute and speak to me, will you?'

The feet shuffled some more. Mark was thinking.

'I just want to help you, Mark, so let me in, will you?' Jo said gently.

'I can't,' Mark told her anxiously, 'Dr Lambourne told me I wasn't to speak to you. He made me promise.'

Jo sighed. Lambourne must have rung Mark straight after her conversation with him.

'Is your mum there?'

'She's asleep,' Mark reluctantly admitted. 'I don't want her bothered.'

He sounded worried, and Jo knew that he was probably covering for the fact that his mother had passed out drunk. Children of alcoholics learnt to lie and make excuses from an early age.

'It's okay, Mark.' Jo didn't want to put him under yet more pressure. According to Helen he was close to breaking point, so she backed off. 'How about another doctor, Mark? Would you let another doctor in if I arrange for someone to visit? Would that be okay?'

'Dr Lambourne said I wasn't to speak to anyone from your surgery as you work for the police and would tell them bad things about me. He's going to see me on Monday, he said.' Mark answered in a rush, knowing that what he was saying wasn't likely to be well-received.

Jo gritted her teeth. She was very cross, but managed to keep her voice steady, not wanting to make Mark think he was the one making her angry.

'That's good, Dr Lambourne's the best person to help you, but promise me you will call the duty doctor if you need to speak to someone before then, will you? It's a doctor from another practice on call this weekend, no one from our surgery, okay?'

'Okay,' Mark responded, although his voice was far from certain. Jo left him, still standing behind the door in his holey socks, panicking quietly about everything.

Jo was fuming, but managed to remain professional when she rang Helen to let her know what had happened. Helen wasn't nearly so restrained in her views of Dr Lambourne.

'It's slanderous. You should sue him. He basically told a patient you and your colleagues would grass him up to the police.'

'I know, Helen,' Jo placated her, 'but we only have Mark's word for what Dr Lambourne actually said, and he could have got it wrong,' Jo didn't really believe that. Mark had seemed quite sure of what he had been told by his psychologist.

'But it's outrageous!'

'Yes, but at least he's done it out of a misguided sense of helping his client, and it certainly wouldn't be in Mark's best interest to force him to repeat what he was told in court, even if I could persuade him to appear. He'd be a wreck.'

Helen had to concede the point, and told Jo that she would visit Mark over the weekend to make sure he was okay, and would decide whether or not she needed to call out the duty doctor.

Relieved to know that someone she trusted was looking after Mark's best interests, Jo walked back up the path and made her way back to her car, watched all the way by the neighbour peering round her net curtains.

9

Saturday turned out to be one of those crisp, sunny, spring days that are just made for a long walk by the sea. Kate didn't agree, however, telling Jo she would rather hang out at the gym. It was late morning before Jo gave up on trying to persuade her and set off for a solo trek across the cliff tops to Fairlight Lighthouse. She had packed a sandwich, an apple, and a bottle of water into a light rucksack, along with a waterproof jacket, an extra jumper, her sunglasses, mobile phone, and some money. She liked to be prepared for any eventuality. Knowing that the path from the East Hill was still closed due to a landslip, she walked along Rocklands Lane to join the path that took her to Ecclesbourne Meadow. The path was steep in parts, both up and down along the hilly route, better than any workout on a treadmill to Jo's mind, and the views were in a completely different league. Jo wasn't sure what it said about her that she liked to look at rolling hills and rocky shores more than well-muscled men in tight vests. She just knew that she did. She couldn't help a small smile of satisfaction as she walked through the meadows and took in the views. She'd passed a few other walkers on her way, but for the most part she had the wonderful scenery to herself. She paused to drink it in, and after a few deep breaths of clean fresh sea air, set off again.

Walking always gave her the space and time to think through problems, sometimes helping her to find an answer, more often just allowing her to come to terms with the fact that there was no answer, and therefore no point in worrying about the problem. The lack of a partner in her life definitely fell into that category. She had tried taking courses and joining clubs of various sorts, thinking that perhaps she wasn't meeting enough men, but the few men who were also joining courses or clubs to find a partner seemed either dense or desperate. The upside was that she could now speak conversational Italian and cook an authentic Indian meal. She had found astronomy and stargazing for beginners fascinating, but had dropped out of the car maintenance course because she hated the dirt and oil under her fingernails, and she certainly wasn't getting her money's worth out of the gym. Once again, she stopped to look at the view and have a drink of water at the top of a particularly steep set of steps that had taken her from a densely wooded valley to a long grassy stretch at the top of the cliffs. The sea looked calm from this height, but the number of white caps on the waves told her that it wouldn't be pleasant if she were on one of the small pleasure boats she could see out there. Sailing was another hobby she had tried, only to discover she suffered from terrible seasickness. Jo would never forget how ill she had felt. The poor man who had taken her out was unlikely to forget either. She moved on, both physically to the next stage of the walk and mentally to her father and what she could do to help him if he refused to help himself. She remained convinced that he was trying to cover up memory problems of one sort or another. The first step would be to get him, and her mother, to admit that there was a problem, be it depression or dementia. Then she could start to get him the help he needed. Although she was aware that her father didn't need help yet, as a GP she knew that there were drugs that could slow the progression of dementia, and therapies and tactics that could help to reduce the impact. She thought about Post-it notes, memory clinics, daily living aids and later, when it got worse, hopefully not for a long time yet, she could organise home help and sitters to support her mother. The first job, though, was to persuade her father that he needed to see a doctor. With a small sigh, Jo accepted that she would need to meet up with her mother and enlist her assistance. Jo put 'speak to mother' top of her mental list of things to do and, as she tackled the final climb up to Fairlight coastguard station, moved onto the next problem; Mark Caxton.

Except that the problem wasn't just Mark Caxton. There was Adrian Lambourne as well. Jo would need to speak to Hugh Grantham and ask his advice about the psychologist and whether they needed to do anything about what he seemed to have said to Mark. He hadn't only suggested that Jo might leak information to the police, but that any doctor in the practice might do so, and she knew Hugh wouldn't be happy about it. The question was, would Hugh do anything about it? The risk was that complaining would only make the situation worse. Having decided that she could trust Helen to care for Mark, and having put speaking to Hugh at number two on her list, Jo reached Fairlight and the string of coastguard cottages, happy to have moved forward with most of her problems, in her mind at least. Feeling satisfied with life, and pleasantly tired after a good morning's walk, she sat on a bench overlooking the sea and ate her lunch.

The intricate preparations he made were part of the thrill. He had spent weeks checking streets and car parks for cameras, both public and private, and logging where they were so that he could avoid them, not just when he took the cars, but as he drove around after he had stolen them as well. Making fake number plates for the cars had also proved easier than expected; the flimsy plastic replicas wouldn't fool anyone close up, but they were good enough to confuse any cameras, either CCTV or the automatic number plate recognition cameras located around the town. For the latter, he always made sure the numbers he used were cloned from cars similar or identical to the cars he stole. Hastings had extensive CCTV throughout the town, and he needed to make it as difficult as possible for the police to track him through the streets. He didn't want to get caught for something stupid like car theft or speeding before he had killed enough to ensure that when he told them why he'd done it, they would listen. That was why he had spent months in preparation, to make sure he killed enough to make an impact, and now he was ready for her, for victim number two. He had the car; a fifteen-year-old Ford, as new cars were harder to steal. He had fitted the fake plates, and put a full can of petrol in the boot with his fold-up bicycle and a drinks can. With a final check that he had the book of matches in his pocket, he smiled and set off for his rendezvous with the lovely Lorraine.

10

'Another Sunday morning, another crispy critter,' Jeffries said cheer-
fully as he suited up, ready to inspect the burnt-out car and its grue-
some contents. Jo, who was just taking her suit off, resolutely refused
to respond, but was unable to stop an angry flush spreading up her
neck, betraying her feelings. Hoping that no one, and in particular
neither Jeffries nor Miller, would notice that he had got to her, she
kept her head high and her back straight as she silently walked to her
car. She was parked a short distance along the track that led to the
cliff-top car park, but as she opened the driver's door to get in, she
couldn't help but glance back. Even from that distance, she could see
Jeffries watching her and smirking as he pulled the suit hood over
his once ginger hair, so he had presumably noticed, but at least there
was a chance Miller, already suited and with his back to her, taking a
closer look at the car and the corpse in the passenger seat, might not
have done.

The dawn had finally arrived while Jo was inspecting the body and
pronouncing death, so once she was sitting safely in her car to write
up her notes, she took the opportunity to look around her and take
in the crime scene. It was similar to the one a week earlier, although
there were fewer trees around, and none between the car park and the
coastguard cottages further along the lane towards the cliffs, just a few
scrubby bushes shaped by the wind. There would have been nothing
to shield the view of the fire if any of the cottage windows had pointed
in that direction, but as they didn't the initial alert had only come after
there had been an explosion, presumably when the petrol tank blew
up, taking most of Fairlight visitor centre with it. From Jo's memory
of her walk just the day before, the visitor centre had been little more
than a wooden shack anyway, but now it was just a pile of burnt planks
and broken glass, with leaflets scattered around it. As in the first case,
the burnt-out car was parked against a line of wooden posts in front of
where the visitor centre had once stood, the posts having presumably
been put there to prevent bad parkers from accidentally ramming the

hut. No one would have envisaged their current use by this murderer, to stop his passenger from getting out of the car. From Jo's brief examination of the body the victim did not appear to have been trying to escape from the blazing car at all this time, as she was sitting upright in the passenger seat with her seat belt still clasped. Perhaps it had come as more of a surprise, Jo speculated. It was also possible she'd had a few drinks and was slower to react or to realise what was happening. Maybe that was a good thing, not knowing that she was about to die, not having time to be terrified. Jo certainly hoped so.

With only these minor changes from the first scene, she felt sure this was the hand of the same killer, and with wooden posts or something similar being used in many country car parks to delineate the area assigned to cars or protect buildings and footpaths, the killer would have a big choice of venues for future killings. With these murders only a week apart, Jo now had no doubt that there would be future killings. She looked across the crime scene, now thronged with investigators and police, and on to the coastguard cottages beyond. To think that she was only up here yesterday, happily admiring the view, and now, well, she would never be able to think of it in the same way again. This was no longer a place of peace and beauty; in her mind it would forever be associated with this horrific crime, and the smell of burnt flesh.

Once home, Jo tried to go back to sleep, but the sight and smell of the body, so awfully contorted in death, were too vivid in her mind to make sleep possible. She couldn't help thinking about the poor woman and how she had died, and of the friends and family left behind to hear the dreadful news of her death. Who was doing this? What sort of a person was capable of setting people on fire and leaving them to die?

She finally gave up on sleep and took a leisurely, scented bath, thinking of ways to distract herself throughout the day in the hope that if she had happier things to focus on, she would be able to sleep better that night. Of course, there was a school of thought that said if she could give herself something different to worry about, like her father, it would work even better, but that would mean speaking to her mother and Jo really didn't think she could face her mother in her exhausted, sleep-deprived state. As she lay in the bath she heard her home phone ring. She let it go through to answerphone, and almost as if she were being punished for thinking that she couldn't face her mother her voice filled the flat with more complaints about her father. Jo had always prided herself on being able to keep her cool even under the most provoking of situations. However, her mother knew precisely how to press her buttons and she was the one person who Jo could guarantee would keep pushing them until she reacted. Calling her back or going to visit was not an option today.

She was just thinking of going to the gym for some mindless jogging on the treadmill or seeking out Kate for a comforting chat over coffee or wine when her mobile rang. Jo hesitated. Could it be her mother? She had been careful not to give her the mobile number; only her father had it in case of life or death emergencies, with the clear instructions that his life would indeed be in danger if he ever gave it to his wife. She checked, and was relieved to see that it was Helen.

'Hi ,Helen, what's up? Is Mark okay?'

'No. Not really. He's been taken in for questioning again.'

It was to be expected, Jo thought. Perhaps she ought to have warned Helen first thing this morning.

'They'll need to check his alibi for last night. There was another car fire.'

'So I heard on the news. Was it another woman? They didn't have any details.'

'Probably. We'll know for sure after the PM,' she checked her watch. 'Do you need me to go in as appropriate adult?'

'No, no. The duty social worker is doing that,' Helen answered quickly, and Jo understood. She hadn't called until she was sure she had it covered.

'Probably for the best, as I'm no longer his GP.'

'Exactly. I knew you'd understand. I didn't want to make things more awkward than they are, but I also didn't want you hearing about it through the grapevine.'

'Thank you.'

Once she had put the receiver down, Jo felt like kicking something and swearing, but decided to vent her frustration with a bit of cleaning instead. Armed with rubber gloves and bleach she set to on the bathroom. She knew that it was only natural for the police to want to question Mark, given that it seemed likely that the same method of starting the fire had been used, but there really wasn't anything she could do to help him since Adrian Lambourne's interference. She had no right to go and see him at the police station as a police doctor unless they asked her to, and she couldn't go as Mark's own doctor because he had effectively dismissed her. After an hour scrubbing the already pristine bathroom, still unable to banish her concern for Mark, and imagining him being railroaded into confessing to a crime he might not have committed, Jo decided to give up and go into the surgery to review his notes.

Once Jo had got over the initial, and wholly unreasonable, irritation she felt when she saw that Gerry Brown had left his car in the car park again, and her subsequent relief on finding out that it really was just his car and that he wasn't hiding anywhere in the surgery, Jo made herself a pot of Dr Grantham's personal and very expensive coffee, and raided Linda's stash of chocolate digestives. There were definite perks to coming in to the surgery when it was closed, beyond getting far more work done without all the usual interruptions.

She took her drink and a couple of biscuits into the office, taking a moment to savour the smell of the fresh coffee, and wonder anew at why some things, nice as they tasted, smelled so much better; coffee, bacon, and roast lamb for starters. Who could resist?

She cleared herself some space at the main desk, opened Mark Caxton's personal electronic record and, having read through her own notes from when she had seen him over the years, she went into the scanned document section, which included the records of his psychology assessments and letters from Adrian Lambourne, along with Helen's case notes.

Jo made notes as she reviewed Mark's files. She hadn't really been involved in any of his court cases, so the detail in some of Helen's case notes in particular was helpful, but if she had hoped that Adrian Lambourne's records of the sessions with his patient would be revealing, she was sadly disappointed. He probably had more comprehensive records at his office, but he had simply sent summaries to her. At least she hoped he had more comprehensive records somewhere, because what she had from him told her little, if anything, useful.

What interested Jo most were the notes that Helen made after the incident where Mark set fire to a car parked outside a house and the fire had spread to the house itself. The old lady living there had needed to be evacuated by the fire brigade, and although she was unhurt she had lost everything and been unable to return to her home.

Mark had been sent to a young offenders institution for a while after that fire. Close as he was to his own grandmother, he had apparently shown profound remorse and anxiety that he had caused the old woman to lose all her belongings and, indeed, that he had so nearly killed her.

Once released, he returned to stealing and torching cars, but he never again set fire to them in residential areas, always taking them to remote locations before setting them alight. While this change of location fitted with the new crimes, it also seemed to suggest that he didn't want to hurt anyone, Jo thought. So why would he suddenly change? Why would he suddenly want to kill, and in such a terrible way? There was nothing in his notes to suggest what might have triggered such a dramatic escalation, but Jo knew that the lack of an obvious trigger didn't mean it hadn't happened.

Going online, Jo searched the local and national news sites and discovered that the second body had been identified. There was a photograph of a smiling Carol Johnson, thirty-four, accountant, married, no children. The photo and personal details looked like they had been lifted straight from her Facebook page, and Jo thought that she recognised her as a patient. A quick check of patient records confirmed it, and also that the Dunsmore family were not, which was a relief. At least the women weren't being targeted because of the doctors' surgery they used. Jo wondered what else they might have in common, apart from being young women in their thirties, but she couldn't think of anything.

The sound of an engine in the car park distracted her, and she looked out of the office window to see who was there. Gerry Brown was collecting his car. It was almost lunchtime, so perhaps he had finally decided to go home, she thought. Seeing him reminded her of her patient with thyroid problems, and that she couldn't remember seeing the results for the thyroid function tests she had asked her to have. She looked up Jill Hollingsworth in the electronic records. There were no results recorded there, so she went through the office pending baskets, but that proved equally fruitless. Knowing that there was nothing she could do on a Sunday, Jo left herself a note to remind her to follow up with a phone call on Monday morning, and a note for Linda to check as well. After that, she decided to call it a day. Suddenly realising that she was starving, she wondered if Kate would be free for a late lunch and a drink in The Stag. It was supposed to be her day off, after all.

It was much later and almost dark when Jo finally opened the front door of her flat and dropped her bag on the table. She closed the door and went and lay down on the sofa without turning the lights on. Drinking at lunchtime was never a good idea, she reminded herself with a yawn, knowing that if she slept now she wouldn't sleep tonight, and would feel terrible tomorrow as well. Perhaps she should write it in her diary: no lunchtime drinking, even on a Sunday. Especially on a Sunday, given how busy surgeries always were on a Monday. She closed her eyes and let the darkness settle around her. There was a blissful, restful silence, and she felt herself slowly drift towards sleep. It can only have been a few minutes later that she opened her eyes again with a start, as the sound of the phone rang through the darkness. With a groan, she rolled over and reached for it.

'Hello?'

'Jocasta? Is that you? You sound half asleep.'

Jo inwardly sighed. Her mother. That was all she needed.

'It's been a long day,' she tried to explain, sitting up and rubbing her eyes.

'And how long have you been home without checking your messages?'

Jo looked at her answering machine. Eight messages, the display blinked angrily at her.

'You've rung eight times?'

'Ten actually, but I only left eight messages.'

Jo sighed, tucked the phone under her chin, and went into the kitchen, flicking on the light as she passed the switch, and then turning it off again; it hurt her eyes too much.

'What's he done now?' Only her father could get her mother into a tizz as bad as this. She opened the fridge, wincing at the brightness of the light and noting the open bottle of Pinot Grigio and the lack of milk.

'He's selfish, thoughtless and obsessive. He doesn't consider my feelings for one minute. Not one minute.'

Jo sighed and closed the fridge door. Wine wasn't going to solve anything at this point, least of all the headache that was fast developing. She needed water, and coffee, so black coffee would have to do. She popped a pod into her coffee maker and filled a glass of water, letting her mother rant for a while about how no one ever gave her a moment's thought.

'So what's new?' she cut in eventually, settling down on the sofa, coffee and water close to hand, only too aware that this was going to be a long phone call.

'It's this motorbike business. That's what's new. I tell you, Jocasta, it's the last straw.'

'Motorbike business?' she had Jo's attention now.

'He's bought himself this absolute wreck of a machine.'

'And he's riding around on it? I didn't know he could ride a motorbike.' Jo had visions of her father, an elderly man, with early cataracts, struggling to cope with an aggressively powerful machine. Had he gone mad? He was a retired orthopaedic surgeon for goodness' sake! He knew that doctors called bikers 'donors' because of how often they ended up donating organs they no longer needed after an accident. It was a bit late for a mid-life crisis, surely? She had been worried about his mental health and the possibility of early dementia, perhaps she had been right.

'Good God, no! It doesn't work. Or do anything useful at all. It's in pieces.' Jo sighed with relief as her mother continued. 'There's bits of it everywhere. He says it's a classic and he's rebuilding it or some such nonsense. All I know is that it's dirty, messy and he spreads black oil everywhere he goes.'

'Well, that's not so bad.' But Jo knew that to an obsessively tidy person like her mother, it was. She knew this because she too had slightly obsessive tendencies; she couldn't abide anything out of alignment, such as towels in the bathroom, clothes in her wardrobe, even the magazines on her coffee table, come to think of it. Everything had its place, be it organised by colour, alphabetical index or size, but her neuroses around order and tidiness were not a patch on her mother's.

'That depends on your point of view, obviously. If I had wanted to marry a mechanic with grubby fingernails and greasy overalls, I would have done.'

'Doesn't he wear gloves?' Jo couldn't understand what had got into him after all those years of protecting his surgeon's hands.

'Of course, but it still gets everywhere. I can't invite anyone back to the house for fear of what kind of state it's in. I shall be ostracised from the bridge club if I don't host an evening soon, but what if they see...'

'What? An oily rag? Will it really be the end of life as we know it?'

There was a short silence from the other end of the telephone and Jo sighed, knowing that in her mother's mind she had let her down again, and that meant one thing and one thing only. Jo's single status was about to be brought up.

'I might have known you wouldn't understand. And that's the reason you will never find yourself a decent husband, Jocasta. You have all the wrong priorities in life. Men expect a wife to...'

Jo rested the phone on her chest and let her mother continue for what was likely to be a very long speech, detailing all of her daughter's faults, not least her failure to marry some rich merchant banker from the city and produce hordes of well-scrubbed grandchildren. It had clearly not registered with her mother that her own husband didn't like her insistence on an immaculate house, so it couldn't be that which was keeping the men from beating down Jo's door. She sipped her water, closed her eyes and waited for the steady drone to finish, before hurriedly picking up the handset.

'Jocasta? Jocasta? Are you there?' her mother was saying.

'Yes of course, Ma,' Jo, while not actually lying, was definitely being economical with the truth.

'So what should I do?' her mother asked.

'Nothing. It's just a fad, he'll get bored with it soon enough.'

'That's easy for you to say. You don't have to live in a back-street garage.'

Jo took a deep breath. There was nothing else she could do; she was going to have to offer to help. She braced herself.

'I'll come and talk to him. I promise.' There. She had said it, she'd offered to go out and mediate, even though she knew she shouldn't. No good ever came from interceding or mediating in her parents' many squabbles. She should know that by now, but equally, she remembered her last conversation with her father. She had suggested taking up plumbing, but he had replied that it was for cardiologists and that orthopods were more like mechanics. Perhaps she was guilty of putting the idea in his head and, if so, it was only right that she should take some of the blame.

'Well, you'd better talk some sense into him soon or I shall start divorce proceedings,' her mother snapped back without so much as a thank you. But what did Jo expect? The woman had never appreciated anything she did.

11

There was a persistent wail coming from the waiting room, and Jo sincerely hoped that the child making the noise wasn't waiting to see her. As a woman she had more than her fair share of families on her list, with mums thinking, quite erroneously, that she would be good with children. She was a single woman, with no children, no siblings, and therefore no nephews or nieces, and it was a sad fact that most of her male colleagues were better with children, simply because they had experience dealing with their own offspring.

Taking a break from seeing patients, Jo popped up to the office to check her basket and to see if Jill's blood test result had come in overnight.

'I count my biscuits, you know,' Linda said as soon as Jo walked into the room.

Jo considered a flat denial of any knowledge of the missing biscuits, but when she had been in over the weekend she had left a couple of notes for Linda, so there was evidence she had been in the office. Deciding that honesty was the best policy, Jo smiled and held her hand up in apology.

'Sorry, I'll buy you a new packet.'

'Make sure you do that,' Linda accepted begrudgingly. 'And before you ask, no, we haven't had any results for Jill Hollingsworth, and I phoned pathology, but they have no record of her attending for the test.'

'Thanks, Linda, I'll give her a call then.' Jo was puzzled. Jill had always been a very compliant patient, and this behaviour wasn't like her.

'Oh, and a patient of yours was admitted to hospital on Saturday.' Linda checked the fax sheet in her hand for the name. 'Mark Caxton. Acute anxiety attack.'

That news stopped Jo in her tracks.

'What time on Saturday?'

Linda checked.

'He was seen by out of hours at five thirty. An ambulance was called and the doctor stayed until he was on his way. Then there's a note that the hospital called to say he was discharged on Sunday morning with a psychiatric follow-up appointment in two weeks, and the out of hours doctor called round on Sunday afternoon to check on him as requested, but there was nobody home.' Linda handed Jo the sheet and she read it eagerly.

'Thank goodness for that.' Jo felt relieved. She had been increasingly convinced that he couldn't be the murderer, but that he might confess anyway. Now Miller would have to drop him as a suspect. He had an alibi. If he went to hospital by ambulance at five thirty, he would have been in the emergency department for at least two hours and more likely four on a Saturday night, and there were security cameras around, and people like nurses, receptionists, and other patients who would be able to testify that he was there. Once on a ward, say by ten o'clock, quite possibly sedated, he would be under the watchful eye of the night staff, who had almost certainly been tasked with checking on him at regular intervals. There was no way Mark Caxton could have sneaked out, stolen a car and killed a woman unnoticed. Miller would have to let him go. Jo hurried down to her consulting room to make the call, just in case Mark hadn't already told them that he was in hospital at the time of the latest murder.

'There is absolutely no way he could have done it.' Jo took a bite of her prawn salad on wholemeal. When she phoned the police station she had been surprised to hear that Miller was already on his way to the surgery to see her, and doubly so when he appeared clutching a brown paper bag holding fresh sandwiches from the local bakery.

'We are doing our best to prove or disprove it.' Miller looked tired, although he was tucking into his ham and mustard roll with obvious hunger. Jo could sympathise. He must have been working every hour since the second body was found, not just trying to find the killer, but also dealing with press and distraught families. Food and sleep would have taken a back seat. 'We're speaking to staff and reviewing CCTV footage to see if there's any possibility of him having left, but I agree, it doesn't seem possible.' Much as he would have liked the opposite to be true, Jo thought, as they both continued to eat. Miller saw Mark as the obvious suspect; she saw him as the easy suspect, and life was rarely that easy. Even if the night nurse fell asleep, getting out of the hospital ward, not to mention back in, before he was missed would be nigh on impossible.

'Particularly as he was sedated soon after he arrived,' Miller continued with his mouth full, and Jo sent up a silent prayer of thanks. They absolutely had to scratch Mark as a suspect now. 'The second victim was identified by her husband, initially from a necklace she always wore, but it's now been confirmed by dental records. She's a Carol Johnson, married, no children, and you are listed as her doctor.'

'That's right. Both Carol and her husband, although I don't think I've ever seen him.'

'Anything you can tell us about her?'

'I looked her up as soon as I realised, but there's little in the records apart from birth control and well-woman checks,' Jo was irritated by the sigh of disappointment from Miller. 'What were you hoping? That Carol might have confided salacious details of her private life with the practice nurse?'

'It would have been nice.' Miller finished the roll and swept the crumbs from his suit.

'Well, sorry, but you've wasted a trip.'

'Not at all,' Miller smiled and looked Jo in the eye. She could feel a flush slowly rising up her neck. Why did her body always betray her in this way? 'I actually managed to eat lunch,' he finished, irritating Jo greatly.

'Do you have any other information for me?' she asked curtly, and was pleased to see that he had the good grace to look slightly embarrassed.

'The pathologist's initial findings are that both she and the previous victim died in the same way. Also, the fire investigator confirms the same method of fire starting.'

'So you think it's probably the same person?'

'It does seem likely.'

'What about the husband?' Jo asked, knowing that family was always high on the list of suspects. 'Could he have done this as a copycat of the first death?' She didn't want this to be the case, as it could still leave Mark in the frame for the first death.

'We never released the details of how the fire was started.'

'Anyone who had access to Mark's historic cases would know that.'

'Well yes, that's true, and there seem to be plenty of people on that list,' Miller conceded. 'But I don't think the husband could have had access, and he had a lot to lose financially. We're checking him out of course, but Mrs Johnson was the main breadwinner, she had no life insurance and they live in rented accommodation, so he won't even get the house.'

'Sounds pretty conclusive, if you think money is important to him.'

'Oh yes. He certainly seemed more upset about being left out of pocket than losing his wife, plus he was out with some friends until nearly two in the morning, and she was already dead by then.' Miller managed to convey his dislike of Mr Johnson. 'And the first victim's husband has a pretty good alibi, too.'

At least he was keeping an open mind and looking at other suspects, Jo thought, even while trying to persuade himself it was Mark.

'I don't suppose there's any evidence the two men knew each other?'

'And colluded you mean? Not yet, but of course we are looking for any connections between the two victims and their families, and where each husband was when the other's wife was murdered but...' Jo understood his uncertainty and agreed. She just couldn't see it. She knew it happened in fiction, she had seen the film *Strangers on a Train*, but in real life? Would two unconnected men really agree to kill the other's wife? It was just too complex.

'Have you managed to trace any men buying cans of petrol?'

'Checking them all out now, but nothing interesting so far, and we are looking at everyone, not just Mark Buxton,' he hastily assured her.

'And no ideas about where the two women were before they got killed?'

'Nope.' If he objected to her quizzing him about what was his job rather than hers, he didn't show it. Jo thought that he actually appreciated someone going through all the possible lines of enquiry, just so that he felt sure he hadn't missed anything.

'What about other leads like CCTV?' she asked.

Miller shook his head.

'Nothing worthwhile so far.'

'It can't be easy to avoid CCTV in a town like Hastings.'

'Almost impossible,' Miller agreed. 'But we haven't found anything even vaguely interesting. So the killer's either highly skilled or incredibly lucky. We're also working through the list of other arsonists in the area, and extending our parameters on that, both geographically and to include those who might be on a trajectory that could lead them to commit this sort of crime.' He finished, hoping that Jo wouldn't see this as an admission that they were combing the haystack in the hope of finding anything that resembled a sewing implement.

Jo nodded and gave Miller a look that told him she had seen right through him.

'And of course we are trying to discover who each of the victims was seeing the night they were killed.'

'What about asking the press to help us with that? Put out an appeal for the men to come forward so you can eliminate them from your enquiries.'

'We have to be careful about that. These women have families we need to consider before we announce to the world that they were committing adultery.'

Jo was surprised that he was showing such sensitivity to the feelings of the families. Maybe he wasn't as tough and no nonsense as she had always thought him to be.

'So we've decided just to ask for witnesses who may have seen them, rather than specifically saying they were out with men. We aren't sure they were, anyway, it's just the most likely explanation. The appeal will go out later today.'

'I'm glad you're thinking about the families.'

'Well, I'm not sure my superiors are,' he confided. 'They just don't want it to come across as though we are in any way suggesting the victims were to blame for their own deaths. That always looks bad, apparently.' Jo could see that Miller was angry about this. 'Personally, I don't think anything should stand in the way of us finding this man before he does it again.'

Jo agreed, but Miller being removed from the case for upsetting his bosses wouldn't help anyone.

'Whatever the reason, the result's the right one. It's the right message to put out,' she reassured him, and was pleased to see him nod in agreement. He gave a long sigh and wiped his face with his hands.

'It's a tough case,' she murmured.

'Pretty full on,' he agreed. 'It's been nice to get out of the office and have a break. Even if we have been discussing the case. It's less frenetic here. More civilised.'

'Huh, you should come during baby clinic. It's not civilised then.' Jo mentally kicked herself. She knew Miller and his wife were trying, so far unsuccessfully, to have a baby. She looked at him closely for any sign that she had hit a nerve, but he had turned quickly away and his face was blank by the time he looked back at her.

'Anywhere without Bob Jeffries counts as civilised,' he said with a small smile, and she had to agree.

Jo had finally plucked up the courage to go round and see her parents after evening surgery. She had pre-armed herself with a box of her mother's favourite chocolates and an appointment to meet Kate in The Stag at nine-thirty, so that she couldn't be persuaded to stay the night. Kate had rung Jo in excitement just as she was finishing her evening list, having seen Detective Inspector Miller on the six o'clock news, and was insistent that they meet later that night to discuss the man she described as the 'hunky detective'. Jo readily agreed, to the meeting up rather than the description of Miller as hunky, so that for once she wouldn't have to lie about needing to leave straight after dinner. Jo was well aware that she was a bad liar and that her mother saw through her excuses, but this time Jo would be able to look her in the eye when she said she had to go.

Her route to her childhood home took her past the farm where Jill Hollingsworth lived with her husband, and she decided to take the opportunity to call in. She had tried phoning but there had been no answer and no facility to leave a message, so an unannounced visit was the only option.

As she pulled up outside the small farmhouse, there was no welcoming curl of smoke from the chimney and no lights on. Jo expected a working farm to be muddy and utilitarian, but even by those standards this seemed uncared for and unclean. The windows were grimy and the woodwork paint was cracked and peeling. A dog barked in the yard, but there was no other sign of life about the place and it felt cold and empty. She could see a car parked by the side of the house which suggested someone was in, and went up to the front door and knocked. There was no response. She knocked again with the same result, but once the dog stopped barking she was sure she could hear some sound inside; the television, perhaps, or the radio?

'Hello?' Jo called out to anyone who might be inside and set the dog barking again. 'Jill? Are you there?' She put her hand on the door-knob, uncertain if she should try and open the door in the hope that her voice would be heard better.

'She's out.'

Jo jumped and gave a little, involuntary scream at the sudden voice behind her. She turned to see a man in his thirties, dressed in dirty overalls and muddy boots, looking at her with deep suspicion.

'I'm sorry,' she said to him, smiling with relief. 'You startled me. Jill's out is she?'

'That's what I said, yes. Who are you?'

'Her doctor. Dr Hughes.' Jo held out her hand and the man reluctantly took it, despite having filthy hands. Jo resisted the temptation to wipe her hand down her clothes. Her hands would be easy to clean with the wet wipes she always kept in the car, her linen suit less so.

'Are you her husband?' She knew that Jill was married, but didn't think she had ever seen him. He was probably on someone else's list or even registered at another practice. There was no rule that said married couples had to have the same doctor.

'Yes. Is something wrong?' he asked. 'Did she call you?' Jo detected genuine anxiety in his voice.

'No, no, I just wanted a word, that's all,' she said reassuringly, but he didn't look like he quite believed her.

'I could hear the television on, so I just thought she couldn't hear me knocking.' Jo gestured towards the door and stood slightly to one side to allow him to open it, but he made no move to do so.

'She's staying at her mother's for a while,' he explained. 'I must've left the telly on when I went to check the cows.' He still made no move to go into the house or to invite her in, despite her smiling and waiting for him to do so.

'Well,' Jo finally said. 'Do you know when she'll be back?' He shook his head and said nothing, but looked pointedly at her car. 'Could you give me her address, then?' Jo persisted. She wasn't sure why, it wasn't

99

urgent after all, but there was something about the man's attitude that had got to her, made her want to be sure.

'I'll be seeing her tomorrow and I'll tell her you've been round.'

'Perhaps I can give you a note for her then.' Jo dug in her bag for pen and paper and scribbled a quick note to her patient, just asking her to get in touch with the surgery, nothing confidential, as she didn't have an envelope to put it in and seal the message from prying eyes. She handed the note to the man, who shoved it in a pocket.

'Bye then,' he said, and turned away, leaving her no choice but to walk back to her car.

'Thank you for calling, Doctor. I'll let Jill know,' he said from the doorway, as she got into the car, friendly now that he was sure she was leaving, but he still hadn't opened the door and Jo wondered exactly what it was he didn't want her to see. She gave herself a mental shake. He probably just didn't want her to see the piles of dirty dishes, as he may not have tidied up while his wife was away. But as she turned the Audi round and drove away, she looked at the man in her rear view mirror; he didn't go into the house, but stood watching until she was out of sight.

As Jo parked outside The Old Vicarage she tried to relax, but there was a tight ball of anxiety building deep down in her stomach that had little to do with her run-in with Jill Hollingsworth's husband. It was more to do with seeing her mother. She knew the dread she felt about it was disproportionate, but it had been there, steadily building, since she had arranged the visit, and the strange incident at the farmhouse had only temporarily distracted her. She loved her parents dearly, but her feelings were complicated by the knowledge that she was a disappointment to her mother. She never stopped telling Jo exactly what her problems were and what she needed to do better. Deep down, Jo knew that she would never please her and that she should stop trying, but it was easier said than done.

She tucked the chocolates under her arm and looked around her as she walked to the front door. She was surprised to see no lights on anywhere. The house had a curiously empty look to it, and her mother's car was not neatly parked to the side of the front door as it usually was. In fact, she couldn't see it anywhere. Jo tried the door and found it locked. She had a key in a drawer at home, but as she had never had to use it, she didn't keep it on her already-overloaded key ring. Mixed in with the relief that she wasn't going to have to face an inquisition into her love life she felt mild irritation that they weren't there, which was highly unfair to her parents, as she hadn't told them she was coming. Having walked around the outside of the house and seen no sign of life, and having got no response to ringing the bell or telephoning the home phone, Jo returned to her car and threw the chocolates on the back seat. She would have to ring tomorrow and find out where they both had been, despite the fact that her mother would use it as an opportunity to give her a lecture about manners and it being polite to arrange visits in advance, even visits to family. And she would have to find the time to visit again.

Kate was already sitting in their usual corner at The Stag with a pint of her favourite Shepherd Neame Spitfire in front of her when Jo arrived. She went to the bar to buy herself a large glass of Pinot Grigio. The barman didn't need to be told she liked it served with one cube of ice, as he had served her many times before. The Stag was a convenient place for the two of them to meet, close to both their homes in the old town; besides which, it had everything you could want from a pub, and a bit more: a warm welcome, an open fire, Kate's favourite beer, and a display case containing an ancient mummified cat.

'Bet you need that after your visit home,' Kate commented on the large glass of wine Jo was carrying as she sat in the chair opposite her friend.

'Yes,' Jo agreed, 'Although no one was in.' Kate looked suitably surprised by this. 'So tell me about the press conference then, I missed the evening news.'

'Ah yes, the scrummy DI Miller.'

Jo rolled her eyes.

'He's not that scrummy.'

'Really?' Kate was unconvinced. 'I'm disappointed in you, Dr Hughes. You need to be on the lookout for fanciable men. Even at work.' Kate drank some of her beer. 'Unless, of course, they are also your patients,' she conceded, 'or in my case, a client.'

'I'll have you know that he's not fanciable, Ms Ward, even if he is good-looking. For me to consider him fanciable he would have to have a nice personality as well, and he hasn't. Not to mention the fact that he is married.' Her point made, Jo changed the subject back to the press conference. 'What did he say, then?'

If Kate was disappointed at her friend's response, she knew better than to show it.

'Well, he was appealing for anyone who might have seen either of the two victims earlier in the evening or on the night they were killed to get in touch. They are trying to trace the women's movements and who they were with.'

'It makes you wonder, doesn't it?' Jo said thoughtfully.

'What?'

'I mean, these were both married women, weren't they?'

'And your point is?' Kate asked.

'Well, if the police are trying to track their movements, it's unlikely they were with their husbands, otherwise the police would know where they were, wouldn't they?'

'I see where you're going with this,' Kate replied. 'You think they were out with their lovers.'

'I wouldn't necessarily go that far,' Jo corrected her. 'I just think they must have been out with someone they didn't want their husbands to know about.' She paused. 'Which quite possibly might mean they were seeing someone else; a lover or a potential lover, at least,' she finally conceded.

'Exactly.'

'But it might be something entirely different.'

'Like what.'

'Like, ooh, I don't know, a surprise. Planning a party for their husbands or something.'

'You think these women were out with a party planner?'

'Well, it's possible, isn't it?'

Kate shook her head at her friend's innocence and drank more of her beer before responding.

'Which brings me onto a bit of gossip I heard,' Kate leant closer to keep the conversation more confidential, although there was no one seated near them. 'A friend told me that a friend of a friend told her that this latest victim, what was her name?'

'Carol Johnson,' Jo told her.

'That's right, Carol, used a dating website to find men.'

'That's awful. She was married, for goodness' sake.'

'Maybe the marriage wasn't a happy one.'

'Well clearly not, if she was looking for someone else.'

'Not necessarily,' Kate corrected her. 'I hate to tell you this, Jo, but sometimes marriages can be, you know, open?'

'No, no, not happy ones,' Jo was adamant. 'I don't honestly believe that, I mean, how happy can a marriage be if that's how they are behaving, and what about the men she met, do you think she told them she was married?'

'Yes. That's the point, Jo, she was using an adultery website.'

Jo was horrified.

'An adultery website?' she said, rather more loudly than expected, and Kate shushed her. They both looked round to see if anyone had heard her exclamation, but fortunately no one seemed to be giving them funny looks.

'I cannot believe such a thing exists,' Jo continued quietly. 'I mean, that there would be people openly looking for affairs like that.'

'I can assure you they do exist.' Kate got out her phone and started searching the internet. 'Look.'

She handed her phone to Jo, who stared at the screen, open-mouthed in amazement.

12

'I'm going to say something really sexist now,' Jo warned Kate as they walked back to Jo's flat, climbing the steep twitten; one of many narrow, unlit passages between the houses that could be found all over the old town. 'I can see that there might be enough men wanting to have affairs to keep a website like that going, but women? It's just unbelievable.'

'Well, it wouldn't work if there were only men registered, would it?' Kate responded, slightly out of breath despite all her time in the gym. 'Or rather, that's a different sort of website altogether.'

'Have you ever tried internet dating?' Jo asked her friend.

'God, yes,' Kate paused for a moment to catch her breath. 'Complete disaster. Why? Were you thinking of giving it a go?'

'Well, yes,' she searched in her bag for her keys and opened the door. 'I have thought about it, but never actually had the nerve. What happened to you?'

'I learnt a very valuable lesson,' Kate followed Jo up the stairs. 'Never give anyone any real details about yourself until you are absolutely sure they aren't some kind of crazy stalker. Good job I'm a lawyer, because it took all sorts of legal threats and an injunction to scare him off.'

Jo stared at her in amazement.

'I'll remove that from the list of things I can do if I get desperate, then!' Jo said as she filled the kettle with water from her filter jug, before asking, 'Coffee or wine?'

Kate looked at her as if she were mad.

'Wine of course. Coffee at this time of night would keep me awake.'

'I do have decaff,' Jo responded with a smile, because she knew her friend's opinion on the point of coffee without caffeine, and the snort of derision from Kate as she settled herself on the immaculate cream sofa showed that she hadn't changed her mind.

The advantage of an open-plan living room and kitchen was that they could easily continue their conversation as Jo opened the wine.

'To be fair, I know lots of people who have managed to find what they were looking for and not had any problems, so I'm not a good example. You just have to be a little more careful than I was.'

'So what happened?'

'We exchanged emails on the dating site and agreed to meet in a wine bar. I had a perfectly nice evening with him, he made me laugh, he seemed like a nice guy, and we agreed to meet again. Then I met Pete, do you remember Pete?'

'The plumber?'

'That's the one. Came to fix a leak and stayed for six weeks.'

'That was soon after I met you, but he seemed nice.' Jo brought two glasses over to where Kate was sitting and put them on the coasters she had placed ready on the coffee table.

'He was indeed,' Kate smiled wistfully at the memory, 'so I cancelled the second date with the internet guy. Of course, he had my mobile number and kept calling and texting, refusing to go away, even when I ignored him.'

'I remember you telling me you were changing your number because some man was harassing you. I hadn't realised you met him online. Didn't he track you down at work as well?'

'Yes. During the evening I'd told him a bit about myself, you know, about being a solicitor working in criminal law, having an office in the main town. I didn't give him my life history, but he had enough to track me down again after I changed my phone number. He turned up at the court to try and speak to me, but I refused to see him and they threw him out. Stupid of him really, there's bound to be security at a court, but he honestly thought I'd change my mind I suppose. Couldn't believe I wouldn't fall at his feet. It got a bit awkward, but fortunately the threat of legal action against him was enough to scare him away.'

Jo brought her laptop over to where they were sitting.

'In some ways it was lucky you found out what he was like early on. Imagine if you'd tried to end it after you had been going out for a while.'

Kate nodded.

'I know, lucky break. Of course, you don't just find nutters like that online. I've dealt with stalking cases a couple of times, and neither of them were from internet dating.'

'Right. Let's take a look at this website, then. What was it called?'

'SusSEXtra,' Kate answered, spelling it out. 'It's a conflation, you know, a word made up of others, in this case Sussex, SEX, helpfully in capitals just to make sure you know what it's all about, and extra, I presume for extramarital.'

Jo looked horrified.

'I know, I know, but I didn't name it, did I?' Kate took the laptop from Jo and typed the name in.

The first page asked for their gender, the gender of the people they wanted to meet, a first name, and an email address. Kate paused.

'Why are we doing this?' she asked.

'If you'd rather not…'

'It's not that, but are we going on the site simply to see what it's like out of curiosity? Or to see if we can find either or both of the victims registered? Only if we want to see if we can find the women we are going to have to register as a man, or as bi or wanting a threesome.'

Jo looked appalled.

'You think they were into that sort of thing?'

'I don't know, and that's the problem. We don't know what they would be interested in, and so we can't put in a profile likely to bring them up as a match.'

Jo looked as if she was rapidly changing her mind about everything.

'But if we did put in a fairly basic profile, do you think we would be able to find them?'

'It's unlikely, in my view. Apart from anything else, they probably wouldn't use their real names.'

Jo thought for a while.

'I just want to have a bit more of an idea about the site, and if it could be where he meets them,' she said finally. 'And I have to admit to a certain amount of curiosity.'

Kate smiled as she clicked and typed. 'Let's say we are a woman looking for a man, then. First name?' She looked at her friend, 'And don't say Jo.'

'Mary?' Jo suggested.

'Nice name, but not really, you know, sexy. How about Vicky, short for Victoria's Secret,' Kate didn't wait for Jo's approval but added the name Vicky.

'Ah, now we have to put in an email address.'

She clicked open a new tab and quickly registered a new Outlook account for Vicky S.

'Have you done this before?' Jo asked. 'Only you seem rather experienced.'

'I told you, I learnt from my first foray into internet dating. Now if I do it, I don't just use a fake name, I have a fake email and a throw away phone, a suitably unrecognisable photo, and I make sure I never tell them anything true about myself.'

Jo thought about this as Kate continued setting up her new persona.

'What if you like them though? And want to start a real relationship. There has to be a time when you tell them the truth.'

'Of course,' Kate said glibly. 'Once you've thoroughly vetted them.'

'Well, don't they object to the fact that you aren't who you said you were?'

'Dunno, I've never got that far.' Kate typed in the new email address. 'And anyway, you have to remember they may not be who they say they are, either. Password. How about 2ladies? Like in Cabaret? Think you'll remember it or do you want to write it down?'

Jo wrote the password down on a notepad.

'Right. Next question. Kate read from the screen, "If we were alone for the night I would like to…" They suggest you try to make it sexy and inviting. What do you think we should write, Vicky?' she glanced at Jo, who was looking bemused. 'On second thoughts, I think you need to leave this to me.'

Jo had no argument with that, she was still struggling to take it all in. She looked at what Kate was writing and decided to drink her wine. She needed it.

'Right. Photo. We can use one we download from the internet or we can dress you up and take one.'

'I don't know, I mean I don't think anyone I know would be on this website but it would be really embarrassing if they were and they, you know, recognised me.' The thought of a colleague or, even worse, a patient seeing her picture was enough to make her blood run cold.

'Relax, Jo,' Kate laughed. 'The advantage of using your own picture, suitably blurred or photo-shopped to ensure your own mother wouldn't pick you out in a line-up, is that photos taken from the internet are so obviously fake, it's got to the point that some models are threatening to sue people who use their pictures on these sites.'

'It's really that common?'

'Yes. It's called catfishing, but most people don't fall for it, and along with not posting any picture at all it just tends to suggest you have something to hide, and you get ignored.'

Jo didn't seem convinced, but Kate filled up her wine glass and sorted out a revealing top, and having rejected all Jo's understated jewellery, insisted Jo wore her own dangly earrings and matching necklace. Then she did Jo's makeup more heavily than she would ever do herself and fluffed her hair up. Kate rifled through Jo's jewellery box again and picked out her grandmother's wedding ring and went to slip it on the fourth finger of Jo's left hand, but she pulled away.

'What are you doing?'

'You are supposed to be married, so you need a wedding ring.'

'No, no, you can't do that, it's bad luck,' and Jo snatched the ring from her and threw it back in the box.

'I didn't know you were superstitious?'

'I'm not,' Jo paused. 'Except about this. Wearing a wedding ring when you're not married means you'll never get married.'

Kate was amazed that her normally rational friend was giving any credence to such an old wives' tale.

'How are you supposed to try it on for size?'

'I suppose that would be okay, provided you were engaged.'

'Well, anyway, if you are right that means I won't ever get married then, because I've done it hundreds of times, whenever I needed a bit of space.'

But Jo wasn't going to be persuaded.

'I know it's stupid, but indulge me. I'll put my left hand out of sight.'

She put one hand behind her back and Kate decided to let it go.

'Okay, now pout like you're taking a selfie.' Jo obediently pouted and Kate took a photo on her phone.

'There you go, no one would ever think it was you,' she showed Jo, who had to acknowledge that she was right. Her normal image was understated, smart, and controlled, whereas the picture Kate had taken was of a far more free spirit, sexy and rather wanton. Jo was surprised and, she had to admit, slightly excited to see this alter ego.

'Never knew you had it in you, did you?' Kate teased as she uploaded the picture, and Jo poured them both another glass of wine.

'Now, what's next, ah yes, your preferences.'

Jo sat down and looked at the new page that Kate had opened.

'Definitely a non-smoker, and he needs to be taller than me.'

'I'll put six foot then, because they all exaggerate their height. And length,' she added, taking a sip of her wine. 'Build: let's say toned. Back to you. Favourite position?'

'For what?' Jo asked and then giggled as she realised what Kate meant. 'Really? I haven't even met the guy yet?' She looked at the list. 'What on earth is cowgirl?'

'Oh for goodness' sake, woman!' Kate took over again, and quickly completed the list of Vicky's preferences. 'And finally, what gets you going?'

They both looked at the list.

'Wow,' Kate said.

'Are they even legal?' Jo asked, astounded.

'Most of them,' Kate replied. 'Between consenting adults, anyway. I suggest we play it safe.' She ticked a couple of the tamer suggestions and submitted them before Jo could object.

Payment and phone number were not required at this stage, only once Vicky decided to contact anyone who was matched to her or who responded to her post, so Kate clicked finish and raised her glass.

'Here's to Vicky!'

They clinked glasses.

'What's next?' Jo asked.

'They'll send through some suggested matches that you can contact or you can wait for a man who has been sent your details in the same way to contact you. I suggest you get a pay as you go mobile ready.'

'I'm not going to actually contact any of them,' Jo said, horrified. 'One of them could be a serial killer.'

'Good point.' The thought made them both feel suddenly sober.

'That's why I need to tell the police about Carol being on here. I mean even if they can't find him through this, they need to warn people.'

'That could be difficult, from a legal perspective. I mean, they don't know the killer meets women through the website, the only evidence we have is that one of the women reportedly used it.'

'I can't not tell them. It might be their only way of tracking him down.'

'I know, but...' Kate paused, before resigning herself to the fact that it had to be done. 'I suppose I ought to be the one to tell them, as the information came from a friend of mine. I just don't want it brought up every time I go in there to see a client. I mean, if those Neanderthals find out that I've been looking at websites like this, I'll never hear the end of it. I can't do it, Jo, I'll never be taken seriously again.'

They both thought for a moment.

'Presumably they gave out a number for people to call with information. We could ring it anonymously, couldn't we?' Jo suggested.

'They get thousands of calls after a press conference,' Kate responded. 'It would be easy for one call to get missed, but you're right, it's better than not telling them at all.'

They both thought about it some more, knowing that it wasn't an ideal solution, and feeling guilty.

'I'm sorry, but I think it's best if we tell them in person,' Jo was suddenly decisive. 'I don't mind doing it.' She thought for a moment. 'There's a sergeant I know from custody, but I saw him in the incident room, I think he was setting it up. Oh, what's his name?' she asked herself, then it suddenly came to her, 'Nugent!'

'I know him,' Kate responded with excitement. 'Nigel Nugent, but they all call him Nerdy Nigel. He's a sweetie, you could certainly ask to speak to him. He'd pass the message on, and might not even involve you at all.'

'Okay. I'll go and speak to Nerdy Nigel tomorrow, as it's my morning off.'

'Thank you,' Kate hugged her, very aware that she had chickened out, and that Jo was doing the right thing for her friend, and the women of Hastings.

13

The office Jo had been taken to by Nigel was little more than a station-ery cupboard, but it offered the privacy she felt she needed to explain about Carol Johnson's use of an internet dating site. She had hoped that he would be as shocked as she had been that it was aimed at peo-ple already in a relationship, but he wasn't.

'I have heard of them,' he said, clearing his throat in embarrass-ment. 'There are quite a few offering no-strings sexual encounters and swinging and such like. At least, I believe there are.'

She consoled herself with the fact that he seemed to be taking it seriously, although she quickly changed her mind when he said she would have to tell DI Miller.

'Can't you?' she pleaded.

'He's going to ask me how I heard and want to speak to you anyway, so it's best to get it over with.' Nigel stood and turned to open the door for her, and she squeezed past him into the corridor. She would have liked to tell him to make sure that she spoke to Miller alone or that at the very least not have Sergeant Jeffries present, but Nigel was already heading off down the corridor at speed, and she had to hurry to keep up with him.

He opened the door of the incident room and ushered her in. Jo reluctantly came into the room behind him and tried not to show her dismay as she realised the whole team was there, in the middle of the morning briefing. A sea of tired faces turned to look at her with undisguised interest, including Miller, who was standing at the front of the room by the whiteboard. She felt a blush of embarrass-ment developing, and turned away. Her heart sank as her eyes locked with Sergeant Jeffries, who was leaning nonchalantly against the wall, clutching a mug of tea and a bacon roll. Did the man ever stop eating? Miller raised an eyebrow at Nigel's interruption, before nodding to the colourless, middle-aged man who was standing next to him to continue his report. As everyone turned back to the front, Jo could feel the redness spread up her neck until the heat was radiating from her cheeks, as she hoped against hope that she wouldn't have to talk about the website in front of everyone. She tried to concentrate on listening to the man who collated all the reports listing a swathe of negatives in a dull monotone: no sign of the car being stolen earlier in the evening on CCTV; no one saw or heard anything from the door to doors, until the explosion, of course; and no car was heard leaving the scene after that. He went on to report on the predictably massive response to the press briefing, and the call for information on where the two women had been on the nights they were murdered, but none of the callers seemed to have any useful information. According to the people who had rung in, Carol might have been in the Hastings Arms although it could have been on another night; the two women were definitely together in Brighton the day after the first woman was murdered, one caller was sure; and according to another caller, the first victim had been at school with a very weird boy fifteen years ago, and he was probably the killer.

'We checked him out.' The collator seemed more animated at this point. 'But it turns out he joined the police and was custody sergeant in Brighton the night of her murder, as witnessed by large numbers of colleagues and criminals, some of whom did agree that he was weird.' There was a ripple of laughter as he continued to tell Miller and the room that some calls were still being followed up, but not one credible sighting of either woman had come to light. Jo was silently praying that Miller would end the briefing and that she could speak to him in his office, but he nodded to a female officer who Jo recognised as PC Jayne Hales, whom she had worked with several times in the past, and she came up to the front.

'The drug screen result is through on victim one.' She paused, and Jo could sense a quickening of interest. 'It's positive for GHB, mixed with quite a high level of alcohol.'

Jo knew that GHB, or Gamma Hydroxybutrate as it was more properly known, lasted in the blood for two to four hours and in the urine for up to twelve hours. It was known as the date rape drug, because when victims were tested for it the next day it was usually negative, but in this case, the victim had died and metabolism of the drug had been halted in time for the test to still be positive.

'So he could meet them for a drink and then slip them the drug that way,' a youngish constable commented.

Jayne nodded.

'That would explain why they went with him.'

'It also explains why they don't do more to try and escape the car when he pours petrol in,' Miller added. 'Between the drugs, the alcohol and parking up against the post so they can't open their doors, these women don't stand a chance of getting away.'

'Let's just hope they were out of it enough not to know what was happening,' Jeffries added sombrely, and while Jo acknowledged that it was a horrific way to die, she was strangely comforted to know that the victims might not have known much about it, and she could tell others in the room were thinking the same.

'Nigel?' Miller called him to the front and Jo felt a spasm of fear. It would be her turn in a minute, and she was vaguely grateful that Nigel didn't go to the front of the room, but stayed where he was to give the report, although in some ways that was worse, because everyone had turned in their seats and they were now looking directly at her.

Nigel cleared his throat and launched into his update.

'As with the first case, the mobile phone was too damaged by the fire for us to get anything useful from the SIM card. I've started the process to get the call log and data from the phone company for the second victim's mobile, but as we still haven't had anything through from the first victim's phone company yet, it will probably be a while before the second woman's data is available.'

'It always takes time, Nigel.' Miller was trying to sound upbeat. 'Anything on their computers?'

Nigel shook his head.

'Not at first look, Guv, but I've sent them off to technical to see if anything's been hidden or erased.'

'Good. Now, last but not least.' Miller looked at Jo expectantly.

Everyone turned their attention to her, and she took a deep breath to steady herself.

'I'm sorry, I didn't mean to interrupt your meeting,' she could have kicked herself as soon as the words were out of her mouth. It wasn't like she had just barged in, Nigel had brought her, although he hadn't explained that a briefing was taking place and everyone was there, but apologising just made her look weak. 'Perhaps we could have a word in private?'

Everyone looked at Miller, and they were clearly disappointed when, after a moment's thought, a moment that seemed an eternity to Jo, he nodded. She let her breath out with a sigh, not having realised that she had been holding it until that moment.

'Right everyone, let's get on with this,' Miller said, and people were suddenly galvanised into action. 'I want all spare hands checking CCTV or back round all the pubs and clubs, this guy must have slipped up and appeared somewhere, someone must have seen him load a drunk or drugged woman into a car. Nigel, chase for phone and laptop info, will you? We need to know where these women met him.'

As people moved back to their desks to get on with their tasks, he turned and gestured for Jo to follow him to an area away from the action, where there was a small amount of free space. It was not as private as she would have liked, and, she noted with dismay, Jeffries followed them. They were only a matter of steps away from the rest of the team, and while this was definitely better than having to give a report to them all, she was sure that they were all feigning a lack of interest and were really listening to every word. Miller and Jeffries were looking at her expectantly, and she found herself feeling just as she had done as a student when singled out to answer a question on a consultant ward round when she was on a surgical rotation. She had the sinking feeling that she was about to disappoint at least half the audience, either by giving a stupid answer and thereby irritating the easily irritated surgeon, or by answering correctly, much to the chagrin of her rivals, who would be desperate for her to mess up so that they could be best student. Of course, in this instance, Miller was the surgeon and Jeffries was her rival student, hoping that she had something stupid to say.

'Um, I wondered if you had checked out dating websites?' she said tentatively, her voice not coming out quite as strong as she would have liked. 'As the place where he might be meeting his victims.'

Miller looked disappointed, but at least that meant he had wanted her to succeed, she thought. Jeffries snorted in derision.

'What do you reckon he puts in the advert, then? Partner wanted for short-term relationship, GSOH and a love of self-immolation required?' Someone sniggered.

'Smokers preferred,' another voice chipped in, proving to Jo that they had indeed all been listening.

'For late night barbecues in the country.'

Jo was livid. She hadn't come here to be ridiculed. This was exactly what she had been hoping to avoid by going to see Nigel. Perhaps she would have been better off speaking to Jayne Hales. At least she was giving Jo a look of sympathy. Miller raised his hand and everyone fell silent.

'Only, you see, the second victim, Carol Johnson, was apparently a user of one,' she persevered angrily.

She could feel the mood change, she wasn't just interfering, she had information.

'How do you know that?' Miller asked.

'Someone told a friend of mine, who told me.'

'Gossip then,' Jeffries said in a tone that spoke volumes.

'Gossip that might help you find the killer.' Jo was trying to stay calm. She knew her information was weak and she would far rather have spoken quietly to Miller on his own or have Nigel pass it on, but he had brought her into the incident room, like a lamb to the slaughter, and she could feel her cheeks burning with a mixture of anger and embarrassment.

'There are hundreds of those websites, thousands even. Trawling through them all would be a massive job,' Jeffries was discouraging.

'We could start by looking at the local ones,' Jayne Hales was trying to be more positive, but then turned away to answer her phone.

'We can narrow it down more than that,' Jo said. 'It was a local website specialising in affairs, called, um,' she steeled herself, 'SusSEXtra, according to my friend.'

A smirk appeared on Jeffries' face and he looked as though he was about to make another suggestive comment when Jayne Hales called out.

'Guv!' She was waving a scrap of paper on which she had been taking notes as she quietly spoke on the phone. 'Fingerprint on a coke can found in a hedgerow near the visitor centre matches Mark Caxton.'

'Yes!' Jeffries raised a clenched fist and grabbed his jacket. Miller was already on his way out as Jeffries hurried after him, both passing Jo without so much as an acknowledgement of her existence.

Everyone in the room was busy congratulating each other and making preparations for Mark to be brought back in. Miller was going to question him again, and maybe this time they had enough evidence to press charges.

Nigel looked at Jo, obviously embarrassed by how she had been treated.

'I promise you we'll follow up on your information, Dr Hughes.'

'I'll make sure of it,' Jayne added.

'Thank you,' Jo responded with as much dignity as she could muster, and left.

Jo went straight round to Kate's office, still flushed, but by the time she arrived it was purely with anger rather than embarrassment.

'He just pushed passed me, with that odious little man running along behind him, and went out to arrest Mark Caxton again. He is absolutely fixated on that poor boy being the culprit, and just isn't interested in anyone else. I mean he was in hospital for goodness' sake. How could he have done it?'

'To be fair,' Kate responded, playing devils' advocate, 'with a solid piece of evidence linking a suspect to a murder scene, Miller has no choice but to pick him up. Imagine if he didn't and another woman was killed? He'd be pilloried in the press, and probably spend the rest of his career directing traffic.'

Jo sighed. She knew Kate was right.

'Why on earth did you march in and tell him about it, anyway? I thought we agreed you would tell Nerdy Nigel on the quiet.'

'I did, and he insisted I tell Miller, but didn't warn me that he was in the middle of a briefing at the time.' Jo put her head in her hands. 'Oh, Kate, it was just awful.'

Kate rubbed her friend's back sympathetically, just as Jo's mobile started ringing. Jo fished her phone out of her handbag and checked to see who the caller was before answering.

'Hi Linda,' she said and then listened. 'Yes, okay,' Jo checked her watch. 'What's this about, do you know?' She listened again, becoming visibly more upset than she already was. 'What? A complaint? From whom?' She listened again. 'Really? Right. Of course. I'll be there in about an hour.'

'A complaint?' Kate queried, concerned for her friend.

'It's a long story. Basically, a patient of mine hasn't been responding to requests to have a blood test, so I popped round to see her yesterday, but she wasn't there, so I left a note with her husband. Apparently that amounts to harassment and they've made a complaint, and now Hugh wants to see me. I was only trying to help.'

'Hugh will see that, Jo, I'm sure.'

Jo had her head in her hands again and Kate gently patted her back.

'This is not a good day,' Jo said, slowly lifting her head.

'No, I can see that,' Kate agreed.

'I seem to be having a problem with men. First Miller and Jeffries, and now Mr Hollingsworth complaining to Hugh, and all because of that stupid, stupid Gerry Brown.'

Kate stiffened.

'What's Gerry Brown got to do with it?'

Jo picked up at Kate's harsh tone and looked at her friend.

'He's our locum. He gave Jill's husband a prescription when he should have insisted that Jill came in. Why?'

Kate bit her lip.

'You know I was telling you about my stalker?' Jo nodded. 'Well, he was a doctor called Gerry Brown. Do you think there could be two?'

'Tallish with thick, wiry brown hair and a beard?'

'You just described him to a T.'

They sat in silence for a moment.

'I think that officially confirms to me that he is a, a...' Jo struggled.

'Twat, I think, is the word you are searching for,' Kate smiled, 'or possibly tosser.'

'I take it you don't want me to send him your best wishes?' Jo finished with a mischievous smile, and Kate laughed.

'No. But you can knee him in the groin for me if you want.'

Jo quite quickly managed to persuade Hugh Grantham that she had done nothing wrong in visiting her patient unannounced; indeed she had been going above and beyond her duty.

He advised that she should stick strictly to protocol from now on, which meant that Jill should not be prescribed any further tablets until her condition was reviewed, and that when she requested a prescription Linda should respond to that effect.

'Worst case scenario is that they'll change doctors,' Hugh said, but Jo worried that it might actually mean Jill would stop treatment, and would become as chronically ill as she had been when she first saw her. Tired, depressed, overweight, losing her hair, she had been so much better once the treatment had taken effect and she had stabilised, she lost loads of weight and had come into the surgery positively bouncing with energy. Jo couldn't understand why she had stopped attending or having blood tests.

'We can't get too involved, Jo,' Hugh advised. 'It's her life and we have done everything expected of us.'

That was all very well, but he couldn't stop Jo thinking that something was wrong for Jill to behave like this. There wasn't anything more she could do, though. A packed clinic soon took all her attention, and Jill was forgotten.

Having finished surgery on time, Jo decided to stop at a supermarket on the way home and stock up with a few essentials. She thought she would make a large chicken casserole, enough for several days, even though experience told her that she would be bored with it after two meals and end up putting the rest in the freezer where it would lie, unlabelled and forgotten, until she had a clear out and threw it away.

As she drove to the end of the lane where she lived, Jo was irritated to see her mother's car already parked in her space. She managed to find another spot and crossly dragged the shopping out of the passenger seat, hoping her mother wasn't planning to stay for dinner. She wasn't sure she could take the constant digs about the standard of the food or the state of her love life for that long. Perhaps she could claim a prior engagement if it seemed her mother might intend to stay for the evening? She had been looking forward to a quiet night in on her own, but what price peace and quiet now? Jo didn't think things could be worse, until her mother saw her approaching the house, got out of her Honda Civic, went to the boot of the car and removed a suitcase.

Jo's dismay must have shown on her face because her mother was on the defensive immediately.

'You can't expect me to live with that man a moment longer. I told him it was the motorcycle or me and he just ignored me and carried on tinkering with that bloody machine.' Her mother's words came out in a rush, and then she promptly burst into tears.

'Oh, Ma,' Jo said, surprised into sympathy, and put her free arm round her mother. 'Let's go in.'

Once inside the flat, Jo got her mother settled with a large gin and tonic, and then poured herself a glass of Pinot. A large glass of Pinot. It was going to be a long night, whether or not she managed to persuade her mother to go home.

Jo sat next to her mother, who had regained her composure after a hefty swig of G&T.

'So come on, tell me what's been going on.'

'You said you'd speak to him, get him to see reason, but have you? Have you done that one simple thing for me?'

'I came round yesterday and no one was in.'

Diana did not look like she believed that for a minute.

'Honestly. I did. Where were you?'

'I was at the church hall, we had a meeting about fund raising,' Diana explained. 'But your father should have been there, in the garage most likely, you can't have tried very hard to find him.'

Jo sighed. She was sure her father hadn't been there, although she hadn't actually gone into the garage, but the door had been closed and there weren't any lights on.

'Maybe he took the bike for a test drive?' she suggested.

'Nonsense, he'll never get that pile of rubbish going. He's completely mad. I suppose he could have gone to see the man who got him into all this, Rob, Roy, something like that. Lives in the next village.'

Jo took a large sip of wine. It was definitely going to be a long evening, she should have known that it would be her fault, hers or her father's, or this Rob or Roy. Nothing was ever her mother's fault.

'The only thing I asked you to do was speak to your father and could you be bothered to make the time?' Diana continued. 'No, of course you couldn't. I'm sure you're far too busy, as usual, although I would bet that if your precious father had asked you to do some little thing for him, you'd have dropped everything to help. But not me. Not your own mother.'

'That's not fair. I did try, Ma.'

'Not hard enough, clearly.' She took another swig of her G&T.

Jo was grateful that at least her mother couldn't speak while drinking, as she didn't seem to need to pause for breath the rest of the time.

'So it's the least you can do, to offer me a bed to sleep in, until you manage to get your father to see sense.'

There it was. The deal. Jo's mother intended to stay until Jo got her father to give up his hobby. She groaned inwardly. Her father was every bit as stubborn as her mother. This could be a long stay. A very long stay indeed.

'How about I cook us some dinner?' Jo said brightly, and hurried into the kitchen to give herself time to think. She wasn't a keen cook generally, but she thought that chopping vegetables might just be therapeutic at that moment.

While she was chopping onions, garlic and mushrooms, the phone rang and Jo let the answering machine cut in so that she could hear who was calling before deciding whether or not to answer. It was Kate, so she hurried over and picked up the phone.

'Hi, Kate.'

Jo could see her mother roll her eyes, as if to say, *'I could have guessed it wouldn't be a boyfriend.'*

'How's things?' Kate asked. 'Did your day get any better?'

'No, not at all. How are things?' Jo answered a little too brightly.

'Fine. What's up with you?' Kate sounded puzzled.

'That's great. Oh yes,' Jo continued in a bright and brittle tone, 'my mother's come to stay.' She had to hold the phone slightly away from her ear as Kate guffawed with laughter at the other end.

14

'They didn't even find the empty can in the car park where the car was set on fire.' Helen Austen confided to Jo the next day over a cup of peppermint tea in her extraordinarily untidy office. Jo wrinkled her nose and tried not to worry about germs as she sipped her tea from the chipped and stained mug in which it had been served.

Helen had been present when Miller and Jeffries interviewed Mark. His legal representative had instructed him to exercise his right to silence and to respond with 'no comment' to every question he was asked, and this time he had managed to do that.

'Where did they find it, then?' Jo asked Helen

'By the overflow car park, about twenty yards up the lane.'

'Not far away then.'

'No,' Helen reluctantly conceded, before continuing. 'I am sure it could have got there at anytime, but the visitor centre manager convinced them that he clears any rubbish lying around the car parks twice a week, Monday and Friday, so he insisted it had to have been left there sometime between Friday afternoon and Sunday morning when the crime scene people found it.'

'What did Mark say to explain it?' Jo asked. 'Apart from no comment, I mean?'

'I wasn't privy to his discussions with his lawyer, of course, but when we were sitting in the interview room waiting for the detectives, Mark just kept saying he hadn't been to Fairlight in years and he didn't know how his fingerprints were found there.'

'It doesn't look good, though, does it? Even if he was in hospital at the time.' Jo believed in Mark's innocence as much as anyone, but even she could see that the chips were stacking up against him.

'No it doesn't, and I know that. But do you really think this is the sort of thing Mark would get up to?' A telephone seemed to be ringing somewhere, but a glance at the telephone cradle showed the handset to be missing. Helen searched under some of the papers strewn across her desk and finally found the handset, just as it stopped ringing. She put it back down on the desk where it would quickly be covered in papers again. Jo had to mentally sit on her hands to stop herself from returning the handset to the base. She did like everything to be in its proper place.

'No, of course not,' Jo hesitated. 'I'm not sure he has the mental capacity to plan it, apart from anything.'

'Absolutely!' Helen agreed emphatically. 'Of course, the police theory is that he's working with someone else. It conveniently covers all the gaping holes in their case if there is some kind of mastermind telling Mark what to do.'

Helen was dismissive, but as Jo thought about it she could see a certain logic to the theory. It could also help explain the second murder having taken place when Mark was in hospital. It really did seem too complex to say that he managed to get out of the hospital without anyone noticing, steal a car, meet a woman and persuade her to go with him, kill her, and get back to the hospital, all without being seen. But a partner would explain a lot. A partner who dropped a can at the scene to incriminate Mark.

'Do they have any idea who this partner might be?'

'None at all.' Helen looked thoughtful. 'One of Mark's problems is that he doesn't make friends easily. He's quite isolated.'

'He has a girlfriend though, doesn't he?'

'Yes,' Helen agreed dubiously. 'But I think it's fair to say she's quite isolated as well, because of her,' Helen waved her hands around a bit, 'um, well she's a funny little thing. Terribly shy.'

'But if he can manage to maintain a relationship with one person, he might just possibly be able to have a partner.'

'Yes, but I still don't see it, why start killing women old enough to be his mother?' There was an awkward silence as they both realised that Mark might well have a reason to hate women of a similar age to his mother. After all, she was hardly going to win any awards for outstanding parenting.

'Yes, well, I still don't believe he has anything to do with this.' Helen finished, and despite the mounting evidence, Jo had to concede that she didn't believe it either.

He knew he hadn't planned this one as carefully as the others, but he just couldn't resist. He normally had to reel them in with promises and sex texts, endless flirting and pandering to their egos, but this one, this whore, needed no encouragement. She was desperate for sex, claiming that her partner couldn't satisfy her needs. She seemed remarkably unworried about who met these so-called needs, treating sex as her right, without any thought for the husband she was betraying.

She hadn't needed any persuading to go out for a drive with him, and had even suggested he could take her to a dogging site, where she might get lucky and have multiple partners. There was no chance of that, of course, not with what he had planned for her. There was no doubt in his mind that she deserved to die, but the price of not planning properly was that things went wrong. Because she had been so happy to comply, he hadn't used GHB. He had thought it would be nice for her to know what was happening to her, and why, but she roared with anger when he threw the petrol over her, and had quickly realised she couldn't get out of the passenger door. By the time he had hurriedly thrown the lit book of matches into the car, she was already climbing across to his side. Despite her hair and clothes catching fire, she had continued her escape, getting the driver's door open. He had already retreated to a safe distance, and by the time he'd rushed back to kick the door shut again she was already out of the car, falling onto the ground, screaming and writhing in agony, so he kicked her in the head instead. It made a satisfactory noise as his foot crunched against her face and her head jerked back. He kicked her so hard he wondered if he'd broken her neck. She certainly stopped screaming after that, anyway, and he moved back a little, watching with satisfaction as she continued to burn where she lay, her body moving jerkily as the muscles and tendons constricted in the heat. Later, when he stopped to examine his shoe, he could see a lump of burnt flesh attached to the leather. Amusing as it was, mistakes like that could be fatal. He knew that only bleach would be able to get rid of the DNA evidence, after he had cleaned the charred skin off the shoes, but bleach would ruin the leather, so he would have to get rid of them somewhere they would never be found. He vowed that next time he would take more care, make sure the chosen whore wasn't in any condition to try and get away. After all, he didn't want to get caught, not yet, not ever if possible, but certainly not yet. There were so many more harlots and Jezebels out there. So many left to kill.

15

'Not a Sunday this time,' Jo commented, as a suited-up Miller and Jeffries joined her in the brightly lit crime scene tent. Miller grunted acknowledgement of her remark, but said nothing. The rain, gently drumming on the roof, was one of the reasons for the tent. Colin Brewer, once again taking the role of crime scene manager, was anxious to protect any evidence from being damaged or washed away, and Miller wanted to keep the increasingly intrusive press at a distance from the more open area that the killer had used for this, his third murder. Jo half expected to hear the sound of a helicopter hovering overhead, filming the activity for the early morning news.

The car was parked as before, with the passenger door against the perimeter fence post of the car park, but this time the driver's door was open, and the body was lying beside the car rather than inside it. The tent was only just big enough to cover both car and corpse.

'She got out,' Jeffries indicated the victim, who was lying in the foetal position on the ground by the blackened, skeletal remains of the car. He crouched down to get a closer look. 'It looks like she just curled up and died,' he added thoughtfully.

'That's the effects of the heat causing her tissues to contract,' Jo explained quickly.

Chris Butterworth strode over to the open door of the tent and leaned in to speak to them. Despite the protective suit and mask, it was clear that he was angry. Very angry indeed.

'Looks to be the same method once again. Have you picked up that little shit yet?'

Miller straightened up and looked Butterworth in the eye.

'Yes. Hence our problem. He was safely tucked up in a cell all night.'

That stopped Butterworth dead, as he tried to assimilate this information. He seemed shocked by the news.

'But…' he shook his head as if to clear it. 'Caxton must be the one doing this. It's his MO.' He looked from Miller to Jeffries, who shook his head sympathetically.

Jo was less supportive.

'I take it you will be letting him go now, or will you be checking the CCTV in the custody suite to see if he managed to sneak out of his cell?' She just couldn't help herself, and was pleased to see a look of irritation flash across Miller's face.

'Been on any good websites recently, Dr Hughes?' Jeffries retaliated. 'Found yourself a boyfriend yet?'

Jo was livid, but not quick enough to come up with a response. It would probably be well into next week before she thought of a decent one.

'Have you finished here, Doctor?' Miller asked, pointedly bringing the conversation to a close.

'Yes. I've pronounced life extinct. Although I'm sure you could have worked that out for yourselves,' Jo responded, then immediately left the tent, pulling off her gloves as she hurried through the light rain towards the officer manning the exit from the taped-off crime scene. She signed out with a worse than usual scrawl, too busy to write legibly as she thought about what she had heard, and started piecing it all together. She quickly undressed and ditched her protective clothing in the bag provided, doing her best to keep dry as she did so, and was relieved to reach her car only slightly dampened, by the weather, at least.

She switched the engine on and put the blowers on full blast to warm up and dry herself out. She sat in the driver's seat, looking out at the drizzle and thinking about what she had heard, all the while wishing that she'd had the foresight to make a flask of tea before leaving the warmth of her home. If Mark was in custody, there was absolutely no way he could have committed this crime, and therefore, perhaps he hadn't committed the others either. So how did a drinks can with his fingerprints on it turn up at the second locus? And who knew his method of starting fires well enough to have copied it?

The drinks can could have been a coincidence, she reasoned, even if Mark said he hadn't been to Fairlight, perhaps he had left an empty can in a mate's car and it had fallen out up there. It was also possible that he had been there and was lying about it; frightened to admit he had visited the site, even innocently, so close to the murder.

The second piece of evidence was that the killer used the same method of fire starting as Mark had in the past, but that might just be down to having read about his previous convictions. The other possibility was that Mark had talked to someone about the way he did it. In which case, it was likely that Mark knew the killer.

On their own, neither fact meant that Mark was being framed, but together they were suspicious, if not conclusive, that he could have been.

Jo looked through the fine rain at the lights on the far side of the car park. The forensic tent glowed eerily in the half-light, but the blue-clad figures seemed slightly faded as they searched the immediate area around the tent now that dawn was beginning to break. She wondered if they would find any further evidence linking Mark to this scene, because if they did, they would know for sure that it wasn't a coincidence, they would know that someone was deliberately trying to set him up. Someone who knew his history and had access to his fingerprints, on used drinks cans at least, but who didn't know he was in custody last night.

A blue-suited man came out of the tent and looked across to where she was parked. She recognised the build and posture as Miller, and she wondered whether the same thoughts were going through his head.

Unable to either go back to sleep or face breakfast after her horrific start to the day, and reluctant to be there when her mother woke, no doubt to complain about being disturbed in the night, Jo decided on a walk to work. She ambled through the streets of Hastings, making her way to the surgery by a very circuitous route, in the hope that it would clear her head and possibly even enable her to eat something before she began seeing patients. The rain had stopped, leaving a dampness in the air that Jo knew would make her hair frizzy, but for once she didn't care. In the greater scheme of things she had to admit that bad hair was hardly a major problem. Besides, she had put some portable hair straighteners in her bag so she could repair the damage once she was at work.

Despite walking for more than forty minutes she still arrived before eight. As she let herself in through the back door, armed with a packet of biscuits she had bought on the way to replace those she had taken from Linda's store, she saw that Gerry Brown's car was in the car park. Wednesday and Saturday nights he left it there. That's what Gauri had told her. She stopped in the hallway as she thought about that. Gerry Brown used internet dating sites. Gerry Brown was a known stalker. Gerry Brown had access to her files on Mark. Gerry Brown left his car at work on Wednesday and Saturday nights. The murders had been committed on Wednesday and Saturday nights.

There was a sudden noise of the alarm going off, and Jo realised she had been too busy thinking about Gerry to key in the code in time. She did it quickly and hurried upstairs to call the alarm company and let them know it wasn't burglars, and to give more thought to her theory that Gerry was a killer. Did it really hold water or was it just that she didn't like the man? And if he was the killer, how could he have got hold of Mark's fingerprints, or rather, a drinks can with his fingerprints on it?

She hadn't been in the office long before Linda arrived and informed her that Gerry Brown had called in sick. The news added weight to Jo's earlier thoughts about whether he was linked to the killings, and the thought occurred to her that he might even be off sick because he had accidentally got burnt. Once the thought was there it wouldn't go away, until Linda thrust a list under her nose.

'So which of his patients are you going to see?'

It was a rare occasion when Jo was able to help out her colleagues by taking some of their patients. It was more often the other way round, so she really couldn't complain that his patients had to be divided between the remaining doctors. With a sigh, Jo was thankful she had first pick, and told an amused Linda which ones she would take.

'I hope he really is sick,' Gauri muttered as she finally appeared in the office at the end of what had obviously been a fraught surgery. 'I was only running slightly late until I had that stupid Mr Herring in, with a list of imagined symptoms and some information he'd pulled off the internet on Myasthenia Gravis. He spent so long complaining about the fact that it was five minutes past his appointment time when I called him through that I never got the chance to sort out what was really wrong with him, if anything, and I was still forty minutes late with the next patient.'

'I take it you weren't overly impressed by Myasthenia Gravis as his disease of the week?'

Gauri's only reply was a snort of derision, as she stomped off to the kitchen to make herself some coffee.

Jo gave Linda a guilty look, because when she had checked the list of extras she had spotted Mr Herring's name and agreed to take more than her fair share of the others provided she didn't get him. She picked up a pile of reports to take down to her consulting room, on the grounds that she was less likely to be disturbed there, but Linda stopped her before she had even left the office.

'Don't forget that Gerry's visits have to be covered as well,' she said, handing Jo a list of names and addresses.

'Right,' Jo took the list and looked at it with dismay.

'I know it's your half-day, but the others have to get back for evening surgery, so count this as one of the days you pay back all the times you've been called out by the police and other people have had to do your visits for you.'

Jo really couldn't argue about it. It was true that Gauri, in particular, had done an awful lot of visits for her, so she took the list and put down the reports. She wouldn't have time to look at them if she was going to manage to do all the visits and still leave time to get over and see her father. After only one night on the sofa, she had come to the conclusion that it could only be a temporary arrangement. It was surprisingly uncomfortable, considering Kate never complained when she ended up sleeping there, which, Jo supposed, wasn't too surprising really, as Kate only ever stayed over when she was too drunk to leave. She had only just got to sleep when she got the call to attend the car fire, so lack of sleep, along with the irritation of her mother staying, and a fuller than usual workload, had left Jo feeling tired, and with a stiff back, as well.

'Are you sure about this, Jo?' Kate asked as she logged into the SusSEXtra website in her office later.

'I know it sounds a bit silly, but I just want to be sure it isn't him and he's off sick because he got burnt or something.'

'Look, I have no reason to defend the man, but from stalker to serial killer is a bit of a leap.'

'But not impossible?'

'No,' Kate hesitated. 'Do you think you should tell the police about this?'

'After what happened last time? No,' Jo shook her head vehemently. 'I don't want them to think I'm even more loopy than they already do.'

'Hmm, are you concerned about what Hastings police in general think about you, or is it just one particular handsome inspector?'

'Of course not.' But Jo knew that she didn't sound convincing, and she also knew that Kate would have spotted it. 'It's a good thing Gerry was off sick, because I wouldn't have been able to stop myself from staring, wondering if it could be him.'

Kate snorted with amusement.

'Watch it, he'd probably think you fancy him.'

'I certainly hope not. He is so not my type.'

'You surprise me,' Kate responded as she navigated to the web page. 'Is it the beard?'

'It's undeniably a factor, but strangely, I just don't find serial killers attractive.'

Kate laughed as she put in the password and went to Jo's page. 'Right. You've had twenty-three responses. Not bad, not bad at all.'

They looked at the messages.

'No one called Gerry Brown and none of the pictures look like him, unless he's changed a lot.'

'No but he could have used a false name and picture, I have heard that people sometimes do that,' Jo countered with a knowing look at Kate.

'Point taken.'

They began to read the details the responders had entered for themselves.

'Why oh why would anyone seriously call themselves The Stud?' Jo asked.

'Maybe it's ironic?' Kate replied as she opened the first response and they read the message.

'Why would he want to know if I can burp on demand?'

'That's clearly his thing. Look here,' Kate pointed. 'Girls who belch get him going. He even asks what fizzy drinks you like best.'

'He doesn't want time wasters, just the real thing. Dear Lord, what is the world coming to?'

'You don't share his eructation fetish then?' Kate couldn't help but laugh.

They continued to read through the message.

'Eeuw!' Jo squealed. 'Fancy actually writing something like that down!'

'Actually, writing down your fantasies can be incredibly erotic,' Kate responded. 'You should try it sometime.'

'Writing them down is one thing, letting someone else read them is another matter entirely.'

Slowly they worked their way through all the messages, with Jo making notes. They found two responders who could possibly match Gerry Brown, if the photo was discounted, and one who actually mentioned that he was bearded, although the photo attached was clean-shaven; at a stretch, he could possibly have been a younger version of Gerry.

'He actually sounds quite nice,' Jo said.

'You're only saying that because he's one of the few not talking dirty.'

'That's very true.' Jo looked at the list she had written down and thought for a moment, then sighed.

'Do you think I'm a prude, Kate?'

'Erm, why do you ask?' Kate prevaricated.

'You do! Admit it! You do think I'm a prude.'

'Well, it's more that you have limits, and perhaps your limits are set at a lower level than mine.'

'I prefer to think of them as standards.'

'Okay, well then your standards are higher than most, Jo. Or at least, they're higher than mine,' Kate continued, anxiously trying not to offend her friend.

'And certainly higher than these people's.'

'I think most of the human race has higher standards than these people.'

'But do you think I should, I don't know, loosen up a little?' Jo asked.

Kate was reluctant to reply, although she had often wanted to say to Jo that she could do with being a bit less uptight.

'Everyone has different ways of living their lives, and no one should ever make fun of them for that or try and push them to do something that makes them feel uncomfortable. You know me; I'm a live and let live sort of person. I don't feel I am in a position to either criticise or advise,' she finally said.

Jo thought about that for a while.

'I just worry that I might be missing out on the fun sometimes.'

'Maybe, but if you wouldn't actually find whatever it is fun to do, you're not missing out on it, if you get my meaning.'

'I do,' Jo readily agreed. 'It's like, you know I hate roller coasters, but everyone tells me how exciting they are so sometimes I force myself onto them, and then I find out, all over again, that all I am missing out on is terror and sickness, and I promise myself that I will never do it again under any circumstances.'

'Until the next time you doubt yourself.'

Jo nodded her agreement.

'That's right. But,' she added, 'there is a difference between not going on a roller coaster and being over-cautious with other aspects of your life. I don't want to be too frightened to live a full life.'

Kate couldn't disagree. Jo sighed and looked at the two possibles on her list.

'So what do I do next?'

'Are you sure about this, Jo?' Kate asked anxiously.

'I'm not going to meet them, just try and get to know them a bit better and see if one of them is Gerry or is in any way giving out serial killer vibes, whatever they might be. Have you got an unregistered pay as you go phone I could use?'

Kate rummaged in her desk drawer and pulled one out.

'The number is on it.'

Jo turned the phone over and saw that Kate had taped a bit of paper with the number written on it to the back.

'You are going to have to pay to contact them. That's how these websites work. It's free up to the point where you want to exchange contact details.'

134

Jo looked anxious.

'I don't really want my credit card details logged here, or SusSEXtra appearing on my statements. It's not exactly subtle, is it?'

'So, in my experience, there are two ways you can do this,' Kate told her. 'We can set up a PayPal account for Vicky and use your credit card to put money into the account, as if you had bought something from her over the internet, making it slightly more than you need for the website so it isn't too obvious. Or if you are still concerned about that we can put in an extra layer of anonymity, by setting up an intermediate false account that you pay money into which then pays Vicky, and she then pays SusSEXtra. If we use different amounts each time and put other bits of money in and out of the accounts to make them seem real it will look kosher, superficially at least.'

Jo looked at Kate in astonishment.

'You've done this before.'

'Yes,' Kate acknowledged. 'Like I said, I learnt after that incident with Gerry. Of course, the police would be able to track it all down, but no one else is likely to be able to connect you with Vicky.'

'Right. Let's do it. Just the first level of anonymity will do. I don't plan to make a habit of it.' Jo handed the laptop to Kate.

'Don't knock it till you've tried it,' Kate winked, and started setting up the account.

Once everything was set up, and Jo had transferred some money across to Vicky's PayPal, she paused to reflect on what she was about to do.

'Sure?' Kate questioned.

Jo nodded, suddenly decisive, and quickly, before she had a chance to change her mind, she paid SusSEXtra. Boxes appeared for her to contact the men who had responded to her original post. She typed in a suitably oblique response to the first man, saying that she liked the look of him. She gave him the pay as you go mobile number and suggested they text each other, then signed off as Vicky and hit enter.

'In for a penny…' she said as she did exactly the same to the second man on her list, and then a few of the others for good measure.

'Promise me you won't do anything stupid?' Kate said.

'I think it's probably too late to promise that,' Jo replied with a weak smile.

'I mean when they contact you, just don't agree to meet up or tell them anything that could identify you.'

'Don't worry. I'm the over-cautious one, remember?'

'I do, but you have to remember it too,' Kate said, and neither of them was smiling.

16

It was four o'clock before she managed to finish all the additional visits and get away. She knew she had to go to see her father, but she was exhausted. What she wanted most of all was to go home; provided her home did not contain her mother. It was a dilemma. She didn't want to confront her father and have what was likely to be a difficult discussion, but if she was to have any hope at all of getting her mother out of her flat, she had to do it. She had to persuade him to take her mother back one way or another, even if she didn't know how she was going to do it. Should she be forceful and insist, appeal to his better nature, or try to charm him? She had absolutely no idea, and she hadn't really had any time to think about the best tactic. There was nothing for it, she would have to drive out to her parents' home and tackle her father.

When she arrived at The Old Vicarage, there was a single car parked outside; her father's aging Volvo. Jo left her sporty little Audi TT next to it, in the space normally occupied by her mother's Honda Civic, a car she religiously changed for a new one, the same model and the same colour, every year.

Jo had always loved this house, if not all the memories from her childhood. In moments when she chose to be fair, she acknowledged that her relationship with her mother had only become a battleground once she hit her teens and began to rebel against the relentless drip, drip of hints about how to catch a good husband: make the most of your looks, darling; try not to be too clever; make sure you can cook and keep house; and whatever you do, don't sleep with them on the first date. The list seemed endless and Jo had broken almost every one of her mother's rules, so perhaps it was not surprising that she was still single.

As she walked slowly, almost reluctantly, towards the front door, Jo could hear the sound of some kind of power tool coming from the direction of the small, detached garage to the side of the house, so she changed direction. The garage door was slightly open and she pulled it wider. Inside, a classic motorcycle, or most of a classic motorcycle, was leaning against the wall, while an assortment of mechanical parts vied for space with all the tools and equipment that her father had bought to help with his hobby. The garage, built in an era when little else other than a car would be kept inside, was full to bursting point. Jo was amazed that her father could work at all in this chaos; no wonder bits had encroached into the house. Charles Hughes was at the back of the cramped space, bent over a piece of battered metal which was clamped to his workbench, and using the wire-brush attachment on his electric drill to buff it up. Jo took a moment to look at him as he concentrated on what he was doing, unaware of her gaze. He was a fit, good-looking man, despite being almost seventy. He was dressed in some battered, dark blue overalls that were covered in dirt and grease marks. His silver hair was still thick for the most part, although Jo could see a thinner patch on the top of his head that she hadn't noticed before. Suddenly, sensing that he was being watched, he looked up. Once he recognised his daughter, he smiled, stopped what he was doing and carefully put the drill down.

'Jo! Good to see you. I was wondering how long it would take.' He grabbed an oily rag and came over to give her a kiss on the cheek, careful to keep his dirty overalls and even dirtier hands away from her. 'Come on into the kitchen, it's time I took a coffee break.'

He peeled off his latex gloves, but Jo could see that they had torn, and oil and dirt had seeped onto his hands. She followed as he led the way through the back and across to the side door of the house, carefully using the rag to touch the door, but still managing to leave a streak of dirt on the brass door knob. In the kitchen, an old *Daily Telegraph* was spread across the kitchen table to try and protect it from the engine parts that covered the surface. Jo was beginning to understand her mother's problem.

'How's your mother?' Charles asked as he washed his hands at the kitchen sink. He began wiping them, although they were still relatively dirty, on a grubby looking towel. There was black grease under his nails and ingrained in the cracks and cuts that covered his fingertips. It was hard to imagine him letting his hands get into this state during his days as an orthopaedic surgeon; he had always been so meticulous about them. The tools of his trade, he had called his fingers.

'Oh, you know Ma.'

'Not driven you round the bend yet?'

'Not quite yet, but not far off,' Jo admitted as she filled the electric kettle at the sink, ignoring the used dishes dumped in there, and now covered in grey, greasy water from her father's hands. She put the kettle on to boil, before fetching two mugs from the cupboard. The jar of instant coffee was already out, and a dirty teaspoon lay on the kitchen counter beside it.

'I popped round on Monday evening, but you were both out.'

'Ah,' he looked at her. 'Your mother and I, well, we had a bit of a tiff and she stormed off, and I followed her. To make sure she was all right.'

Jo could imagine the scene. Her mother would have been drinking, and would probably have been over the limit, so her father would have felt honour bound to ensure she came to no harm, no matter how cross he might have been feeling with her.

'I have to tell you, Dad, I hate it when you two fight.'

'Every marriage has its bad patches. It's a part of married life, Jo.'

'I know, but that doesn't make it any easier to deal with.'

She poured some hot water into each of the mugs, stirring as she did so, and went to the fridge for some milk.

'You have to let us sort it out for ourselves.' He took the proffered mug from her and sat down at the kitchen table.

'Of course, and I'm not interfering or taking sides. I just want to know what you're doing to sort things out, because there is only so long I can have Ma living with me before one of us kills the other,' she smiled encouragingly at her father. 'So what will it take to get you back together again?'

'Oh we'll be back together before too long, don't you worry, I just need to finish this little project off, and then she'll come back.'

'And do you have any idea how much longer it will take? It looked pretty much done to me.' It hadn't, but she lived in hope.

Her father shook his head.

'There's still a lot to do. Maybe another month.' Jo couldn't help but feel a little dismayed. A month? No way could she have her mother living with her for a month.

After they had finished their coffee her father took her back to the garage to show her the work he was doing to restore the motorcycle. She tried to seem interested, but it was a struggle.

She handed him back the now shining and perfect exhaust.

'You've done a good job on it, it looks almost brand new.'

He took it from her, beaming proudly, and carefully put it down on a piece of clean linen that looked as if it might have recently been a good quality bed sheet.

'I can't tell you how much I'm enjoying doing this, Jo. I've been thinking that once I've finished it, I might try and build myself one of those kit cars.'

Jo sighed as she thought about how long that would take, and where her mother was likely to live while he was doing it.

'But don't worry, I'll give your mother a bit of a break before I start on that,' he added, with a small smile and a twinkle in his eye, 'so you can have a bit of time to yourself.'

A small wave of relief washed over her, as she contemplated what looked like a lot of her mother's company in the future.

'I know I suggested you take up a hobby, but did it have to be such a messy one?' She gestured at the bits and pieces strewn across the garage.

He thought for a moment before answering her.

'When I retired it was a big shock, Jo. I went from being head of a busy department, working all hours, with my patients' lives in my hands, to having very little to do at all, and what I did find to do was of absolutely no use to man nor beast.'

She could only imagine what a shock that must have been for a man like her father. She had seen the same problems adjusting to retirement in patients who had worked all their lives, and it didn't seem to matter what sort of job it was, even people who had been cleaners or worked on assembly lines, if they had never had much in the way of leisure time, they ran into problems once the unending stretch of retirement lay ahead; they just didn't know how to deal with it. Jo knew that it was a similar problem for mothers when the last of their children left home, a sudden awareness that your useful life is over. She had always urged her patients to take up a hobby, something that gave them a purpose again, and wasn't that exactly what her father had done?

'I felt useless. I suspect I was a little depressed. My brain began to stagnate,' her father continued. 'I began to forget things, have difficulty with the crossword, find myself falling asleep in the afternoon. I honestly thought I had Alzheimer's.'

Jo put her hand on his and gave it a sympathetic squeeze. For a man like her father, senile dementia was the ultimate fear.

'So you suddenly decided to take up motorcycle maintenance.'

'It wasn't such a sudden thing, Jo. I even went to a couple of evening classes, but they were full of very boring people, apart from the tutor Roy, who spends his spare time doing up old cars. He showed me what he was up to and I began to get interested. He really knows what he's doing. I saw an advert in the Parish Magazine for this old wreck of a Triumph Bonneville. It was being offered free for spares or repairs, and I thought I'd find hands-on learning more interesting. The rest is history, as they say.' He pointed over at the motorbike. 'Someone painted it red at some point, but I chipped away at the paintwork and I'm pretty sure it was black originally, so that's what I'm going to make it. Back to black. What do you think?'

She smiled. She had to concede that this new hobby of her father's was definitely good for him, if not for anybody else.

Later that night, after her mother had gone to bed, as Jo waited to see if she would get any responses to her expressions of interest on the website, she passed the time by searching for information about the use of fire to kill people, and specifically to kill women. Once again she was stunned by the amount of information available on what she had considered to be an unusual way of killing.

Sadly, she was wrong. It was quite a frequently used tool. By far the most common cause of death was arson of buildings in which people may have been killed because they were there at the wrong time or because they were firefighters, but fire was quite often used to cover up a murder, and to destroy DNA or other evidence, which was plausible as a reason in the current killings. It had certainly caused problems for the police. Continuing her search, she found a considerable amount of immensely sad information about bride burning and honour killings that were a form of domestic violence practised in Pakistan, India and Bangladesh, and which had certainly occurred amongst those communities in England as well. However, none of the local victims were of Asian ethnicity, so this seemed an unlikely explanation for the current murders.

She read discourses on the Koran stating that death by burning was a martyr's death, and an equal number saying that it was expressly forbidden. News websites talked of Buddhists who had been known to douse themselves in petrol and set themselves on fire as a form of protest. The Old Testament was cited as saying that the sentence for adultery was death, and on at least two occasions, death by burning, when combined with exacerbating circumstances such as prostitution. So the murderer could be some sort of religious fanatic, but it was hard to know which particular religion, and it seemed it all depended on your interpretation of the various texts on which the beliefs were founded.

Carrying on with her research, Jo then read about Tristan and Iseult, in which some versions have King Mark sentencing the lovers to death at the stake. Burning at the stake was apparently mentioned as a punishment for sexual immorality in old Irish literature, possibly because it had taken inspiration from the Old Testament. She found that many societies have used death by burning as an execution method, usually for treason, heresy or witchcraft, but sometimes also for adultery or other sexual transgressions. It was common for the condemned to be bound to a wooden stake, sometimes alone and sometimes in groups. She also found a chilling reference that burning alive for murder in England was abolished in 1656, but that burning for adultery and heresy remained a legitimate form of punishment for a while longer.

She stopped at that point, because it was all getting too horrible. There were even videos of people being burnt to death if she wanted to see them, but she didn't want to. She didn't want to see them at all. She had seen the results in real life three times now, and that was more than enough.

She looked through her notes. The first two victims were both married and would appear to have been actively unfaithful. The cars were parked up against wooden stakes to stop them escaping, and they were then burnt to death.

To Jo's mind, the case was made, even if she didn't have all the evidence. The murderer was killing these women for committing adultery, using his own variation on the medieval punishment of burning them at the stake.

Jo jumped as Kate's throwaway phone pinged, letting her know she had received a text from one of the men she had given the number to.

Her hands shook slightly as she opened the message.

Hey Vicky, thx 4 msg. U look hot. Txt me wot UR doing. Lee xx

Jo was tempted to text back that at that moment she was reading his message, and to ask how old he really was, but she controlled herself and texted back:

Just playing on internet. Waiting for you to message. What RU doing?

She was quite proud of herself for sounding quite flirty, but would Gerry Brown really use textspeak like this, she wondered?

The phone pinged again.

Watching porn like U :) we shd do it 4 real. Im nkd, what RU waring? smthg sexy?

There followed some descriptions of what Lee was currently doing and would like to do to/with Vicky. Jo shuddered. There was no way she could continue this conversation, so she turned the phone off.

She couldn't believe Gerry would ever use such bad punctuation or spelling, but at least Lee had taken her mind off the horrific images of women being burnt at the stake. She made her way to bed, hoping that they didn't come back to haunt her dreams.

17

Jo was incredibly nervous as she approached the police station, because she suspected the only reaction she was going to get would be laughter. In the cold light of day she had to admit that it did sound ludicrous. What sort of madman would kill women to punish them for committing adultery? And resurrect a medieval punishment for it at that. But try as she might, she couldn't come up with an alternative motive to fit the murders as well as this one did, and she was determined to tell Miller, and anyone else who would listen, even if they discounted it out of hand. She could never forgive herself if she didn't tell them and she turned out to be right. She had given up on the idea of approaching Nigel after he had dropped her in it the last time, and anyway, Miller was the person who would be able to authorise the checks that would be needed if they were to discover whether any of the other women had used the dating website. She didn't know if Nigel or anyone else on the team had already started that process, and if they had, with what success.

She had been anxious ever since she had decided on this course of action at about four in the morning, having woken from a nightmare. Her rational mind told her it was just a combination of sleeping on the sofa and the problems with her mother, but as she tossed and turned she had finally come to the conclusion that she had to tell the police her theory, if she was ever going to be able to sleep again. Having made that decision, she promptly fell asleep.

She slept soundly and didn't wake until her mother came in to make her early morning hot water and lemon juice, something she always had first thing, claiming it cleansed her system. She managed to make Jo feel that she had failed, firstly for not having brought her mother a drink in bed, and secondly for not replacing her own English Breakfast tea with hot water and lemon. As Jo hurried out of the flat she resolved to set her alarm to ensure she was up and out of the house before her mother woke. She was in a rush, because she wanted to make good her resolution to tell the police about her theory and she needed to do it before morning surgery, as there was a practice meeting at lunchtime. She also needed to do it before she had second thoughts.

As she parked her car and headed towards the modern office block that housed the main police station, Jo wished she had a couple of beta blockers she could take. She had used them before as a student, for practical exams and stressful situations, to try and help her maintain her cool professional image and stop her getting flustered or flushed, but she didn't have any on her, so she would just have to breathe deeply and hope that, if nothing else, Jeffries was not in yet.

Despite her role as a forensic physician, Jo wasn't allowed to roam the building freely and had to be escorted, so she waited in the reception area, and was surprised when Miller himself came down to fetch her and take her up to the incident room. She was even more surprised when he led her into his office, rather than speaking to her in front of everyone else. She had been dismayed to see the room so full at that early hour, but there had been no sign of Jeffries, thank goodness.

As he held the door for her to enter the office she could smell a subtle mix of sandalwood and shaving foam for a few moments when she passed him, before the office odours of stale food and bodies brought her back to earth.

'Sorry about the mess,' Miller apologised, as he cleared some files off a chair and invited her to sit down. 'Can I get you anything? Tea? Coffee?'

'No thank you.' She took a seat, and was just formulating what to say when the door crashed open again and Jeffries barged in carrying a chair, which he managed to bang against several items of furniture, as well as Jo's leg.

'Oops, sorry Doc. The room's a bit small,' he said as she rubbed her leg. She was gratified to see that Miller looked annoyed, but not annoyed enough to ask Jeffries to leave.

'So,' Miller looked at her. He seemed genuinely interested in what she had to say and, like her, seemed slightly anxious about what his sergeant might say in response. She found herself for the first time looking directly into his eyes, which were a very lovely soft shade of brown, with amber lights. She quickly looked away. This would never do. She cleared her throat and with an apprehensive look at Jeffries, explained why she was there.

'I know that my simply telling you the gossip that the second victim had used a dating website was not enough, but I have been thinking about the women who have been targeted. You haven't identified the last one yet, have you?' She looked for confirmation from Miller.

'Not yet.'

'It seems likely that at least the first two women were married and on a night out with a lover.' Both Miller and Jeffries nodded.

'And it's possible the third one was married as well. We obviously don't know that yet.' She hesitated. This was the point of no return; her last chance to stay quiet about her theory and leave with her dignity intact, albeit with a guilty conscience. 'I have been thinking about motive.' Jeffries looked as if he was about to interrupt, but Jo held up her hand to stop him.

'I have been looking at the use of fire as a murder weapon around the world, and discounting arson for monetary gain or to cover up a murder that has already taken place, death by burning is most commonly used as a punishment. A punishment for heresy, treason or adultery.'

She let that sink in for a moment and was pleased to note that Miller was giving it some serious thought.

'Come off it, Doc.' She might have known Jeffries wasn't going to be persuaded. 'That's an Asian thing. None of these women are...'

'That's very interesting,' Miller interrupted his sergeant before he could say something politically incorrect.

Jo glared at Jeffries before continuing.

'It isn't only Asian cultures that have used it as a punishment. We used to burn women at the stake for adultery in this country, and the car park posts could be interpreted as symbolic stakes.'

Jeffries snorted with derision.

'Blimey, if someone is out there killing people as a punishment for committing adultery, why aren't they killing men rather than women? After all, there's a lot more men fucking around out there than women. Trust me, I know.'

Before Jo had time to respond that it has traditionally always been the woman who pays the price there was a knock at the door and Jayne

Hales came in, with a glance of apology at Jo, although she wasn't sure if Jayne was apologising for interrupting her or for how she had been treated the day before.

'Got an ID on the latest victim, Guv,' she said, and both Miller and Jeffries jumped to their feet and headed for the door.

Jo stood as well. She had said what she wanted to say, and if they chose to ignore it then more fool them, she thought crossly, as she followed them out of the office.

'Thank you, Doctor,' Miller said to her as she headed for the incident room door. 'That's a very interesting theory.' Before Jo could reply he had turned his attention to Jayne, keen to hear what she had to say.

'Teresa Hardwick, aged twenty-seven, freelance hairdresser,' Jayne began, as Jo opened the door to leave.

'Married, no children. Husband didn't report her missing straight away because she often stayed out overnight, apparently. He said it was for her work, but I'm not sure why a hairdresser would need to work overnight.'

Jo smiled to herself. Another married woman, lying about where she was and what she was doing. She knew she was right about the motive for these murders, but it wasn't any great consolation if Miller wasn't going to take it seriously.

'Yes, Linda, I do understand, but given the problems we have recruiting locums who are on the approved list, we have no choice but to do everything we can to keep him.'

Hugh Grantham was digging his heels in about Gerry Brown in the face of growing complaints, not just from his medical colleagues and the practice nurses, but from the administrative staff as well. Apparently over his illness, and with no signs of burns as far as a disappointed Jo could see, he had been rude to one of the receptionists this time, and she had been so upset she had left work early, leaving her colleagues having to cover at short notice.

'It's not easy to find good reception staff either,' Linda countered.

'Of course not. I admit that Dr Brown needs to brush up his social skills, and I will remind him to be polite to practice staff at all times.' Hugh looked round the room. He knew the weight of opinion was against him. 'But he is a competent GP,' he held up his hand as Jo looked as if she was about to interrupt, 'not good, but competent, and I shouldn't need to remind you that if he leaves we will all need to pull together and cover his work load.'

There was a sulky silence. Everyone knew he was right and no one wanted any extra work when they were struggling to cope with what they already had.

'Perhaps it would be a good idea if we were to at least look at the alternatives out there.' Gauri suggested. Hugh's agreement to this might appease some people, even though they all knew there were no alternatives and it had taken them several months to find Gerry.

'And to have a plan for if he decides to leave us,' Jo chipped in. 'I get the impression he doesn't like it here very much, and we all know there are plenty of other locum jobs going.'

Hugh looked round at the senior team to confirm that a consensus had been reached. There didn't seem to be any dissenting voices, so he nodded.

'Of course.' He turned to Linda. 'Can I ask you to ring the agencies again and see if there is anyone available?' Linda made a note of his request. 'And I will speak to Dr Brown about not upsetting the staff. I will also draw up an emergency rota to circulate for comment.' He checked that there was no other business and left, signalling a mass exodus from the meeting, leaving just Jo, Gauri and Linda behind.

'The man has the social skills of a gnat,' Linda complained. 'I'm not sure Mo will come back after what he said to her.'

'What did he say?' Jo asked.

'He said there was no point in him telling patients to lose weight if the receptionists weren't going to follow such basic advice.'

'Ouch!' Jo said. There was no denying that Mo was morbidly obese, but she was a good worker and the patients loved her. There was, however, a little part of Jo that felt Gerry Brown had a point. Mo was hardly a good example of a healthy lifestyle. Looking at Gauri, Jo could see that the same thought was going through her mind.

'My concerns are about how he is with patients,' Gauri said. 'Not that I am belittling how upset Mo is, of course, but if he is as bad with the patients as he is with the staff, they may choose to find a new surgery.'

'Losing a few patients might actually be a good thing,' Linda sighed. They all knew they were over-subscribed. It was the same story for most of the surgeries in the town.

'Do we know anything about his personal life?' Jo asked, trying not to sound too interested.

'He put married as his status on his personal details form,' Linda said with a slight sneer. 'But I'm not sure how much that means.'

'In what way?'

'Rumour has it he's got a bit on the side. Stays with her every Wednesday and Saturday. That's why his car's always left here on those nights.'

'You wonder what his wife makes of it.'

'He probably tells her he's working. Staying in the hospital on call or something. I knew a surgeon who did that.'

'I have no time for gossip,' Gauri stood up. 'There are some visits I must make.'

Gauri left and Jo felt a little guilty. Everyone knew that Linda loved to gossip, and Jo encouraged her, so long as it never crossed the line into breaching confidentiality. Her view was that it sometimes paid to know who was sleeping with whom, if only to avoid putting your foot in it.

'She must live in the old town then, if he leaves his car here,' Jo remarked to Linda, fishing for further details. 'Do you know who she is?'

'No, I have asked around but got absolutely nowhere, and short of following the man there's not much more I can do to find out.' Linda's voice was tinged with genuine regret, and Jo felt much the same. If he genuinely was having an affair and seeing someone regularly, it would potentially rule him out as the killer.

Jo looked at the picture of Teresa Hardwick, victim number three, which Jayne Hales had printed off from her Facebook page. The photo was clearly a selfie. Her face was angled up to prevent a double chin, her eyebrows were slightly raised to make her eyes look larger, and the obligatory pout looked forced. The result was unnatural, and un-attractive. Not for the first time, Jo wondered what possessed people to post pictures like this online. No doubt she got lots of likes for it on her status and deluded herself that her virtual friends genuinely thought she looked good.

She handed the photo back.

'Is the DI okay with you talking to me?'

They were in a small café just down the road from the surgery that Jo sometimes used for lunch when she wasn't able to get home because of pressures of work or, more recently, because her mother was there. It was after the lunchtime rush, so she and Jayne had the place to themselves, apart from the lady behind the counter.

'Of course! Don't worry, I'm not about to jeopardise my career by going behind his back. I'm sure he would talk to you himself but he's a bit busy at the moment.'

Jo could imagine he was. With three murders almost certainly committed by the same person the press were pouring into the town, and the pressure on him to find the serial killer before anyone else died was intense.

'He wanted you to know that he wasn't dismissing your theory that this is some kind of punishment for adultery but he's not sure how to investigate that, although he's got me checking to see if anyone connected with Mark's past had a particularly bad divorce, and cross checking to see if they have any current contact with him using the TIE process. Unfortunately, that's still quite a few and I'm only a quarter of the way through the very long list of policemen, firemen, social workers, judges, and so on from his past. And that list includes Sergeant Jeffries, by the way.' A fact which seemed to please Jayne.

Jo knew that TIE stood for trace, interview and eliminate, and she could sympathise with the frustration Jayne was feeling. Too often medicine was like the TIE process – doing investigations to rule out diagnoses one at a time until you hit on the right one.

'Although,' Jayne continued regretfully, 'Bob's wife divorced him for his adultery, not hers, and he knew Mark was in custody, so if he really was the killer trying to frame Mark, he would have known not to leave his fingerprints at the most recent scene.'

'Another soda can?' Jo asked and Jayne nodded. Jo was surprised to hear that news. It definitely looked like someone was trying to frame Mark, unsuccessfully, and she filed that particular piece of information away.

'Oh, congratulations on your promotion to sergeant, by the way.' Jo changed the subject. 'And your move out of uniform.'

'Thanks. Unfortunately, the secondment to CID is only temporary, but I'm hoping that I do well enough on this investigation to make it permanent sometime in the future. Although I don't think Bob Jeffries will be very happy if that happens.'

Jo nodded sympathetically. Bob Jeffries probably didn't think Jayne could possibly be a good addition to the team, because she was neither pretty nor male.

'I'm surprised you have the time to come and see me.' Jo still wasn't quite sure why Jayne had contacted her and suggested this meeting.

'The boss knows it's not easy for you to come and see him in the incident room,' Jayne gave her a sympathetic look, 'what with Bob and his attitude, but he does value your opinions. He says you are sometimes spot on, and he's also concerned that if you think we aren't taking you seriously you might go off and investigate on your own.'

Jo cleared her throat guiltily, took a bite of her hummus and salad sandwich and tried not to look pleased that he had listened to her, that he wanted her to know he had taken her crazy theories seriously, and also that he wanted to stop her from putting herself at risk, as she had indeed done in the last case she was involved in, but she didn't feel quite able to admit to Jayne that she had been carrying out a bit of investigating on this case as well.

'What about the internet dating site?' she asked instead.

'Not being very cooperative at the moment. As you can imagine, they really don't want any sort of rumour started that a serial killer is working his way through their clientele.'

'Then they should cooperate. If I'm wrong they can prove it, if I'm right swift action is their only hope. No chance of forcing their hand with a warrant, I don't suppose?'

Jayne shook her head.

'Insufficient grounds, apparently.'

'I take it the identification has been confirmed?' Jo asked.

'Yes. The body is definitely Teresa Hardwick,' Jayne sighed. 'I'm not sure how she would feel about the way her husband described her, though.'

Jo raised a quizzical eyebrow and waited for Jayne to finish her mouthful of bacon and egg roll. She swallowed, then glanced round to make sure no one could hear what she was about to say, but even the serving lady had disappeared out to the back room, where they could hear her washing up the dishes from the lunchtime rush.

'Mr Hardwick knew his wife looked elsewhere to supplement the sex she had at home. He said she was very physical and active and had a high sex drive. He even admitted that he'd suggested she should seek treatment for sex addiction.'

'So she's another one who might have used the website.'

'I know. It's frustrating, isn't it?'

As she hurried back to the surgery Jo gave more thought to the meeting, and how useful her burgeoning friendship with Jayne could be. Useful for Steve Miller, because she could give him her ideas and any medical input and explanations he needed, useful for Jayne because she had a hotline to her boss's ear and it could further her career, and useful for Jo because she had a way of getting news of how the investigation was going and a way of helping where she could without getting herself into danger, and without having to listen to Sergeant Jeffries' sexist or inappropriate comments. It had indeed been a clever move of Steve's to send his ambitious new sergeant to her. Jo just hoped that it didn't also mean she had no need to contact him directly any more.

18

'They've only gone and questioned Mark again,' Helen had called Jo to tell her the news as soon as she had the chance.

'What?' Jo was astounded. 'But they know he couldn't have done it! He was in custody for goodness' sake.'

'At least this time they questioned him at his house rather than at the station. Honestly, I think the boy's going to have a complete breakdown.'

'Do you know why they questioned him?' Jo was cautious about letting Helen know she'd already been told about the fingerprints, in case she felt she ought to have warned the social worker, and Mark.

'Apparently they found another drinks can with his prints on.'

'I can see why they wanted to talk to him. I mean, the killer has to be someone Mark knows well enough that they can get hold of his discarded drinks cans to leave at the scene.'

'Quite, but they could have done it more gently, rather than treating him as though he's stupid or lying when he says he doesn't know who it is.' Helen hesitated. 'Look, I suggested he come and see you, and he wasn't averse to the idea.'

'I thought he was going to change doctors?' Jo queried.

'I think I convinced him that you weren't really anything to do with the police thinking he was a suspect. Besides, he wouldn't have a clue how to find a new doctor, poor lamb.'

'Has he been to see his psychologist again?' Jo couldn't even trust herself to mention Adrian Lambourne's name after his insinuations.

'He was supposed to see him last week, but he kept Mark waiting so long that the poor kid gave up and walked out. Please Jo, he needs all the support he can get. At least give him a call, just so he knows you don't hold anything against him, if nothing else.'

'Okay, I'll do that tonight, and offer him an appointment tomorrow morning, as it's my turn to do Saturday. But it depends on him agreeing to see me, and on the police not picking him up again,' she added.

'I wouldn't put it past them,' Helen agreed.

Once Jo had hung up, she took a deep breath. What on earth was Miller thinking? Why was he still hounding Mark? He couldn't possibly still think that he had anything to do with it. She couldn't help feeling that the boy's crimes were rooted more in his inadequacy than any real badness. Jo wondered if she should mention to Lambourne her worries that Mark might have been abused at some point, but decided that now probably wasn't the time to tackle that particular issue. It could wait until he'd recovered from all the police attention. She was so angry that she had to wait a while to calm down before ringing Mark. There was no answer, so she left a message on the machine saying she would hold an appointment at the end of morning surgery for him the next day. It would have been better if she could have spoken to him in person, but he was probably too anxious to answer the phone, and who could blame him? She just hoped he listened to her message and felt able to come and see her tomorrow, or she would have to find time to visit him at home again.

It was a Friday evening, and the pubs in the main town were surprisingly packed with people celebrating the end of another working week and the prospect of two days of rest. Even with the persistent rain, groups had spilled out of the bars and were huddling under the limited cover, smoking, shouting and laughing. Most of them were already so drunk that Jo suspected they wouldn't remember much of the night at all, unless friends helpfully reminded them with photos of their most embarrassing antics. She was interested that women were still socialising, seemingly unworried that there was a serial killer around; something they were unlikely to forget given that a number of journalists were making the rounds and asking people if they felt frightened. But even the journalists were growing tired of the endless stream of people saying that yes they were frightened, but no they weren't about to change their habits and stay at home, as that would be like letting him win, wouldn't it? Jo wondered if the pubs would be as busy tomorrow night, or would these diehard fun-loving women take the risk even on a Saturday?

Kate was just locking up her office, juggling her keys and umbrella, as Jo arrived to meet her. They too were going for a drink, but they would stay together, and then they were going home. Early. Perhaps

Jo misjudged the giggling women in the bars around her. Perhaps they had also made plans to stick together and make sure they all got home safely and were tucked up in bed nice and early.

'Ugh.' Kate looked at the scenes around them. 'Let's hurry over to the civilisation of the old town, quick.'

'I thought you liked the bars round here?' Jo queried. 'You said they were a happy hunting ground, as I remember.'

'Well yes,' Kate agreed, unabashed, 'it rather depends on what you are hunting though, and right now I want relaxation, good beer, and intelligent conversation. None of which are likely to be found in a sports bar.'

Jo had to agree. The noise level in most of the places was such that you couldn't hear yourself speak, let alone what anyone else was saying. Not being a beer drinker, she couldn't comment on that particular aspect, but she had found that most places stocked a decent enough Pinot Grigio these days.

Once they were settled into the warmth of The Stag, drinks and crisps in front of them, they both certainly felt more relaxed.

'Well,' Kate asked, almost beside herself with curiosity, 'have you heard from any of them?'

Jo fished the cheap mobile phone out of her bag.

'Four, so far,' Jo told her, and Kate leant closer to see as they scrolled through the various messages that Jo had received from her SusSEXtra matches.

'Ooh, he's a charmer.' Kate was reading the short conversation she'd had with Lee, and the many, many further messages he had sent trying to persuade her to meet him. Kate was being sarcastic. At least, Jo hoped she was being sarcastic.

'And a dick pic from this one! What a surprise!'

Jo grabbed the phone back.

'This one sounds nicer.' Jo showed her a message she'd had from someone who called himself Lance, and took a little while to understand why Kate was sniggering.

'Honestly I do wish people would just use their real names,' she said crossly.

'What? Like Jocasta?' Kate responded. 'Are you looking for someone young enough to be your son?'

'No! I would never use that name, because of the whole Oedipus thing, but Jo or something else normal, all these names with innuendos are just so… puerile.'

They sifted through the various messages.

'Which one was this Lance, then?' Kate asked.

'He was the one who said he had a beard even though his picture was clean-shaven.'

'I think you should try and draw him out a bit. See if it could be Gerry.'

Jo sighed.

'I'm not sure this will work.'

'Why's that?'

'Well, I don't know how I could tell if it was him. I mean, it was fairly clear that Lee wasn't Gerry. He was virtually illiterate.'

'Pretty imaginative, though,' Kate said with a smile.

'Behave!' Jo threw a cushion at her.

'Seriously, I do know what you mean. And even if we do recognise him, it isn't evidence that he's the killer, is it?'

'I'd be pretty convinced.'

'But would Miller be?'

'Maybe we would do better to pretend to be a bloke and see if we could find the victims? That way we'd have some hard evidence to take to Miller.'

'Right. I suggest you try and draw Lance out, see if he says anything that makes you think he might be Gerry. And I'll register as a man and see if I can find any of the victims. Okay?'

'Okay.' They clinked glasses. 'We have a plan!' Jo smiled.

'Not necessarily a good plan,' Kate qualified, 'but still a plan.'

Jo checked her watch.

'Do you reckon your mum is safely tucked up in bed by now?' Kate asked with a mischievous grin.

'I wish. It's more likely that she's stayed up and is counting every minute I keep her waiting.'

19

Saturday morning surgeries usually ended at twelve thirty, but Mark still hadn't shown up for his appointment by quarter past one. Jo was just getting ready to go home, having decided he wasn't going to come, when the receptionist rang through to say he'd arrived, hinting that Jo should refuse to see him, but there was no way she was going to do that to him. He was anxious enough without her adding to his problems, so she turned her computer back on and went out to the waiting room to collect him, bumping into the practice nurse as she did so. The practice nurse took one look at Mark still waiting to be seen and nipped out of the surgery door before Jo could ask her to stay and help.

The receptionist gave Jo a disapproving look, and knowing the woman was probably keen to get back to her family, Jo suggested she went home.

'I'll make sure everything's closed up, don't worry.'

The receptionist didn't look in the least bit worried as she grabbed her coat and hurried out. If Jo was mad enough to see patients on her own after the surgery should have closed, then it was her own lookout.

Jo smiled at Mark as she let him back into her clinic room and gave him a little time to get settled, hoping he would speak when he was ready. She hoped she hadn't made a mistake seeing him in an empty surgery. She had a panic button but it only rang at reception, and now no one was there to come running if she needed help. She had to admit he didn't look aggressive, he just looked tired and worried, with blue smudges under his eyes. He was wearing torn jeans, the inevitable fake designer baseball cap, and a grubby, misshapen short-sleeved T-shirt, revealing the tattoos that covered every inch of his arms. He must have been cold walking around without even a jumper, Jo thought.

'How are you feeling?' she asked gently, when she realised they would be there all day if she waited for him to speak.

He shrugged and examined his cuticles.

'It's been a difficult couple of weeks, hasn't it?' she encouraged him.
He nodded.

'But the police know that the fires weren't anything to do with you, don't they?' she persisted. Mark still didn't answer, just plucked at imaginary bits of fluff on his trousers.

'Are you managing to sleep at all?'

He plucked harder at his jeans.

'I didn't do nothing,' he suddenly blurted out, and once started there was no stopping him. 'They keep banging on and on about who knows about my past, where I've been, who I've been with, and all stuff like that. It's doing my fucking head in. On and on, they go. What do I drink, where did I drink it. I can't think anymore. I just can't fucking think!' He banged the desk as he finished and then looked guilty.

'Sorry,' he said, straightening the pen holder that had fallen over at his blow.

'That's all right. I can imagine how frustrating it must be.'

He nodded.

'They ask the same stuff, over and over, and I don't know the answer. I can't remember and I can't even remember what I said before.'

'That's okay. That's normal. None of us remembers everything, not when we have no reason to think it's important at the time.'

'I wish I could. But the more they ask, the more I dunno, I mean, I feel like maybe I should, like, make it up to get them off my back…'

'No!' Jo interrupted quickly, then continued in a more even, reassuring tone. 'That wouldn't be a good idea.' She paused, she didn't want to say anything that might alarm him further, so rather than telling him he could get in trouble if he lied she took another line. 'It could stop them finding whoever is doing this, and that's the most important thing. They will leave you alone once they have this guy.'

Mark looked at her, unsure.

'They don't fucking believe me, but I just, like, don't remember stuff. Sorry.' Jo was surprised that he was apologising for swearing, and it reinforced her opinion that despite the clothes, the terrible home life, and the tattoos, Mark was a good lad at heart.

'I can talk to them, if you like. Make sure they understand?'

Mark nodded.

'Thanks,' he mumbled.

'Now,' Jo was back to being briskly businesslike, 'how are you coping? Have you had any more panic attacks?'

Mark shook his head.

'I hear there were some problems with Dr Lambourne running late for your last appointment. Have you made another one?'

Mark nodded.

'He sent one in the post, but I don't see the point. He don't do no good. The man's a prick, and I never believed what he said about you.'

Mark looked out from under his floppy fringe, checking that Jo believed him.

'I am sure he was doing what he thought was for the best,' Jo was determined to remain professional and not let Mark know just how much she agreed with him. 'And I think it would be a good idea if you continued to see him. He may be able to help. After all, Helen seemed to think he was doing some good before. Okay?'

'Okay,' Mark agreed.

'I don't want to change your pills if you've not had any more attacks, especially if you're going back to see Dr Lambourne.'

Mark nodded.

'I'm alright really. Now I know they ain't gonna lock me up again.'

'Good, that's settled then. Now, don't forget, you can call anytime if you need to see me or the duty doctor.' She showed him out and watched him walk down the street, jeans hung so low she could see the make of his slightly grey underwear. Once he was out of sight she heaved a sigh of relief, knowing that seeing Mark in an empty surgery could have so easily gone horribly wrong.

Having checked that the doors and windows were all locked on the ground floor, Jo carried her basket of notes up to the office and checked every floor was empty and clear, including the toilets. There had once been an embarrassing situation when an old dear had come out of the toilet only to discover she was locked in and alone. She had called the fire brigade to come and free her, and spoke lengthily of her ordeal to a local journalist. Embarrassed by this adverse publicity, Hugh had threatened immediate dismissal for anyone caught not checking every nook and cranny before setting the alarm and leaving.

As she pulled out of the car park and drove down the High Street towards home, she saw Gerry Brown signalling to turn into the street and, presumably, park his car in the surgery space. She was tempted to go back and confront him, to ask him what he did every Saturday night, but an impatient toot from the car behind reminded her that she was blocking the road, and she drove on, thinking about the fact that today was a Saturday, and wondering if there would be another murder that night.

She was almost home, and could feel herself growing tense in anticipation of seeing her mother's car in her space when her phone rang. She pulled in to the side of the road and was relieved to see it was the police station. One of her regulars had been picked up and needed attention. Dani was in his thirties and was originally from an Eastern European country, but no one was quite sure which one, just as nobody knew how long he had been in Britain. He said he came to find work, but whether he had ever found any was unclear. He had lived on the streets of Hastings, begging and drinking, for many years now, and was regularly picked up for being drunk and disorderly. He was considered a nuisance more than a threat but, despite offers, he resisted all attempts to help him dry out or to re-house him, claiming he needed his freedom, not a roof. Today, he had apparently relieved himself in George Street, in full view of a number of tourists, and had unfortunately splashed a basket of lavender bags on display outside a craft shop as he did so. Once arrested, he fell asleep in the van taking him to the police station and they had difficulty rousing him, hence the call to Jo. Having checked that Dani really was just drunk and had no signs of injury or illness warranting transfer to hospital, Jo left him to sleep it off and persuaded the desk sergeant to take her through the locked door to CID, where she made her own way up to the incident room. She had been unsure whether speaking to Miller about Mark would actually do any good, but being called in to see Dani had made the decision to try easier.

The incident room was quieter than she expected. She hoped that meant everyone was out following up leads, warning any women who hadn't got the message yet, and doing their best to find the killer. The only person she knew in the room was Nigel, who looked up from his computer and quickly shut down the page he had been looking at, but not before Jo had seen the distinctive logo of SusSEXtra.

162

'How's it going?' she asked him. 'Have you managed to find any of our victims on there?'

Nigel cleared his throat and looked round the almost empty room guiltily. No one was paying them any attention.

'We've confirmed that the second victim was on there, Dr Hughes, like you told us, but, um...'

Jo had a slight panic, what if he had found her on there and recognised her?

'That was because her name came up as a possible match for me, and she had used her own picture and her middle name,' he continued. 'But I haven't been matched with any of the others yet, as far as I know.' He looked round guiltily.

'You've gone on as a client?' Jo was surprised, and quickly went through the list of people she had contacted from the site. The last thing she wanted was for her alter ego Vicky to be having covert conversations with a policeman.

'Um, yes, well the website owners haven't yet responded to our request for a client list, so in the meantime...'

'And did you find anyone else interesting on there?' she fished, hoping not to see a guilty look pass across his face, but all she saw was confusion and then relief that he was saved from having to reply, as Miller came in to the room.

'Jo?' He seemed surprised to see her, and she was saddened to see how tired he looked. He had loosened his tie to undo the top button of his crumpled shirt, his sleeves were rolled up, and his hair looked as though he had been running his hands through it. The strain of this investigation was definitely beginning to take its toll.

'I was seeing a prisoner and I just thought whilst I was here, well, um, could I have a word?' She could have kicked herself for being so tongue-tied. Why was it that every time she saw this irritating man she lost her cool?

He ushered her into his office and cleared a chair for her.

'What can I do for you?' he asked.

'I promised Mark Caxton I would speak to you.'

He couldn't disguise a flash of irritation.

'Please tell me you haven't been seeing him alone.'

'He is my patient, and we have a very good system for summoning help in the surgery.' She didn't add that it only worked if there were staff there to be summoned.

'He's told you he is no longer a suspect, hasn't he?'

'Yes, of course. He knows that you just keep asking questions because you think he must know the killer or have had some contact with him.'

Miller relaxed.

'Good.'

'But he is still finding it quite stressful having to answer all your questions. He feels you don't believe him when he says he can't remember.'

Miller sighed and rubbed his face.

'I know. It's not that I don't believe him, it's just incredibly frustrating that he can't seem to tell us what he was doing only a few days ago.'

'The more pressure you put on him to remember things, the less he'll be able to help. He gets into a panic and his mind goes blank. Look, if you want to talk to him again, why don't you get Helen or me to be with him? Just so that he feels like there's someone there to support him.'

'Of course. Yes, I'll do that. Where it's possible, that is.'

'I realise it won't always be practical,' she conceded, 'But please, don't let Sergeant Jeffries anywhere near him,' she added, with what she hoped was a disarming smile.

He nodded his understanding and stood to show her out, but hesitated when she didn't immediately stand herself.

'I was just wondering how things were going?' she asked. He hesitated for a moment, uncertain quite what she was asking. She wasn't sure herself, but was relieved when he chose to believe it was a work-related question rather than personal.

'We're trying to get a warrant for the records of the company that runs the website, but with only one confirmed victim on there, well, who knows if we'll have any luck with that.'

'Won't the company cooperate without a warrant? Surely they don't want to be the reason another woman gets murdered?'

'I spoke to the owner, a Ms Hepton-Lacey, but she felt her hands were tied. Her lawyers had advised her that without a warrant she could be sued by anyone who felt she had breached their right to privacy by letting us see their details.'

Jo could see the problem. She knew all too well that in today's society everyone was worried about being sued by everybody else. As a doctor, the insurance premiums to cover her against legal action were substantial.

'Could you not issue a warning? That you think he meets his victims online, even if you can't name the specific website?'

'Apparently not. We don't want to frighten the public or damage anyone's business, do we? We might end up being the ones getting sued.'

Miller was unable to keep the bitterness from his voice.

'That's ridiculous,' she retorted angrily. 'The public are already scared. If a woman dies tonight and the police haven't done everything possible to stop it, I would imagine you might be sued anyway.'

Miller threw his hands up.

'You don't need to tell me.'

'Who do I need to tell, then? Because believe me, I am quite happy to give the Chief Constable a piece of my mind if that's what it takes.' Miller smiled at her righteous indignation.

'What?' she asked, angry that he didn't seem to be taking her seriously.

'God, but she's beautiful when she's angry, isn't she Boss?'

Both Miller and Jo turned guiltily at the sarcastic voice that had interrupted their conversation, then scowled when they saw Jeffries standing there.

'But don't let me stop you, Doc,' Jeffries continued, coming into the office. 'I'd pay good money to see you give the Chief Constable a piece of your mind, especially now that the CPS have turned down our request for a warrant to get SusSEXtra's client list.'

'The women of Hastings are locking their doors and staying in tonight. With the body count now standing at three, they are too frightened to go out, knowing that a vicious killer is stalking the streets, picking them off, one by one.' The reporter finished her piece, and the camera panned across the near empty streets of the town centre.

Jo pushed her plate of prawn stir fry away from her in disgust. It wasn't that it tasted bad, it was the endless ghoulish speculation about the possibility of another death that seemed to be on every television channel that was putting her off her food. Would there be another Saturday night murder? She sincerely hoped not, but she knew she wouldn't sleep tonight, expecting to be called at dawn to pronounce another woman dead. At least people had got the message and were staying in, if the report was true. Apart from her mother, that is, who was not going to have her plans changed by something so tawdry, and had gone out to a whist drive or something equally tedious. Jo switched channels as the special feature news programme cut back to the studio. She didn't want to watch the picture parade of victims she had come to know too well, and the endless sanctimonious platitudes about them: good wife, perfect mother, best friend ever, I'll never find anyone like her again. The women had become saints overnight, with no one willing to speak ill of the dead. Everyone who had ever met any of the victims was queuing up for their moment in the spotlight, weeping and wailing in an effort to convince the world how traumatised they were. Jo chastised herself for being so cynical and began channel surfing, hoping to find something to distract her from her tense wait for the phone to ring, but she couldn't find anything, so she switched the television off and resigned herself to an evening of silence.

She would have liked to chat to Kate, even over the phone, but she was out at a dinner party given by one of her many friends. Kate was funny and gregarious and found herself in almost constant demand at dinner parties, to balance any single men who had been invited. Jo found herself invited by friends as well, but usually because they were trying to pair her off with some completely awful relative they were desperate to see settle down, so she rarely accepted. Kate believed no one bothered trying to palm some loser in-law off on her because they knew she would frighten most of them to death. Jo thought she was probably right.

Jo checked her watch. Nine o'clock and the killer was probably meeting his victim, buying her drinks, GHB at the ready, planning how to get her into the stolen car he would have waiting outside. A thought occurred to her; if he was busy with his fourth victim, he wouldn't be very likely to respond to a text from anyone else. She hurriedly fetched her laptop and signed in to the SusSEXtra website, sending messages to everyone who had contacted her, and then texting the ones she had exchanged numbers with, including the unlovely Lee, to see which of them got back to her.

By ten thirty she had chatted with ten men, mainly using WhatsApp, which seemed to be most people's favourite. She was surprised that the list of men responding included Lee, who seemed completely unabashed by her previous put downs. Like a puppy he was up and bouncing, full of energy, wanting to meet, and do a lot of other things which he described in great detail, but which Jo quickly deleted. She kept on her flirty sexting with each of the men long enough to convince herself that it was unlikely they were also holding a conversation with a woman who was with them. Not a woman they were trying to chat up, anyway. Jo checked her watch. Her mother would be back shortly, as Jo had made her promise not to stay out late or go anywhere other than the village hall, not that she thought for even one moment that her mother was a possible victim. Apart from anything else, the killer would have to be mad to pick on a woman who could repel any advances with a single withering look. Jo drew up a list of all the men who had contacted her and crossed off the ten names she had managed to get responses from in the last hour. Only another twenty-two suspects then.

He sat, furiously playing with his glass. How dare she be late. The bitch. How dare she stand him up like this? He checked his phone again. At least he had developed his relationship with Vicky while he waited, but that was scant consolation for a wasted night. He stood up to leave the packed pub. It seemed full of people who were there because it wasn't a town centre pub, and for some reason they thought that meant they would be safer. Such stupidity. He had never used a venue in the town centre because of the ubiquity of CCTV. He checked his watch again. He'd given the whore enough time. She clearly wasn't coming. He ignored the comments from the couple who had been waiting for his table as they slid into his seat the moment he left it. Perhaps it was a good thing the bitch hadn't turned up, sitting alone and blocking a table, they would have been able to remember him if she had eventually arrived, and he made a note to himself; if the place was packed, do not occupy a table until the date arrives, even if that meant there were none free. They could always find a space outside.

He had to think about what to do with the car. He could leave it somewhere, open, hoping that it would be stolen, but what if it wasn't? It would have his DNA all over it without the cleansing effect of fire. If he held onto the car and hid it in his garage for the next time then that was a risk as well. What if anyone saw it there? Or saw him driving it back? How could he explain away a stolen car with fake plates? It was too direct a link to the murders. No, he had to get rid of the car, stick to the plan, and burn it like the others. Only this time, the car would be empty.

20

Jo woke with a start and looked at her watch in surprise. It was nine o'clock on a Sunday morning and she could hear church bells, as well as the usual raucous screech of the seagulls. And the noise of the shower running in the bathroom. She reached across to the coffee table and quickly checked her phone. Perhaps she'd slept through the ring or the battery had died overnight, but no, the screen burst into life and showed she hadn't missed anything. There had been no early morning call to pronounce life extinct. She sighed and lay back again, before realising that she had better take the opportunity to get into her room and collect some clean clothes before her mother had finished in the bathroom. Groaning slightly and rubbing her sore back as she levered herself off the couch, she hurried into her bedroom.

As she picked out her clothes for the day she thought through the implications of her unbroken sleep. There had been no call. Therefore there had been no killing. Unless they just hadn't found the body yet. The killer might have chosen somewhere so remote that it would take a while before the body was found.

She picked up the pile of clothing and hurried back into the living room, grabbing the remote from the coffee table and switching the television on. She wasn't sure why she was checking, as there wouldn't be anything on the news if they hadn't found another body yet.

She watched the headlines as she made a pot of English Breakfast tea, using loose leaves and warming the pot carefully in her regular Sunday morning ritual – one she shared with her mother, who would no doubt want a cup as soon as she was up and dressed. With a bit of luck her mother would go to church, leaving her to have a civilised start to the day. She might even walk down to the seafront for a leisurely coffee and a read of the Sunday papers. Except that the papers would be full of the murders.

'Television? In the morning?' Unnoticed by Jo, who was concentrating on the news, her mother had come out of the bathroom dressed in a floor-length pink dressing gown and with her hair in a towelling turban. Jo straightened her own robe and made sure all her essentials were covered.

'Just checking there haven't been any more murders,' she explained, handing her mother a cup of tea, hoping she would take it through to the bedroom to dress, and feeling relieved once she did.

On the television news channel, a lengthy discussion was taking place on whether the killing spree had stopped. The debate consisted of more speculation than fact, and Jo was just pouring herself a second cup of tea when there was some breaking news and they cut to a reporter rushing breathlessly into a country car park. Jo sat forward and gripped her bone china mug so tightly that there was a danger it would break.

Having got the wreckage of a burnt-out car into frame behind him, the reporter continued his story. Jo looked closely and could make out the blackened remnants of what appeared to be a small hatchback. She tried to work out where the car park was, but didn't think it was anywhere she knew.

'Another Saturday night, another burnt out car, and as the fire brigade and police responded early this morning, they feared there had been another murder. Thankfully, when they got here, they found out that this time, there was no body inside.'

Jo hadn't realised she had been holding her breath until then, but let it out in a huge sigh of relief, and put her tea down. She imagined Miller must have reacted in a similar way when he was told there wasn't another burnt corpse.

'Are the police connecting this to the previous incidents?' The anchorwoman was asking her colleague.

Jo could see Colin the crime scene manager in the background, well away from the car and indicating to a constable that he should move people back. The moment he realised he was on camera Colin ducked out of sight, and a police constable appeared, rolling out crime scene tape, forcing the reporter and cameraman to move further away from the car. As they moved back Jo saw Chris Butterworth, the fire investigator, looking around the area intently. Then the camera moved, focusing on the reporter again.

'The car park venue, in an isolated area of the countryside, would suggest that this is the work of the same man, but the police are keeping an open mind at this stage.' Somehow, Jo doubted that any police officers had spoken to the reporter, let alone told him that they were keeping an open mind, and she suspected that the only reason he knew there was no body in the car was the lack of a mortuary van or police doctor at the scene. And remote car parks were often where cars were dumped and torched. The killer wasn't the only arsonist to use them.

'Thanks, Giles,' the anchorwoman said to the reporter before turning back to the studio camera, with a serious look on her face. 'We will keep you updated on developments in Hastings as they occur,' she said, before finally allowing herself a little smile, 'And now over to Casey for the weather.'

Jo switched the television off and wondered why the killer hadn't added to his victims. The car could have been left by a bunch of joy riders this time. If so, it wouldn't take Colin and Chris long to uncover the discrepancies. Jo rubbed a hand across her forehead. If this one was just a straightforward case of arson she hoped Mark wasn't involved. He torched cars for pleasure and to relieve stress, and he had undoubtedly been under stress recently. If the killer was copying his methods, then it stood to reason that torching cars in remote car parks was exactly how Mark worked. The more she thought about it, the more it seemed possible that if this car wasn't the work of the killer then Mark might be the culprit, and she knew he would find himself under a whole lot more pressure pretty quickly if that was the case, and even if it wasn't. Although she wasn't on call as a GP this weekend, perhaps a pre-emptive visit was in order.

She quickly dressed, and just as her mother came out to ask if she wanted to come to church with her, grabbed her bag, said she had an urgent appointment but that she hoped to be back in time for lunch and suggested they go out somewhere. Her mother readily agreed. At least that would stop her mother from insisting on doing all the cooking herself, but meanwhile, she had to see Mark and make sure he wasn't responsible for this latest arson attack.

Jo knocked at the door of Mark's home and waited. She could hear him inside and called out to let him know it was her. There was a bit more shuffling from inside, then the door opened and Mark peered out. He looked relieved to see she was alone and opened the door wider to let her in.

He showed her into the untidy sitting room and she perched on the worn and stained sofa. Jo had got used to the state of some people's homes over the years. Visiting the sick was always a risky business, and she had learnt to take care to dress in clothes that could be easily cleaned or washed. Her love of pastel colours had caused problems on a number of occasions, and she had resigned herself to having to throw some of her favourites out when they became stained by blackcurrant squash or bodily fluids. The need for hardwearing and machine washable clothes was not something she had ever seen mentioned in a job description for doctors.

Mark sat on an armchair and began an in-depth study of his cuticles again.

'I wondered if you had heard the news this morning?' she asked tentatively.

He shook his head, but looked up for a moment, interested.

'Was there another one? Another woman burnt?'

'No, well there was another car fire, but there wasn't anyone in the car this time.'

Mark nodded.

'That's okay then,' he went back to picking at his fingers.

Jo was more than a little anxious about her next question.

'Um, I don't want you to take this the wrong way,' she started, and leant forward with what she hoped was a reassuring smile as he looked at her at last. 'I don't suppose it was you this time?'

For a moment he didn't understand what she was saying, but then his eyes widened as it finally registered.

'What!' he jumped up. 'You think I done this?'

'No, no. Not necessarily,' she tried to reassure him as he started pacing the room in agitation. 'I don't think that, but I just need to be sure so that I can head the police off...'

'The police, no!' He was really agitated now, and too late, Jo realised her visit was having the opposite effect to the one she had hoped for. 'Dr Lambourne was right. You're trying to stitch me up!'

He jumped up and Jo forced herself to sit still, hoping that this would help cool the situation down.

'Calm down, Mark. I came here to help you. The police are going to have to question you. They are probably already on their way, but if we can...' before she could finish her sentence he had run out of the house, slamming the door behind him.

With a sigh, Jo got up and headed for the front door to leave, berating herself for having made matters worse rather than better. She heard some shouting, and as she opened the door she came face to face with Miller and Jeffries, the latter holding a struggling Mark in a bear hug.

'Dr Hughes!' Miller looked surprised to see her.

Jo nodded to him but headed straight to her patient and went to touch him gently on the arm, before hastily dropping her hand as she remembered this might trigger a more violent reaction.

'I didn't call them, Mark, but I did know they would want to question you. That's why I came to speak to you. To help you.' Her words seemed to have a calming effect on the boy and he stopped struggling, while he tried to think about what she was saying.

'Why don't we go inside and get this cleared up?' She turned to Miller. 'He didn't even know there had been another car fire,' she explained. 'He got frightened when I told him, that's why he was running away.'

Jo didn't think it would help if she said he was running away from her because he thought she was trying to help the police frame him.

Miller decided to emulate Jo's quiet reassuring tone.

'We just want to ask where you were so that we can rule you out, Mark.' He gestured to Jeffries to let the boy go, and, reluctantly, he did.

'Like Dr Hughes said, why don't we go inside?'

Miller and Jeffries quickly established that Mark had been staying with his girlfriend overnight, and that he had only just got back home when Jo arrived. Jeffries went outside to get the alibi confirmed and Miller continued to question Mark, with Jo there as his appropriate adult.

'You know what we talked about? That we found a drinks can at each scene?' Miller asked Mark gently.

Mark shrugged.

'They were from a brand of energy drink that we know you like.'

'Lots of people drink it,' Mark said, anxious to make sure Miller wasn't trying to put the blame back on him.

'Of course. But your prints were on the cans at the previous sites, and we will find out soon enough if that's the case with a can we discovered near the car this morning.'

Jo registered this new fact. The killer obviously didn't know that Mark had been eliminated as a suspect if he'd left another can there to implicate him.

'But I didn't put the cans there,' Mark was beginning to get agitated, and Miller hastened to calm him.

'We know that, but whoever did put them there is trying to get you into trouble. Do you understand what I'm saying, Mark?'

Mark nodded.

'Do you have any idea why anyone would want to do that?'

Mark shook his head.

'It seems mad,' he said, clearly not having any idea why anyone who wasn't mad would do this to him.

Miller reached into his pocket and pulled out a piece of paper. He unfolded it and showed it to Mark. It was pictures of what looked like three matchbook covers.

'Do you recognise these?' Miller asked Mark gently.

Mark nodded.

'They're matchbook covers,' he leaned forward. 'Nice ones.' Mark looked closely and then turned to Jo. 'They're pretty, aren't they?'

'Yes,' she agreed.

'I've got that one, and that one,' he pointed to two of the pictures, 'but not that one,' he pointed to the third and then looked at Miller. 'Will I get them back?'

'I don't know, Mark, probably not,' he admitted, thinking that there was absolutely no chance of him getting them back. Mark looked saddened as he realised his collection had finally gone.

Miller pointed back at the paper.

'These are the matchbooks used in the three murders. The lab managed to bring up enough detail with infrared photography to identify them.'

Mark looked at the pictures and shook his head in dismay.

'I never used nice ones,' he told them. 'I used the boring ones and the ones I had more than one of. I would never have used ones as nice as these. That's mental, that is. And I never had that last one. I never even seen one like that. I would've kept it if I had.'

Miller changed tack.

'When you set cars alight, did you ever leave an empty can behind, as a sort of calling card?'

Mark looked at Miller as if he was now the madman in their midst. 'No!'

Miller just looked at him.

'I mean, I might have left one by mistake, but I wouldn't do it on purpose. I didn't want to get caught.'

'So,' Miller persisted, 'where do you think he gets these cans with your prints on?'

'I don't know,' Mark seemed genuinely perplexed. 'I mean, I drink them all the time, but I always bin them. I don't litter.' This simple statement confirmed to Jo that he really was a good boy at heart.

At that moment Jeffries came back into the room and nodded to Miller. The alibi was solid. Mark couldn't have torched the car.

As they left Mark's house, Jo turned to Miller.

'Were you asking about the drinks cans from previous fires because you think someone has got hold of them and is leaving them at the current sites?'

'Are you suggesting a copper nicked them from the evidence store and planted them at the scene?' Jeffries came back aggressively.

'No, but…' Jo retorted angrily, but Miller stopped her before things escalated into a full-scale row.

'Even if he had left them in the past, which he says he didn't, these cans couldn't be from then, because they're the new design and the batch numbers show they must have been purchased recently.'

Jeffries and Jo both glared at each other, neither willing to apologise.

'Can you narrow it down to where they were bought?' Jo asked Miller.

'Only to a local cash and carry that supplies about forty different shops in the area.'

'Pretty much every corner shop in Hastings,' Jeffries added grumpily, and Jo could relate to his unhappiness this time. They had obviously tried hard to find the source.

'If it's not something Mark used to do when he set fires, then the killer has simply invented a calling card, and he must be someone close to Mark, because he seems to be able to get drinks cans with his prints on them without any trouble,' Miller continued. 'We need to check who has access to his rubbish, both here and at places he frequents like the youth centre.'

'What about the matchbooks? As Mark said, they aren't common or garden ones. Can you trace who bought them?' Jo added.

'It's hard. There are so many collectors out there. Jayne was checking them out, but we will need to escalate that search and check if anyone even remotely connected to Mark has bought any online or from a dealer.'

'And then cross check those people with the people who know the MO, have access to the rubbish and are divorced,' Jeffries added with obvious dismay. 'Which could take a sodding lifetime.'

Miller nodded and added with a slightly malicious smile, 'The joys of modern policing, Bob. It's all about the data searches.'

Jo was pleased that they were checking names against so many criteria, searching for connections. Surely one name would come to the fore soon? The trouble was, as Sergeant Jeffries had pointed out with the unnecessary expletive, it could take a very long time. A very long time indeed.

'The killer must realise by now that you no longer suspect Mark, so why continue to leave the cans?' It seemed peculiarly vindictive to Jo.

'That's a good question,' Miller responded.

'Just to fuck with us,' Jeffries added, seemingly indifferent to Jo's wince at his use of another swear word.

'And to let us know he's still out there, that he hasn't stopped.'

Jo couldn't suppress a slight shiver at Miller's words, and the thought that more women could, and probably would, die before they caught this man.

'Right,' she said, 'I'm off to enjoy the rest of my Sunday in relative peace, I hope. Goodbye.' She walked back to where she had parked her car, with Jeffries glaring daggers at her retreating back, and Miller looking at her with an altogether different expression on his face.

The plan for the rest of her day was for lunch with her mother, and a frank discussion about her long-term housing plans. Jo had thought about inviting her dad as well, in the hope that they could sort their problems out, but she didn't feel ready for it just yet, and she was pretty sure they weren't either. It would have to happen, and soon, because much as she was loath to get involved in other people's arguments, there was a limit to how long she could sleep on the sofa.

'It was a total disaster,' Jo admitted to Kate later. 'The moment I mentioned the possibility of Ma talking to Dad or moving out of my place she went off on one. Any hopes I may have had about her not making a scene in public were shattered. She told me I was an ungrateful and unloving daughter who wouldn't even give her homeless mother a place to stay for a few weeks. I swear the entire pub was listening in and condemning me for my heartlessness. And then she refused to speak again for the rest of the meal. I can't believe I got it so wrong.'

'Perhaps you should have spoken to her at home or chosen a posh restaurant; I bet she wouldn't have created a scene in Claridge's or somewhere like that.'

'I'll remember your wise words if I ever try and do anything like that again. I have never sat through such an excruciating meal in all my life.'

'Not even with that Doug guy? You know, the one who wouldn't sit at a round table and then wanted reassurance from the chef that nothing had garlic in, and then wanted to change how things were cooked and what they came with.'

'Believe me, his fussiness pales in comparison to what I went through today.'

'So, I take it your mother is still staying with you?'

Jo nodded and pulled a face that said pretty much how she felt about it, causing Kate to laugh.

'I don't know what you're laughing at! If this goes on much longer I'll be turning up on your doorstep with my suitcase.'

'Seriously though, Jo, you know you are always welcome, and you can stay as long as you like.'

But they both knew Jo wouldn't do that. She valued her privacy too much, and it would mean admitting that she couldn't live with her mother, and in spite of the fact it was true, admitting it felt like too much of a betrayal. Besides which, her mother would never let her forget it.

21

Having spent what was left of her Sunday cathartically cleaning her home in an effort to get the murders out of her mind, as well as to impress her mother, and failing on both counts, Jo had come to a decision, about the murders at least. She needed to find out if Gerry was involved, if only to put her mind at rest. She couldn't very well voice her suspicions to the police, because she had no real grounds for them. She could imagine Miller's reaction if she told him that she suspected Gerry to be a serial killer because he was a creep or because he wasn't a very good doctor, let alone because he parked his car at the surgery every Wednesday and Saturday night. No, she had to find out if there was any basis to her suspicions first. It seemed pretty hopeless trying to prove or disprove Gerry Brown's involvement through the website. Especially since she couldn't even rule out the ones who had responded on Saturday, as no murder had taken place. How could she ever know if any of the men she had been talking to was Gerry? Unless she agreed to meet them, and there was no way she was going that far. It had been while cleaning her oven that she had decided to stop trying to talk to him through the website and to take the radical step of speaking to him in person. She wasn't going to ask him outright if he was a serial killer, of course, but just generally get to know him better and see if she could find any other indications that he was the murderer. Something concrete she could take to Miller without him laughing at her.

Once she got to the surgery on Monday morning, Jo checked Gerry's morning list and worked out when he would be finishing. There was no point trying to speak to him before he started surgery as he wouldn't want to begin late, but if she could catch him once he had finished and before he rushed off to wherever it was he disappeared to between clinics, she might just get to speak to him. Of course, that meant she would have to take a break from her own patients, as her surgery was longer, but if she could just try and get a bit ahead and then nip up at the relevant time for a cup of coffee, it could work. The important thing was to ensure that she wasn't already running late by that time.

Her plan started well. Her first three patients were all on time and only had one problem each for her to deal with: a blood pressure check, a medication review and a referral, but then the fourth patient came in armed with a list and Jo's heart sank. There was no way she was going to get through a list of problems in the allotted ten minutes. And she didn't, so she missed Gerry. He had disappeared for his lunch break long before she made it up to the office.

'Why did you want to see Gerry?' Linda asked when Jo checked if he was still there.

'Oh, you know, I just thought I'd try and get to know him better.'

Linda raised an eyebrow, clearly not buying that explanation.

'It's this thing about leaving his car here twice a week. My curiosity is getting the better of me and I really want to know why he does it. So I thought I'd try asking him, in a roundabout way, of course.'

Linda laughed. Curiosity was something she could understand.

'I don't suppose you know, do you?' Jo asked, hoping Linda had managed to find out, but she shook her head, disappointed not to be able to shed any light on the matter. 'I mean, you'd think his wife would object.'

'Ah, well! I might not know why he leaves his car here, but I do know that he and his wife have split up. That's one of the reasons he left his previous practice and came to us as a locum.'

'One of the reasons?'

'The other being the cause of his marital split...' Linda leaned in confidentially and checked no one else was listening before whispering, 'he had an affair with a patient.'

Jo was genuinely shocked. That was an absolute no-no for doctors.

'I think Dr Grantham felt a bit sorry for him, you know, given his own history, so that's why he came here when no one else would touch him with a barge pole.'

Jo knew that Dr Grantham had fallen in love with a young and beautiful patient many years ago and there had been a whiff of a scandal. But in his case, the patient had left the practice and got herself another doctor in town so that there was no barrier to them seeing each other, and they had been happily married for twenty-seven years now. So, even though Hugh had taken great care to do things the right way once he knew the depths of his feelings, she could understand his sympathy for Gerry.

'That explains a lot,' Jo told Linda. 'He's probably still seeing the woman, too.'

'Not sure about that,' Linda said. 'According to the practice manager at his old surgery, the affair only came to light when the patient complained to the surgery that she had chucked him but he wouldn't leave her alone.'

That fitted in well with how he reacted when Kate had tried to break free. He was not one to take rejection lightly.

'And then his wife threw him out. Unsurprisingly,' Linda continued. 'She's some high-powered internet millionaire with a very good legal team, not to mention something that she can hold over him and threaten to get him struck off for if he didn't do as she wanted. So he lost his wife, his girlfriend, his home, his car and his job. Everything. In one fell swoop. He's probably ended up having to pay her maintenance as well.' Linda seemed to take great delight in this, and Jo did too, if she was honest. It was nice to hear of someone getting their comeuppance like that, but had it tipped him over the edge and turned him into a killer? It seemed a possibility that she couldn't discount.

'And I'll tell you the final irony,' Linda had really got into her stride now, and Jo certainly wasn't about to stop this useful flow of gossip. 'His ex-wife made her money out of one of those dating websites that encourages people to have affairs. It's got a really tacky name, now what was it?' Linda thought for a second, struggling to remember.

'SusSEXtra?' Jo asked helpfully.

'Yes, that's it!' Linda agreed. 'How did you know what it was called?' she added, suddenly suspicious.

'Oh, it cropped up in another conversation,' Jo tried to sound innocent, but she wasn't sure she had convinced Linda, who looked as if she was about to question her more closely.

'Anyway, I must get on,' Jo grabbed her basket of paperwork and hurried into the doctors' office.

Once she was alone in the office, she logged onto a computer and opened up a web browser. She needed to find out more about

181

SusSEXtra, or SSE as some of the users seemed to call to it. Companies House gave her the information she needed. The owner of the company was listed as Amelia Hepton-Lacey, and gave the registered address in Brighton. Using these details Jo had little difficulty getting a contact number.

Before she had time to do any more Gauri came in, laden with notes and papers, and settled herself at another workstation. Jo quickly flicked back to the surgery software system and picked a letter out of her basket, to make it look as if she was working.

'Please tell me there isn't a partners' meeting today?' Gauri plaintively asked Jo.

'I don't think so,' Jo quickly checked her calendar. 'No, it's next week Gauri, you're alright.'

'Thank goodness for that.'

They worked on in companionable silence as Jo despatched with her paperwork in record time and hurried out to the main office.

Linda had allocated her three visits, none of which would be too onerous with any luck, and Jo collected the notes.

'I'm just popping home for lunch, then I'll do these visits,' she said, putting the notes in her bag and waving at Linda and the secretaries as she hurried out before they could find anything else for her to do.

Saying a silent prayer of thanks that her mother had gone out, Jo sat at her dining table holding her phone, with the SusSEXtra company contact number and an untouched sandwich in front of her. For once she was not distracted by the spectacular view out of her window.

She took a deep breath and dialled.

'Hello, SSE, can I help you?' A woman's voice answered after only two rings.

'Oh hello. Could I speak to Amelia Hepton-Lacey, please?' Jo replied.

'I'm afraid she's not in the office at the moment, can I take a message?'

For a moment Jo was floored. She hadn't really thought through what she was going to say next.

'Um, my name is Dr Hughes and I'm with the police,' she finally said, crossing her fingers. It wasn't actually a lie. She was, after all, a police FME, but there was no way her role covered what she was currently doing. 'Can I ask who I'm speaking to?'

'Jenny Harris. I'm the office manager. Who did you say you were?' Jenny countered.

'Dr Jo Hughes. I work as a consultant with the police, I can give you a number to contact to check my credentials if you would like?' Jo hoped Jenny would decline, because she wasn't quite sure who she could ask to do that for her.

'No, that's okay Dr Hughes, I can see you listed on the website.'

'Of course,' Jo had to stop herself from sounding surprised. She had no idea she was listed on the Hastings Police website. Jenny was clearly very efficient if she had found her so quickly. That was probably bad news for Jo, but she pressed on regardless. 'As you know, we are looking into the possibility that the murdered women were accessed through the website. It's obviously vital that we are sure if this is a real possibility or if it's a dead end, so to speak, and I wonder if you could help me?'

'It's terrible, isn't it? To think of what happened to them?' Jenny seemed genuinely distressed.

'Which is why it's so important we know how he is contacting these women. Of course it may not be through your website, but we have to eliminate it.'

'Of course, and I'm honestly happy to do what I can,' Jenny said helpfully. 'But Amelia has left clear instructions that we are not to divulge the names or details of any of our clients to the police without a warrant. We could be liable if we did.' She sounded quite upset at not being able to help more.

'I quite understand and I wouldn't want to put you in a difficult position,' Jo agreed, and decided to push that little bit more, as Jenny seemed to want to help, if she could. 'But I am sure that since you knew of our interest, you will have done a bit of digging and checked the victims' names against your client list, wouldn't you?'

'Well, our clients usually use aliases, so the client list isn't much help, but the payment details are more accurate,' Jenny admitted, which suggested she had been checking out the victims. 'I can quite understand how important it is for you to know, and I'd really like to help.' Jenny left that hanging in the air as a hint to Jo that she was willing to cooperate.

'So would it be possible for me to say the names one at a time, and if that person is a client you might find you need to cough?' Jo suggested.

'How about I might need to cough if they aren't a client?' Jenny countered.

'Okay. Sarah Dunsmore,' Jo waited, but there was no cough, 'Carol Johnson,' as expected, there was no cough after Carol's name, 'Teresa Hardwick.' Jo held her breath. This was the crunch moment. No cough again. Jo waited, just in case, but the silence lengthened and there was no doubt in her mind.

'So all three were clients?' Jo just wanted to be certain.

'You might like to think that, but I couldn't possibly comment,' Jenny paraphrased the well-known quote from House of Cards. Jo thanked her profusely for her help and ended the call.

She sat there, with the phone in her hand, knowing that she should call Miller, but at the same time looking for reasons not to. In the end, she couldn't think of any that really stood up to scrutiny, so she dialled his number and was slightly relieved to get an answerphone message.

'Hi, this is Jo,' she said quickly, as she hated speaking to machines and felt she always came across as incoherent. 'I have had confirmation that all three women used the, um, the SSE website.' Somehow she really couldn't come out with its full name. 'I also wanted to talk to you about the website owner's husband. Can you give me a call back?'

She ended the call and looked at her sandwich. She really wasn't feeling very hungry. She checked her watch and realised she'd have to get a move on if she was going to do her visits and get back to the surgery on time. She grabbed her bag and, after a moment's hesitation, picked up the sandwich, popping it into a plastic bag as she hurried out of the door.

22

Jo was surprised that Miller hadn't called back by the time she'd finished evening surgery, but not half as surprised as she was to see him sitting in the waiting room when she came out with her basket of notes and papers.

'Dr Hughes.' He stood, formal and professional as always in front of the public, even though that was only the receptionist and a couple of Gauri's patients, 'I wondered if you had time for a word?'

'Um, of course, do you want to come in?' She indicated her consulting room, but he didn't move towards it.

'I thought perhaps we could go out, if you don't mind. I could do with something to eat.'

He looked at her basket and Jo realised that the uneaten sandwich was still there, clearly visible, proof that she hadn't had lunch either. Again.

'Of course, that would be good, actually. I'll just sort these and I'll be with you in five minutes, if that's okay?'

Jo hurried up to the office and dealt with her paperwork in record time, chucked the sandwich in the bin, nipped into the ladies to make sure her hair wasn't a mess, and headed back down to the entrance where Miller was waiting for her.

'Ready,' she said, slightly breathlessly, and went through the door that Miller was holding open for her, ignoring the raised eyebrows of the receptionist who was watching her intently, making sure she remembered every detail of the encounter to share with Linda, no doubt.

Miller hardly said a word as they walked down the High Street, only giving Jo monosyllabic answers to her questions about how he was and how the investigation was going. By mutual consent they never mentioned his wife when they were together, Jo because she found it too uncomfortable and Miller because it would seem like a betrayal, somehow. It was only a short walk to Porters, where he ushered her in and sat her at a corner table before going to the bar to order a glass of Pinot Grigio for her and a beer for himself. Jo was getting quite nervous about his unusual recalcitrance by the time he returned with the drinks.

'So,' he finally said once they were both settled. 'Tell me how you know all three victims used the SSE website?'

'Well, I spoke to someone who works there and got her to confirm it.'

Jo was glad he was referring to it as SSE, as she really didn't want the other customers getting the wrong idea about the two of them if they happened to overhear the conversation.

'And is this person willing to make a statement to that effect?'

Jo cleared her throat and fiddled with the stem of her glass. Despite his rigid control, she could tell he was angry.

'Um, no, she can't because she is under express orders from her boss not to.'

'And what, exactly, do you expect me to do with this piece of unattributable information?'

'I don't know,' she snapped back. 'I had thought you would be grateful that you were at least on the right track as you tried to get a warrant to see the client details. Maybe I thought that this information might help you get that warrant.'

He paused for a moment, to collect his thoughts and let her cool down.

'Which it did, thank you. But ...'

'It did?' she interrupted, a smile lighting up her face. 'That's brilliant!' For once she really felt that she had been useful. So often, in both her jobs, she felt that she was just putting a sticking plaster over a major wound. She very rarely felt she had made a real difference.

'Yes, but as I was saying, Dr Hughes, Jo, you can't go around interfering like that. It may have helped this time, but what if it had gone wrong?'

'How could it? All I did was persuade the office manager to cough if I mentioned the name of someone who wasn't a client, and she didn't cough.' Jo was cross that he didn't seem pleased with this breakthrough. She felt she deserved some praise for helping.

'And how did you get her to agree to do that? How did you manage to persuade her that you weren't a journalist looking for some dirt on the company?'

Jo had a nasty suspicion that he knew very well what she had done.

'I said I was from the police which, strictly speaking, is true. She checked on the website and saw my name and was happy with that.'

'You impersonated a police officer.'

'No, I never said I was a police officer. I said I was with the police. I am very well aware of the difference, and when she checked my name with the website, she would have seen my job title. And yes, I was surprised she agreed, as I could have been anyone, even a journalist pretending to be me.'

'Believe me, any self-respecting journalist would have rejected such a weak plan. I mean it was hardly likely to work, was it?'

'Well, it did, because I think she really wanted to help. She knew the information might save a woman's life.'

He said nothing, just glowered at her.

'And I didn't impersonate a police officer,' Jo was childishly cross that he wasn't impressed.

'What you did was as good as impersonation. You can't expect members of the public to differentiate between someone who works with the police and a genuine policeman.' He was unable to contain his anger any longer and banged the table as he spoke, causing a few other customers to look up and the barmaid to start wondering if she was going to have a problem with the couple arguing in the corner.

'I was quite clear. I said I was a consultant with the police, and my title is doctor, not constable or detective whatever,' Jo said quietly despite her anger. She was angry, in part because he was being so ungrateful, but also because a little bit of her knew that he was right and that she was in the wrong.

'But that was what she thought you were, a policewoman, and that is what she would say if she gave evidence. And what if your source hadn't wanted to cooperate and instead had told her boss and they made a complaint? You could have ended up losing your job with the police or worse, getting disbarred or whatever it is happens to doctors.' Thankfully, he was keeping his voice down as well.

'Struck off,' she corrected him.

'Struck off then.'

There was an uneasy silence for a few moments, and the people around them returned to their conversations.

'I know you're right,' she conceded. 'I did take a chance, and it could have gone horribly wrong, but it didn't. I don't think it would have been grounds for anything more than a rap on the knuckles from the General Medical Council, and yes, I might have lost my job with the police, but that wouldn't be the end of the world, not in comparison to what it delivered. It gave you that little bit of help you needed to get the investigation moving in the right direction, didn't it?'

She was so desperate for reassurance her hand reached out to him, and he couldn't bring himself to resist. He rested his own hand lightly on hers and she felt a frisson of electricity. Looking at his face she was sure he felt it too.

'Yes, I know, I just don't want, I couldn't bear if ...' he said gruffly, but couldn't finish the sentence. All his anger had gone now, and he looked as if he really wanted to lean forward and kiss her. It was Jo who broke the moment first. She looked round and realised that the middle-aged couple who were sitting nearest to them were watching avidly and smiling at this apparent reconciliation. She pulled her hand away quickly and a look of hurt passed momentarily across his face. At least she thought it did, and she was glad he still cared.

'Thank you,' she said quietly. 'I know, and I promise I won't do anything like that again.'

They both sat back in their chairs and concentrated on their drinks, trying to forget the moment that had passed between them, and at the same time not wanting to forget.

'So,' he cleared his throat so that he sounded less husky. 'There was something else you mentioned in your message? Something about the website owner's husband?'

'Oh yes.' Jo had forgotten all about that and had to think for a moment or two to make sure she could tell the story in a coherent manner. 'This is more of what your Sergeant Jeffries would call gossip.'

Miller raised an eyebrow.

'Go on,' he encouraged her. 'Gossip can be helpful, even if it can't be used as evidence.'

So she told him Linda's story about Gerry Brown.

'And I happen to know one of the people he dated from the website, or a website, anyway,' she suddenly realised that Kate hadn't said exactly where she had contacted Gerry, but it couldn't have been SSE, could it? Because then they wouldn't have needed to set Jo up as a client, would they?

'Anyway,' she repeated, while she collected her thoughts again, 'he refused to accept that she didn't want to see him again, and basically stalked her, even arriving at her workplace demanding to see her, until she threatened to take legal action against him, which could have led to him getting struck off. She didn't know about his transgressions with a patient of course, but it's just,' she paused again and realised that he was showing considerable interest in what she was saying. 'I just think he could be a person of interest, that's all.'

'Would he have access to information on Mark?' Miller asked.

'I don't think so,' she admitted. 'I didn't get Mark's full notes from Helen until a few days ago, so he could only have accessed my own notes, which didn't have any details about his method of starting fires.'

'That's a shame,' Miller said, 'I don't suppose he could have got hold of the drinks cans either?'

'I don't see how he could,' she admitted. 'His consulting room is on the first floor, so even if Mark did throw away a can in the waiting room when he came to see me, he would have had no way of knowing that, and Mark hasn't been to see me enough times for him to have got as many as you've collected. Three or four isn't it?' He nodded and she sighed, aware of how flimsy her case against Gerry was, but thankful that Miller hadn't laughed outright at her information.

'It's just that if you are putting together a list of men who have connections to SSE, have had acrimonious divorces, and who perhaps have abnormal attitudes to women, he's got to be on it.'

'Quite,' he smiled. 'Unfortunately, I think we'll find that's true of a lot of men using that website.' He looked up at the menu board. 'Have you decided what you want to eat?'

Jo looked at the board as Miller stood, ready to go to the bar and order their food.

'The sea bass, I think.' She quickly checked the rest of the board. 'Yes, definitely the sea bass.'

Miller pointed at her still almost full glass, but she shook her head.

'No, this is fine thanks.'

Jo checked her phone while Miller ordered their food and got another beer for himself, and thought about what people on their own did before the invention of smart phones. It seemed that no one was allowed to just sit anymore, they had to be busy, connected and communicating with friends or work at all times. She was as guilty as everyone else, but in a way it felt as if people were losing independence and space for reflection in this mad quest to be connected twenty-four hours a day. Fortunately, Miller returned quickly so she didn't have to think about it too long.

'When will you be able to get the client details from SSE?' she asked once he was seated again.

'Already have. Nigel's going through the list as we speak.' He took a swig of beer. 'They had everything ready for us as soon as we served the warrant, so I think you're right, they really were happy to cooperate. Either that or, as my cynical sergeant said, they wanted to make sure no one could accuse them of not cooperating fully in case they got sued.'

'He has a point. They'll need to cover themselves as much as possible if they want to continue in business.'

'I got the impression that Amelia Hepton-Lacey has already decided that SSE won't survive this. She was busy planning to close the site down and re-open under a different name, with different branding.'

'It would be too much to suppose the new website would also have a different ethos, would it?'

'I rather think it would,' he smiled, but then his phone buzzed and he pulled it out to check who was calling. Clearly it wasn't from someone he could ignore, because with a rueful smile and a wave of apology, he took the call and hurried out into the street where there would be less background noise.

Jo went back to examining her own phone, but Miller soon hurried back to her.

'Sorry,' he apologised. 'I have to go, something's come up.' He grabbed his jacket from the back of the chair before pausing. 'Will you be okay?'

'Of course,' she assured him, 'but you need to eat.'

'I'll pick up some fish and chips on my way back to the station.'

A waitress arrived at that moment with cutlery and condiments.

'I don't suppose you know anyone who might want to eat my steak and ale pie?' he asked ruefully. 'I've already paid, and it would be a shame to waste it.'

'I'll call Kate.' Jo said with a smile. 'She only lives round the corner and I'm sure she'd be delighted to join me.' She reached for her bag. 'Let me give you the money.' But by the time she had pulled out her purse, he was already on his way out of the door and the waitress was giving her a sympathetic smile.

Jo smiled back at her and the diners at the surrounding tables, who clearly thought that he had walked out as the result of their argument. She could hardly tell them that it was work calling him away. At least she thought it was. It could, of course, have been Lizzie calling him, but she thought not as she reached for her phone to ring Kate. No, she was sure that he had deserted her because he was urgently needed at work, trying to stop a serial killer, rather than because his wife had called him home. That was what she was going to tell herself, anyway, even if no one else in the restaurant would have believed it. She reached for her phone and called Kate.

'Mmm hmm! Nothing tastes better than a free dinner,' Kate wiped her lips with her napkin. 'Particularly when it's steak pie.' She scooped the last mouthful onto her fork.

'It's lucky you were able to get here before it was served.' Jo had sat for several minutes, suffering sympathetic looks from fellow customers and servers alike, before Kate had breezed in and saved the day. She had seriously considered walking out, and would have done if Kate hadn't said she would drop everything and rescue her friend, but she hated the thought of leaving the food to go to waste, and where would she go? Home, where her mother was waiting? No. Far better to wait for Kate.

'I can move pretty quickly when I need to,' Kate agreed. 'Nothing worse than a cold and congealed pie.'

'Yes,' Jo replied, although they both knew that she would never willingly eat a steak pie, whether hot or cold. Jo indicated Kate's nearly empty glass of red wine. 'Wine or coffee?'

'Wine please, and some cheese and biscuits would be good.'

With a shake of her head, Jo went to the bar to order wine, cheese, and a decaff for herself. Kate need never know.

When she returned to her seat, Jo pulled out the mobile phone Kate had lent her to text the men from the SSE website, and pushed it across the table to her friend.

'Thanks for lending me this, but I won't be needing it anymore.'

'Why?' Kate asked, as she spread lashings of butter onto a cream cracker and added a generous chunk of Stilton, completely ignoring Jo's look of disapproval.

'The police are on it now. They got their warrant and Nigel is going through all the SSE clients as we speak.' She paused, and suddenly looked panicked. 'Oh my goodness!'

Her sudden outburst caused Kate to stop, with her cheese-topped biscuit halfway to her mouth.

'What?'

'He'll find me! My details will be on there.'

'Relax, we put in fake ones, remember?'

'Yes, but once he realises they're fake, he'll check the profile, won't he?'

'He won't recognise you from that photo. No one would.'

'But what if he does? What should I do?'

'Look, Jo. Calm down. He'll be concentrating on the men anyway, once he's identified the three victims. What Miller will want to know is who has contacted all three of them – and then they'll be busy arresting anyone who has, I should imagine. They are not going to be looking at all the other women on there.'

'You're right,' she took a deep breath. 'I know you're right. I'd still be happier if we took my profile down, just in case.'

'That's fine, I'll do that for you, I promise. Tonight. Although Lee and Lance will be heartbroken.'

Jo was relieved. Kate had convinced her that all would be well.

'I really don't care how disappointed they are.'

'You swapped to WhatsApp after the initial contact, didn't you?'

'Yes.'

'So, once I've deleted your profile all you have to do is delete the conversations and their contact details and ask them to do the same, then no one will ever be the wiser. Except…'

Kate paused as she finished the cheese and biscuits and sipped her red wine as Jo looked at her expectantly.

'I mean, Nigel will definitely play by the book, but I can imagine that Sergeant Jeffries bloke going through all the profiles and contacting any women that he thought he might get lucky with!' Kate ducked as Jo threw a napkin at her and managed to at least smile as Kate guffawed at her own wind-up.

'That is my worst nightmare,' Jo told her once Kate managed to stop laughing. 'Promise me you'll take my profile down tonight or I won't sleep a wink.'

Kate finished her wine and grinned.

'Don't worry. Of course I'll take it down. Why don't you come back to mine and we can do it now?' Jo agreed, relieved that her SSE adventure was going to be over.

23

The sun was shining and the air had a clear, clean feeling to it after the overnight rain. As Jo walked to work, quickly heading down the narrow steps that led to All Saints Street, she was feeling positively light-hearted. She had slept unusually well, safe in the knowledge that her profile had been taken down from the SSE website and that she almost certainly wouldn't have to confess to Nigel, or Miller, that she had posed as a client. While she knew she had done nothing wrong, she also knew it would be embarrassing if they ever heard about it, and, in particular, if Sergeant Jeffries ever heard about it. She knew that he would never, ever let her forget it. She still had a slight worry that they would trace her through the client list, but Kate had reassured her that the police would be concentrating on the men using the site, not the women, and Jo hoped that Jeffries hadn't got it into his head to check out the ladies, including those who had removed their details. It would be just like him to do something like that, taking advantage of his professional role to find willing and available women for himself, but even that small, niggling anxiety wasn't enough to dent her good humour. She was sure that the police would quickly discover who the murderer was now that they had all the contact details. After all, there couldn't be too many men who had contacted all three of the victims, could there?

Jo's mobile rang and she stopped walking to search for her phone in the depths of her bag, her heart beating slightly faster when she saw that the call was from Miller.

'Dr Hughes speaking,' she answered, mentally kicking herself for sounding so formal and unfriendly.

'Hi, Jo,' Miller said, and Jo could immediately detect some embarrassment in his voice. She began walking again; putting her slight breathlessness down to the speed she was going, rather than because she was speaking to Miller. 'I wanted to apologise for last night and to, um, let you know that Mark was arrested again this morning.'

'What?' Jo stopped dead, her good humour fading fast.

'Nothing to do with the murders. Apparently he torched a disused barn last night,' Miller told her. 'He confessed. Said he needed to stop the roar in his head.'

Jo took a deep breath.

'I told you this would happen if you kept pushing him. I told you he couldn't take the pressure.'

'I know, I know, and for what it's worth, I'm sorry.' Jo believed him, and she knew it wasn't his fault. He hadn't, in all reality, had any choice but to focus the investigation on Mark.

'Is he at the station now?'

'Yes,' Miller confirmed. 'I told them not to interview him until either you or Helen were there, and I went down to see him, just to check on him, and he seemed okay, calmer than I've ever seen him before, in fact.'

'That's the effect it has on him. Setting fires releases all his stress.'

'Maybe I should give it a try.' Miller sounded tired. Jo knew he must be under an awful lot of pressure with three women dead, and the press, his bosses, and the public all demanding he find the culprit. She would have liked to say something comforting, if only she could think of anything that might help.

'Was anyone hurt?' she asked instead.

'No, no, the barn was in the middle of nowhere. No chance of him hurting anyone, and it was pretty much derelict, so I think the farmer's actually quite pleased with the idea he might get some insurance money out of it.'

'I told you he wouldn't deliberately hurt anyone.' She couldn't help adding what amounted to an 'I told you so'.

'I know.'

Jo checked her watch.

'Look, I've got morning surgery, so I can't make it to the station until lunchtime, and much as you say Mark is pretty chilled at the moment, it might be better to see if Helen can come in before then. Can you ask her?'

'That's fine. I thought you would be busy. I was just letting you know as much as anything else. It's not my case, but I'll ask them to call Helen, okay?'

'Thanks, and sorry.' Jo would have liked to ask him about the contact list from the website and if they had found anyone with links to all three women. Had Lee, Lance or Gerry contacted them? While she was still trying to work out how to put the question, he said goodbye and hung up. She would have to wait to hear. Unless, she thought, she managed to finish surgery quickly so she could fit in a trip to the station during her lunch break. The plan appealed. Even if Helen had already sat in for Mark's interview, he was unlikely to have been released by then, as the paperwork always seemed to take hours. She could say she was just checking up on him. A welfare visit to one of her patients would be perfectly reasonable, and it would be polite to drop in on Miller while she was there, wouldn't it? After all, he'd had the courtesy to let her know Mark had been arrested.

Having convinced herself that this plan was in everyone's interest and not just idle curiosity, Jo hurried to the surgery. Although she had plenty of time before her morning list was due to start she wanted to try and catch Adrian Lambourne and find out if he had managed to see Mark before the boy had imploded. If Lambourne hadn't, despite all her requests for him to do so, she thought that she could insist he make room to see Mark as an emergency as soon as he was released. Of course, Lambourne would also be a good target for her pent-up frustrations. She was in the mood for a good argument.

Before Jo could ring Lambourne, she found another reason to get upset. A quick check of her paperwork basket revealed a request for her to forward on the electronic records for her patient Jill Hollingsworth, and also for her husband David. It seemed they had recently registered with a new surgery in a village many miles from their home. Jo was surprised they had applied to join such a distant service, and even more surprised that they had been accepted. She looked to see what address they had given in case they had moved in that direction, but their address remained at the farm where they had lived for as long as Jo had known them. A quick look at her watch told her it would be a bad time to call the new surgery and enquire exactly why they were taking a couple who lived more than an hour's drive away, as they would just be starting their own morning surgery. Most practices insisted patients lived within a reasonable distance, in case they needed a home visit, and it was surprising that the doctor had elected to ignore this. So, instead of trying the surgery, she decided that she might just have enough time to call Lambourne and vent some of her anger without being too late for her own patients. She hurried down to her consulting room, switched on her computer in preparation for work and reached for the phone.

'Dr Hughes here, I'd like to speak to Adrian Lambourne immediately, please,' she said as his receptionist answered the phone, and was gratified when she was put straight through.

'Dr Lambourne speaking.' His insistent use of the title of doctor irritated Jo intensely, as she felt it was done to deliberately mislead patients. She knew he was entitled to call himself Doctor as he had a doctorate, a PhD in some obscure aspect of psychology, but he hadn't been to medical school or taken a degree in general medicine as most people assumed. While Jo knew he was still highly skilled at treating patients, it did mean he couldn't prescribe at all or treat anything other than psychological disorders. It didn't take an in-depth knowledge of psychology to know that he insisted on using the title because he had some kind of chip on his shoulder about not being a medical doctor and wanted his patients to think he actually was. Now wasn't the time for her to tell him her feelings on this, but she added it to her list of reasons to be angry with him and decided she had no intention of pandering to his ego.

'Adrian, it's Dr Hughes here. I was just wondering if you had managed to see Mark yet? Or if you would be able to get him admitted any time soon?' She knew, of course, that he hadn't, and also that she was being unfair in asking about admission, because it was most unlikely he would have been able to find a bed yet, even if he had tried.

There was a moment's silence before Lambourne responded. She could almost hear him counting to ten before speaking in a well-practised and measured tone.

'He has an appointment to see me, I believe. Let me just check my records. Ah yes, tomorrow. As I am sure you know, we would love to have the resources to fit patients in and to admit them at the drop of a hat, but we don't, and I am doing my best, Dr Hughes, I really am. You might not think it good enough, but it is honestly the best that I can do.'

Jo took a deep breath and told herself to chill. Much as she would have liked to rant at him, she knew that he was right.

'I'm sorry, Adrian, I know I'm being a tad unfair, but Mark was arrested again this morning and has been charged with arson.'

'Not another murder, surely? I didn't hear anything on the radio this morning.'

'No, not a murder, they know he's not responsible for those, but he did set fire to a disused barn, probably because of the stress of being treated as a suspect.'

'Oh, have they definitely ruled him out for the murders, then? That's good news.'

'Yes, yes, he's been ruled out. He was actually in a police cell when one of them took place so that's no longer the problem, it's more about the continued questioning that he's been subjected to, about people who might know his methods. That sort of thing.'

'Oh right, yes, that would still be upsetting for him. Do you think he'll be released today?'

'I should think so, but there's the worry that if the pressure starts building again...'

'Quite. Look, I'll ask my receptionist to call him later and see if she can get him to come here today, and I'll check to see if there are any beds available anywhere. If not, I'll get my colleague Dr Johanssen to up his medication, and try to get him seen by one of us daily for a while. How does that sound?'

'Thank you.' Jo was genuinely surprised he would offer to do that much. Dr Johanssen was one of the psychiatrists who practised at the sleep clinic where she knew Lambourne regularly did sessions, and she was also aware that they had an arrangement whereby Johanssen would prescribe medication for Lambourne's patients when it was needed urgently, rather than having to wait for the patient to make a separate appointment to see their GP. 'That's more than I could reasonably have expected of you. I'm sorry to have been a little abrupt earlier.'

'Not at all. I really do want to try and help the boy. After all, we were doing so well before all this. Goodbye, Dr Hughes.' And he had hung up before she had a chance to say goodbye, leaving her feeling guilty for having been so unfair on him.

Jo had rushed through her morning patients with indecent haste, and despite having found a note in her basket telling her that Helen had been able to drop everything and go to be with Mark for his interview she hurried out of the office, leaving paperwork and visits for her partners. She had promised to make it up to them later in the week, claiming that she was needed urgently at the police station, and once her partners heard about Mark's arrest they were more than happy for her to go. He was, after all, a patient of hers, not simply a police case. Sometimes, she thought it might be nice to be a Roman Catholic and assuage her guilt by confessing and saying a few Hail Marys for penance, but she suspected that deliberately sinning in the expectation of getting forgiveness was probably against the rules.

She arrived at the police station, having nipped home to collect her car, at about the time she thought most doctors would be finishing up paperwork and taking calls after their morning clinics. She fished in her bag for her notepad and phone and keyed in the number for the surgery that had requested the Hollingsworth's notes.

'Hello,' she said once her call was answered. 'My name is Dr Jo Hughes from The Bourne Surgery, Hastings. I received notification today that some patients of mine from Croft Hill Farm in Westfield have registered with you. Is that correct? I have their NHS numbers if that will help?'

Jo waited patiently as she was first passed to the practice manager, who insisted on checking her identity with Linda, who she knew from the practice managers' support group, before answering cautiously in the affirmative. The Hollingsworths had indeed registered at the practice, but she wasn't happy to say more than that.

'Thank you,' Jo persisted. 'What I am at a loss to understand is why they have left our practice and why they have re-registered somewhere so far from where they live, not to mention quite why you would have accepted them, under the circumstances.' Jo waited while the beleaguered manager put her on hold, presumably to discuss her questions with someone else. It was several minutes before she was taken off hold, and this time she was speaking to a Dr Simms, the GP who had accepted the couple's registration.

'It's a delicate matter, Dr Hughes,' he spoke with a soft Scottish burr, 'and I'm hesitant lest I break confidentiality.'

'I certainly wouldn't want you to do that, Dr Simms, and I have to say that I am not surprised they decided to move practices. It's no secret that Mr Hollingsworth made a complaint against me. I am just concerned that they have chosen a doctor so far from where they live, and puzzled that you would take them.'

'Well, I have to say it was not without a good deal of pressure from the husband. He seemed to think that all the doctors in Hastings would have it in for him because of that complaint.'

'That seems rather excessive.'

'Indeed. I was wondering if he might have a history of paranoia. I don't suppose there's something of that sort that I should know about?'

'He's hardly been to the surgery the whole time he's been registered with us. Although,' she added as an afterthought, 'it would explain how he's been behaving recently.'

'Aye, well, he was very persuasive, I'll have you know. I felt I had to take them.'

'I'm sorry it's come to this, and I hope for your sake it's just a misunderstanding and he isn't a problem. I'll forward their electronic records as soon as possible.'

'Thank you for that, Dr Hughes, I'm obliged.'

'Oh, and Dr Simms?'

'Yes?'

'Please don't hesitate to call me if you need any clarification about any health matters, particularly about Mrs Hollingsworth's hypothyroidism.'

'She has myxodoema?' He sounded surprised. 'Her husband assured me they were both in good health.'

Jo sighed.

'I'll send you a copy of the complete records directly, Dr Simms, as well as sending them through the proper channels, and you can see for yourself.'

Jo felt increasingly disquieted as she ended the call, which was the opposite of what she had hoped. She actually had more unanswered questions now than before. What on earth was David Hollingsworth up to? Did he have difficulty accepting that his wife had a long-term condition and needed monitoring and treatment? How did Jill feel about it? There were so many questions, and none that Dr Simms had been able to answer, but they would have to wait, for now. She got out of her car and headed into the police station.

She checked with the custody sergeant and found out that Mark had been charged and was being bailed to appear before the magistrates the following morning. It was moderately quiet in the custody suite and the sergeant was happy to take her to the cells to see Mark and satisfy herself that he was okay. She explained to him that his psychologist would try and see him that day and would probably want to increase his medication as well. Mark seemed indifferent to what was going on and she tried to impress upon him the need to see Lambourne, but she left by no means sure that he would bother to go. Setting the fire seemed to have calmed him to the point of apathy.

Back at reception, Jo asked to speak to Miller and was escorted up to the incident room. Miller looked up as she walked in and hurried over to divert her straight into his office, clearly worried she was about to lay into him about Mark's arrest. She let him stew for a moment or two before smiling and thanking him for letting her know her patient was in custody. He looked relieved, but Jeffries, watching surreptitiously through the window, couldn't hide his disappointment, which pleased Jo.

'I was just wondering how you were getting on now that you have all the contact details from SSE? Have you found a common link?'

Jo had been expecting Miller to be enthusiastic and upbeat but instead he seemed to slump slightly.

'I wish.' He paused, as if he was unsure how much he should confide in her. 'There are no contacts in common between all three women and no one even remotely connected to Mark, as far as we can tell.'

Jo felt a spasm of disappointment and anxiety.

'I thought it would all be over as soon as you had that information. That it was only a matter of time before you made an arrest.'

'I know. We all did. But life just isn't that easy.'

'No. You're right. It's never that easy.' She thought for a moment. 'Did anyone contact more than one of the women?'

'Yes, we have five men who each contacted two out of three. Nigel is checking them out.'

'Good.' She smiled again, but then had a sudden thought. 'Does the list include people who might have contacted the women but have since left the website? I mean, he might be trying to cover his tracks?'

Miller looked thoughtful.

'I assume so. I mean it's a list of all the contacts they have had, but…' he got up and opened the door into the incident room. 'Nigel?'

Nigel looked up from his screen.

'People who have left SSE are still on the list, aren't they?'

'Yes, Guv,' Nigel nodded vigorously. 'There are several clients who have since left.' He looked round the room. 'None of them contacted more than one of the women. Jayne is calling them to find out why they left, so I'll check with her and find out how far she has got.'

'Thanks, Nigel. I thought you'd have it covered.'

'Of course,' Jo had followed Miller to the door, so that Nigel and Jeffries could hear her. 'He might have more than one profile.'

'I've checked methods of payment and none of them use the same ones.' Nigel assured her, and Jo didn't want to go further and point out that there were ways round that, in case they asked how she knew. Perhaps she could call Nigel and put the idea into his head. He was much more open to suggestions than either Miller of Jeffries.

'What about phone records?'

'We have the details of all calls and texts for numbers registered to the women, but we have nothing that connects them to any of the men on SSE, and we haven't been able to find your Dr Brown on there, either. Although we did bring him in for questioning. You might want to steer clear for a while, I think he knows someone from the surgery put his name forward.'

Jeffries snorted.

'He won't do anything, he was just a dickhead.' For once Jo agreed with him, but she still thought it would be prudent to give Gerry a wide berth.

'Do you think the women had more than one phone?' Jo queried. 'Or just swapped out the sim cards for a pay as you go one not in their names.'

'It's possible, we haven't found anything to prove it though.' No wonder Miller seemed so defeated. Information that had seemed guaranteed to lead them to the killer was looking like a dead end.

'And um, from what I can tell, after the initial contact they would probably have used something like WhatsApp, and with their handsets pretty much destroyed we have no hope of getting those messages from the company,' Nigel added morosely.

'Not unless we get GCHQ or MI5 involved,' Jeffries continued, and Jo silently thanked Kate for making her use WhatsApp.

'We are working our way through everyone on all our lists,' Miller tried to sound upbeat, but failed.

'We'll still be tracing, interviewing, and eliminating well into next century,' Jeffries brought him down to earth with a bump. 'What we need is a faster way to eliminate them. Who's for a cuppa before we get back on the phones?'

Jo took the hint and left them to their work.

24

Gerry Brown was in the general doctors' office rushing through a stack of repeat prescriptions, barely checking them to see if they were correct before adding a scrawled signature to the bottom, when Jo came in and watched for a few seconds before he realised that he wasn't alone and turned to look at her. She swallowed her irritation at his slapdash work and smiled, despite Miller's warning that he might suspect her of having given his name to the police. He would hardly have been likely to remain in the room with her if he really did think she'd done that, would he?

'How's it going?' she asked vaguely. He looked up, as if only just registering that there was anyone else in the room.

'Okay.' He shrugged, seemingly unsure what she was asking, and in truth, she wasn't sure herself. She was just trying to strike up a conversation, so that she could get to know him better. Now that the SSE website seemed to be a washout she was wondering again about the locum GP, and was curious about what he did on Wednesday and Saturday nights.

'I was wondering, now that you seem more settled here and are spending more time in Hastings,' she began, 'if you wanted me to show you round one night? Introduce you to the pubs or the jazz club? I mean, I know you don't live that far away, and have probably had nights out in the town already, but I thought it might be fun.' She knew it sounded like a desperate pickup, but she ploughed on. 'Maybe next Wednesday? The comedy club has an open mike night on a Wednesday that can be quite fun,' she finished lamely.

'Wednesday's not a good night for me.' Gerry looked a bit like a rabbit caught in the headlights. 'I have a standing commitment on a Wednesday.'

'Oh? What's that?' she tried to sound innocent, but he just glared at her and went back to his work.

'Some other night, then,' Jo persisted.

'Um, maybe. Let me think about it.' Gerry seemed more irritated than flattered at being asked out by Jo. 'Thank you.' He added as an afterthought.

'Assuming your wife doesn't mind,' she added maliciously.

'We're separated.'

'I'm sorry to hear that,' Jo lied.

'I doubt it. I mean, you don't seriously expect me to believe you would make a pass at me if you thought I was still married, do you?'

'Busted,' Jo smiled. 'I heard on the grapevine that you were working here because you had left your wife, but I wasn't sure if you already had another girlfriend and, you know, that that was the cause of the split.'

Gerry abruptly switched off his computer and stood up.

'I don't know what your game is, but I don't believe for one moment that you haven't heard all the gossip. Everyone in the office must know very well why I have ended up in this God-forsaken job.' And he stomped out of the room and straight down the stairs, without even bothering to take his signed prescriptions into the office.

'Touchy subject,' Jo said to herself as she gathered up both of their paperwork and took it all through to the girls in the office to deal with.

'Dr Brown gone?' Linda asked her when she saw Jo had his work as well as her own.

'Yes, I may have upset him,' Jo admitted.

'Well, that's not exactly hard these days.' Linda looked round the room conspiratorially and then continued in a quieter voice, 'You know his wife has really taken him to the cleaners?'

'That's hardly a surprise, under the circumstances.'

'No, but he was a partner in their website business and now he's had to resign from that, as well as having to give her the family home. It seems she had a controlling interest in the company and has voted him out. Good job he's got his stellar medical career to fall back on,' Linda laughed.

'Ooh, who would have thought you were so cruel, Ms Crompton.'

'It seems that she's happy to make her money from adultery but not so keen on her husband doing it. That's irony for you.' Linda paused and gave Jo a meaningful look. 'You should have told me that his website was the dating agency that's been in the news.'

'I wasn't sure I was allowed to.' Jo did feel a bit guilty about it. 'And anyway, I didn't know for absolute certain that it was them.'

Linda gave her a look of disbelief before moving on.

'They were probably both having affairs left, right, and centre. Mind you, he's probably quite glad he's not on the board anymore. He doesn't need any more scandal, and I can imagine it's not going to be bringing in quite so much money now it's been linked to a killer.'

'Linda?' One of the other staff called to the manager and she hurried away, leaving Jo to think about the implications of what she'd said.

Gerry had lost pretty much everything when he was forced to give his wife their healthy and profitable business, not to mention the house, but the situation had changed. He no longer had a financial interest in the success of the business, and the murders now meant that it was not the cash cow it had once been. In fact, it was in ruins, and so his wife had lost her money too. If that didn't shout motive, nothing did. Jo hurried back into the now empty doctors' office and grabbed a phone.

There was no answer from Miller's mobile so she rang the incident room and got through to Nigel. She told him that Gerry Brown had not only been a director of SusSEXtra but that he had been forced to give up his position in the company as part of the separation agreement. She told him that revenge on his wife by destroying the business rather than revenge on all adulterous women could possibly be a motive for the murders.

Nigel took careful notes of what she was saying and said that he would pass it on to Jayne, so that she could add Amelia Hepton-Lacey to her interview list. If anyone would know how to get round the website financial systems and checks, it would be Gerry, he pointed out.

'And I wanted to thank you for your information about how someone could hide their identity, Dr Hughes,' Nigel continued. 'I'm following that up now myself.'

Jo was relieved that her information was being acted on, and began to feel renewed hope that the killer would be caught, possibly even quite soon.

Jo had barely put the phone down after her conversation with Nigel when it began to ring again.

'Hello?' she said as she answered. 'Dr Hughes speaking. Oh, Adrian, how can I help?'

She listened as Adrian Lambourne explained that he had seen Mark and started him on some relaxation therapy and also changed his medication again. His colleague at the clinic had issued him with enough of his increased strength tablets to last him a week, but he wanted Jo to write a prescription to continue them from then on. He had also booked Mark in for weekly sessions so that he could be monitored more closely moving forward.

'Of course,' she agreed. 'I'll do it straight away. Oh, and Adrian? Thank you.'

She had more than a twinge of guilt that she had been so rude to him, but was pleased that it had finally made him sit up and take notice. The result had been better care for her patient, and that was a good result in her book.

As she walked out of the surgery door, Jo was surprised to see Jayne Hales waiting for her in the car park.

'Hey Doc,' she greeted Jo casually. 'I thought you'd be finishing about now.'

'Why didn't you come in and say you were here? I would have been out sooner.'

'I didn't know if your patients knew about your work with us, and didn't want to risk one of them taking it amiss if they saw the police hanging round their doctor.'

'I shouldn't worry. Most of my patients would enjoy the gossip. Anyway, it's not like you're in uniform.'

'True,' Jayne hesitated. 'Do you need to rush off or have you got a minute?'

'I've finished for the day, thank goodness. I was just going to walk home. How can I help you?'

Jayne looked relieved.

'Well, maybe I could walk with you and pick your brains as we go, if that's alright?'

'Perfectly.' Jo started walking towards All Saints Street and the twittens that climbed between the houses. 'I hope you're fit, it's a steep climb!'

'Everything's a steep climb in Hastings,' Jayne laughed. 'I wanted to ask about a colleague of yours.'

'Gerry Brown? I spoke to Nigel as soon as I heard about his connection with SSE.'

'That's right, he's passed it on to me as I am interviewing the wives of anyone connected with Mark, because the killer has to be someone who knows him, and the boss wants to know if they also have any marital problems or whatever, because of your theory about the motive being adultery.'

Having paused to ensure Jo had followed her explanation, Jayne continued.

'So, I have an appointment to speak with the ex-Mrs Brown tomorrow, to get her side of the story. I just thought I'd speak to you first and get the low-down from your point of view.'

Jo quickly ran through everything she knew as they walked.

'I really don't know any more, except that he's not a very likeable man and I'm not exactly impressed with his skills as a doctor, either.'

'So,' Jayne said, breathing deeply as she struggled to keep up with Jo as they climbed the twisting steps. 'I'm betting you don't need to go to the gym if you're doing this every day.'

'It certainly helps,' Jo agreed. They had reached the top of the hill and were outside her building.

'Do you want to come in for a cup of tea?' she asked.

'No, no. Resuscitation possibly, but I'll pass on the tea and get back to my car. I've been trying to get hold of someone without success, and I thought I'd try catching her at home. Well, I thought I'd doorstep her, in fact, as she doesn't seem to want to speak to me.'

'I don't envy you that job, but it's hard to know why someone would try and avoid speaking to you.'

'Embarrassment, probably. I'm asking about their divorces, and I am learning that people don't always behave well during a divorce. I don't suppose you know anything about the background to Dr Lambourne's divorce, do you?'

'I didn't even know he was divorced,' Jo admitted. 'I really don't know anything about him. Apart from the fact that he's Mark's psychologist.'

'Oh well, worth a punt,' Jayne smiled, and looked down the steps they had just climbed. 'At least going down is easier,' she laughed, and called goodbye as she set off back down the hill.

It was early evening when Jo walked into The Stag. She was pleased to see that Kate was already seated at a table by the window, a pint and a packet of crisps in front of her, and a glass of Pinot Grigio with one cube of ice slowly melting into the wine, ready and waiting for Jo.

'Excellent. Just what I need,' Jo said by way of greeting, and sat on the bench opposite Kate.

'Bad day?' Kate asked, and Jo paused before answering.

'No not really, just long, and a bit disappointing, that's all. How about you?'

'Dreadful,' Kate admitted.

'Oh dear, what happened?' Jo looked at her friend with sympathy as she listened to an account of having to explain to a magistrate that there was a legitimate reason why her client might have failed to show up in court, despite her being unable to even get hold of said client to find out why he had decided not to appear. The day had then been made up of her trying unsuccessfully to track the client down, as well as barristers she wanted to get responses from on behalf of other clients, and policemen who failed to answer her queries on cases or even acknowledge that they had received them.

'In the end I gave up and went home early, even though I had achieved absolutely nothing. So tell me about your long day. What, in particular, was disappointing about it?'

'Well, in all fairness, the disappointing bit actually happened yesterday. Apparently they are no further forward with finding the killer, because there are no contacts in common between the three women.'

'That could be for all sorts of reasons...' Jo held up her hand to stop Kate.

'I know, and I called Nigel last night and gave him chapter and verse about how people can cover their tracks, so he is following up on that, but it's a delay I hadn't anticipated. I was so sure they would find the killer as soon as they had the information from SSE. I'm just glad we deleted my account before he started looking more closely at the clients.'

'I told you, they won't be looking at the women,' Kate said in exasperation. 'At least I hope not or they'll find me pretty quickly.'

'Please tell me you aren't meeting any of the men who contact you. Not while the killer is still out there.'

'Of course not! I'm not that stupid. But as soon as he's behind bars I want to be ready. There are some really dirty men on there,' she said, with a smile that could be described as pretty dirty as well.

'But, by definition, if they are looking on that website they are not looking for a meaningful relationship. I mean, they are either married or think you're married.'

'I know, but a bit of fun without strings while I wait for Mr Right will keep my sexual organs in full working order.'

Jo sighed. There was no way she could think like that. She wasn't interested in a no-strings relationship. She wanted one with all the strings; engagement, marriage, children, everything.

'What about your friend and mine, Gerry Brown,' Kate asked, 'do you still think it could be him? I mean that he could be doing this as a sort of act of revenge against his wife?'

'It doesn't really fit, but the police are checking him out as well.'

'Good.' Kate thought for a moment. 'As well as what? Or rather whom?'

'Well, I can't claim to know everything they are following up on, but I do know that Jayne Hales is interviewing the wives and ex-wives of anyone connected to Mark Caxton.'

'The kid who likes to burn cars, but not with people in them?' Kate queried, and Jo nodded.

'I think she's more likely to get a true picture of their relationships and break-ups from the women involved rather than the men.'

'Ain't that the truth,' Kate agreed, a little too readily, probably thinking about her version of various past relationships and how they wouldn't match the accounts of the men involved.

'I think it's depressing that so many people have unsuccessful marriages. Jayne was saying that most of the people had been divorced or separated from long-term partners, and that it would be a lot quicker for her to interview the happily married ones.'

'But we're talking mainly doctors, healthcare professionals, and policemen, and they are all well known to have a high divorce rate.

'Comes with the job.' Kate thought for a moment. 'Lawyers are as bad, probably because of their association with police.'

'That would account for psychologists as well, I expect.'

'Thinking of someone in particular?'

'Adrian Lambourne, Mark's psychologist. Jayne was asking if I knew the story there, but I hadn't a clue he was divorced. It's not something you ask people you work with, is it?'

'Why do think it is?'

'Why do I think what is?'

'That some professions have higher divorce rates than others.'

Jo gave it some thought.

'Long hours, stress, and having to deal with death, I suppose. It makes you want to live life to the full yourself.'

'So you think that's why they sleep around?' Kate queried. Jo shook her head.

'I think it's more that they don't want to put up with being unhappy or to put up with second best if they think they have ended up with a relationship they can't put right. They don't want to waste the one short life they have.'

Kate sighed her agreement that this was probably the case, and they drank in silence for a moment or two.

'Mind you, you would think a psychologist would be able to make his relationships work, wouldn't you?'

'I agree, but I seem to remember they have a pretty high divorce rate, just like psychiatrists.'

'Maybe it's because they're all a bit mad.'

'That's simply not true!' Jo chastised her friend gently. 'A few, maybe, but not all,' she laughed.

'It makes you want to find out why though, doesn't it? See if there are any salacious details?'

'Like what?'

'Is he into dressing up in women's clothing? Or is he an obsessive compulsive who organises his sock drawer by colour?'

'It's more likely that his wife just realised he's a jumped-up little twerp who has a chip on his shoulder about not being a proper doctor.'

'Miaow!' Kate squealed, and they laughed together until Jo felt guilty.

'Actually, he's not that bad. He's been very helpful with Mark since I managed to get him to take notice.'

Kate sighed.

'One day, Jo, you are going to be able to say something truly horrible about someone who deserves it without feeling guilty.' Kate shook her head, knowing that it would never happen. 'How about another?' she nodded at Jo's empty glass.

'My round.' Jo stood to go to the bar. 'You know, I am going to have to find a way of getting my parents back together again. At this rate I will become an alcoholic.'

Jo laughed with Kate, but she knew that it really wasn't a laughing matter.

Later that night, once her mother was safely in bed, Jo began to make a list of things that might help her to get the flat back to herself. Her first choice would be for her mother to move back home. For that to happen her father would have to give up his hobby, and he was clearly not going to do that just yet. Another option was for her mother to move into a flat of her own, even if it was only temporary. She picked up the local paper and began looking in the properties to rent section, circling any she thought might be suitable. After a while, her mind wandered and she thought more about Adrian Lambourne and, in particular, Jayne's difficulty in getting hold of his wife. She wondered if Jayne had been successful in doorstepping her. Perhaps she was away? If so, how else could Jayne get the information she needed? Jo had an old classmate from medical school who worked as a psychiatrist in the local NHS trust where Lambourne also spent some of his time. Perhaps he would be a good source of information. Before she had a chance to change her mind, she called his office number and left a message, asking him to give her a ring when he had a chance.

He smiled to himself as he put down his latest pay as you go mobile phone. He knew the police had worked out that he met his victims through the website. He also knew that since a link with dating websites had been hinted at on the news, people were bound to be more careful. It was lucky that he had a number of women already prepared and communicating with him offline. He'd even joked about being the killer, telling them that they'd better beware, making light of it so they would feel confident it couldn't be him. He'd got one lined up for tonight. He was sure she'd turn up, because she was stupid. She was barely able to read or write, and seemed pathetically desperate for sex. Anything to make her feel loved or at least wanted. In that respect, her desires would be fulfilled. He wanted her. He really wanted her. He just hoped he wouldn't have to waste too much time talking to her first.

25

The rain was lashing down by the time Jo arrived at the farm track, which she had been told was the easiest way to the crime scene. She knew from her previous walks along the cliffs that the track led to a farm and camping ground. From the farm there was an unofficial, and often impassable, route down to Fairlight Cove, where there was a naturist beach. Jo parked her car at the top of the track as instructed by a cold, wet, and miserable-looking constable, who was trying to ignore the water dripping steadily off the peak of his uniform cap, and walked the rest of the way on foot. As she picked her way along the rutted track, she passed a field that was used as a campsite in the summer, but which was empty now. She could see the farmhouse beyond the field, with lights ablaze. She imagined that they must have seen the flames and alerted the emergency services. Jo shivered as an ice cold drip of rain ran down her neck. She hadn't bothered with an umbrella, as she knew she wouldn't be allowed to take it into the crime scene, so she pulled the hood of her cagoule up and tightened the cord in an attempt to stop the rain getting inside. She hoped they had at least managed to set up somewhere out of the rain for her to get her coverall suit on before checking the body, or else she would be soaked through in no time at all. She stumbled slightly on the uneven track and wondered if she should have brought a torch, but once she rounded the final corner there was light from the headlamps and blue flashing lights of the fire truck and police cars that were already at the scene. She could see a lone figure in a crime scene suit standing and watching the fire crew check the burnt-out car, and realised it was Miller.

He turned as she suited up, trying to keep herself as dry as possible, but finally giving up because it was a fight she just wasn't going to win.

'Sorry to get you out on a night like this.'

'I'd completely forgotten that it was a Wednesday.'

'I know,' Miller agreed. 'I'd thought with all the publicity around the killings and the dating website that no one would be so stupid.' He shook his head in frustration.

'Yes. It does make you wonder how he persuaded anyone to get into his car, let alone to come to such an isolated spot, doesn't it? Especially in this weather. I mean, you'd get drenched if you wanted to go for a quick... you know, if you wanted to urinate.'

He smiled briefly, amused by her inability to use even faintly crude words and then frowned and turned quickly away. Jo was disappointed that it had been such a brief smile, but they were at the scene of another woman's death; a death that would no doubt have left him feeling guilty, because he hadn't stopped this maniac before this latest victim lost her life.

'Exactly, he must really know how to turn on the charm.'

'Speaking of which, no Sergeant Jeffries?' she asked, looking round as if expecting him to pop out from behind a bush. Miller looked at her again, his features softening.

'Not yet,' he replied, before turning away a little too abruptly and continuing briskly, 'he's on his way. It's pretty much the same as the previous scenes. We just need you to confirm life extinct once the firemen say it's safe for you to do so. I'll go and have a word with them.' He walked off in the direction of the fire appliance.

Jo watched him go with a quizzical expression on her face as she tried to work out what on earth she could have said to upset him.

'Hi, Dr Hughes.' A voice startled her, as she hadn't been aware anyone else was there. Jo turned and saw a figure in a protective suit and mask that pretty much could have been anyone.

'It's me, DS Hales. Jayne,' the voice said helpfully, much to Jo's relief.

'Oh hi, Jayne. I didn't recognise you. Do we know anything about this one?' Jo nodded at the still smouldering car.

'No, not yet. The fire bods won't let us get anywhere near until they've finished. If you'd asked me half an hour ago I would have said I hope they hurry up, but I'm so wet now that it won't make any difference how long they take.'

'I know how you feel,' Jo replied, as a trickle of icy water made its way down her spine, despite all her precautions. 'I'll be straight in a hot shower when I get back.'

They stood and waited in companionable silence.

'Did you manage to get hold of Mrs Lambourne?' Jo asked after a while.

'No, she seems to have gone away on a cruise around the Med. I'll try and contact the cruise line later, once I've confirmed which one it is, and see if they can get a message to her, but to be honest it might have to wait until she gets back.'

'I've contacted an old friend who might know them, just to see if there's any gossip. If I hear anything, I'll let you know.'

'Cheers, Jo, that would be great.' They watched the crime scene team rig up some lights before Jayne turned to Jo again. 'We checked up on your Dr Brown as well, and he has a pretty good alibi.'

'Oh yes?'

'You didn't hear this from me, right?'

Jo nodded, trying to appear indifferent, when in reality she was all ears.

'Seems that as a condition of his GMC hearing he has to attend a sex addiction clinic. Group therapy every Wednesday and Saturday night.'

'But they can't go on very late?' Jo couldn't see how it was an alibi.

'Yes, but he goes home with one of the other patients afterwards and spends the night with her.'

'Nice to know the therapy is working,' Jo said, and Jayne giggled.

'Well the clinic now know, because of the questions we were asking, rather than us actually telling them straight out,' Jo was quite sure that wasn't true. She could imagine Sergeant Jeffries taking great pleasure in telling the psychotherapist in charge of the sex addiction clinic just how well the therapy was working, 'and it's up to them whether or not they report him to the GMC.'

'Oh heavens,' Jo hadn't thought of that. Her life wasn't going to get any easier if Gerry Brown was suspended for breaking the conditions of the GMC's ruling.

Suddenly, the floodlights came on, bathing the scene with their fierce illumination.

'Also, Nigel checked the clinic where Dr Lambourne worked, and the receptionist confirmed that he doesn't allow patients to take food and drink in with them,' Jayne continued. 'Something to do with an incident in the past when a patient assaulted him with an item of food.'

'Nothing too hard, I hope?'

'A banana, apparently,' Jayne told her, and they both couldn't suppress a giggle as they thought about it. Jo wished that Jayne was around at more crime scenes, not only because she was a fantastic source of information, but she also managed to take Jo's mind off the grisly reason for her being there.

'Look,' Jayne pointed to a helmeted fireman who was beckoning them forward. 'I think it's okay for you to go and check the body now.'

Later, once Jo had finally managed to warm up and dry out, she sat in her fluffy towelling dressing gown and sipped a cup of hot milk. It was four in the morning and everyone, except for a few very late night revellers, was asleep. Including her mother. Most of the streetlights had been switched off, so the old town lay in almost complete darkness. Only a very few lights, spilling from club and casino doorways, gave clues as to where the roads and houses were laid out in the streets below. She knew she should try and sleep, but it was impossible. The thought of another poor women burnt to death was enough to prevent her from sleeping. That and the smell. She had showered and washed her hair, even squeezing some fresh lemon juice into the final rinse, a trick a colleague had once shared with her, but the smell seemed to remain. She knew it was because microscopic particles were probably caught in the hairs of her nasal passages, and even though she had tried snorting some water up her nose, the smell persisted. So she sprayed some more perfume on her wrist and breathed in, deeply, hoping to displace the foul smell with a new, nicer one.

Before she had left the crime scene, before dawn had even begun to break, Miller had asked her if she would be free to be with Mark, so that he could ask the boy more questions. She had agreed to meet him at Mark's house at eight that morning. Jo switched the television on to a 24-hour news programme and turned the sound down low, so that the voices were little more than murmurs. The news of the fourth murder didn't seem to have reached the press yet. With the lights off, and only the flickering of the screen as background, she closed her eyes and finally drifted off to sleep.

She woke suddenly to the shrill ringing of her mobile. It took her a few moments to register what the noise was, and why she was sleeping on the sofa. She grabbed the phone but just missed the call. She could see from the display that it was six o'clock and that the call was from the friend she had contacted for gossip about Adrian Lambourne, so she rang back immediately, yawning and rubbing her eyes as she waited for him to pick up.

'Hi, Johnny? It's Jo. I'm sorry I didn't get to the phone in time,' she said when he answered.

'No problem, Jo,' came the reply. 'Sorry to call so early, but I've a full day ahead. It's been such a long time since I last heard from you. Much too long.'

'I know, I know. I've been really busy.' Jo didn't point out the obvious fact that it wasn't just down to her, he could just as easily have called to see how she was doing. 'Look, I need to ask you something.'

'Of course. How can I help?'

'I was hoping you were still as much of a gossip as you used to be, Johnny.'

'I think that's slanderous, Dr Hughes. I'll have you know I never gossip, I simply pass on news about my colleagues in the interest of freedom of information. Speaking of which, did you know Mary Hilton? You would remember her if you'd ever met her, long mousy, unstyled hair, an earnest expression and pre-loved clothes that definitely weren't genuine vintage or charity shop chic if you know what I mean, just old? She left the NHS and set up an alternative healing centre in Dungeness. All yoga pants and organic vegan food.' Jo smiled in spite of her tiredness.

'In Dungeness? I wouldn't have thought that having a nuclear power station in your backyard made selling clean living easy.'

'But it does make property cheap, and I rather think she might have managed to exclude the nuclear plant aspect from her advertising.'

Jo had forgotten how much she enjoyed Johnny's particular bitchy style of gossip and resolved to meet up with him soon, but she would have to make sure she never gave him any personal ammunition, as she would hate to be the subject of his conversations with others. She was tempted to ask if he'd heard about her recent disastrous affair with a consultant at the general hospital, but she was sure he would have done and didn't want to hear his take on it.

'Listen, Johnny, I wondered if you had heard anything about Adrian Lambourne's divorce?'

'Please tell me you're not interested in him, Jo? The man goes round with a face like a slapped arse.'

'No, no,' Jo hastily reassured him, 'it was just something I heard that might have influenced a decision he made recently.'

'Thank goodness for that. For a moment there I thought the world had stopped turning. I couldn't imagine a more unsuitable boyfriend for you than our Dr Lambourne. If you are on the hunt I could name a dozen more suitable candidates, and even put in a good word for you if you wanted?'

'No, thank you,' Jo hastily interrupted him, remembering previous men Johnny had set her up with. Even her mother had better taste in men than Johnny, who thought that all straight men were boring and unimaginative. 'I really do just want to hear about Adrian's divorce for work reasons.'

'Well yes, you do have to feel sorry for the man.'

'Do you? Why?'

'His wife felt neglected because he worked too hard, poor lamb, so she took her revenge by sleeping around, mainly with his patients, including some of his private ones, and a smattering of his colleagues as well.'

'I can see that would be upsetting.'

'Upsetting? The man didn't just lose his dignity once it all came out; he lost most of his income, too. He must have been absolutely fucking livid, excuse the bad language, I know you're not a fan, but I would have been beside myself with anger if anyone had done that to me.'

'Right. Yes, it does explain a lot.'

'I mean, he's had therapy and says he's put it behind him, moved on and everything, but I'm not sure I could. Could you?'

Jo thought about some of her past boyfriends, and in particular the doctor she most recently fell for, who turned out to have forgotten to tell her about his wife. It had taken a long time for her to get over the fact that he had tricked her into a relationship, she who had always sworn that she would never go out with a married man.

'No. I couldn't,' she said at last. 'Look, thanks for the call, Johnny. We must meet up for a drink sometime.'

'That would be lovely, and don't let's leave it so long this time. I could bring Dan and you could bring your significant other. Make a night of it.'

Jo made her excuses and ended the call with many promises to keep in touch, but the thought of inflicting an evening of Johnny's salacious mix of gossip and sexual innuendo on a boyfriend, even if she had one, did not appeal. That and the fact that he thought an evening was a disaster unless everyone got roaring drunk, despite Jo telling him time and time again that she didn't like it. She hated the feeling of being out of control, and she hated the hangover she inevitably had the next morning. Kate, of course, would enjoy every minute of an evening with Johnny. Perhaps that was the answer. She could go with Kate and, better still, she could arrange to be called away nice and early and leave them all to it.

The information she had got from Johnny had, however, been very useful, and Jo started to dial Jayne's number before noticing that it was still only six o'clock. Perhaps the news of Adrian's awful divorce could wait until after she'd had breakfast, or at least a cup of tea.

Jo parked her car and hurriedly got out, checking her watch as she did so. She was a few minutes late and could see Miller's silver saloon car already parked a little further up the street. As she locked her car she saw, with relief, that Miller had waited for her and was only now getting out of his car.

'Sorry,' she hurried over to where he was parked. 'Last minute problem with a patient,' she lied. It had, in fact, been her mother who had delayed her, full of complaints about the disturbed night she'd had because Jo had been moving around, using the bathroom, and even chatting with her friends on the phone. Even if Jo had tried to explain, her mother would not have been interested, so she had just apologised profusely and made her mother a nice pot of Earl Grey tea by way of a peace offering.

'No problem, I had some calls to make,' Miller answered.

She was pleased to see that he had come alone. The last thing they needed was for Jeffries to make some crass remark and upset anyone.

'Have you identified the latest victim?' she asked, as they walked towards Mark's home.

'No. Not yet.'

'Someone must have missed her by now, surely?'

Miller shrugged.

'Her husband could be away, or perhaps they're separated. We just don't know.'

'She might not even have been married,' Jo mused.

'I think that's rather the point of the website, isn't it?'

'Yes, but people lie online, which is also rather the point, isn't it?'

And he had to concede she was right.

'Was there a can at the latest scene?' They had reached the short path to Mark's front door.

Miller hesitated before answering.

'No. At least, not that we've found so far.'

'Well, they weren't hard to find at the previous scenes, so it's likely there isn't one.'

'Yes.'

Jo thought about what that meant. Either this latest murder wasn't connected with the previous ones, which seemed unlikely, or the killer knew that his ruse to implicate Mark hadn't worked and was no longer bothering with the misdirection. As the presence of the cans had not been revealed to the press, it once again pointed to the killer being someone close to Mark or close to the investigation. Jo was about to say this to Miller, but one look at his thunderous face told her he was very much aware of the fact, so she kept quiet.

They reached the front door and Miller knocked.

The door was opened almost immediately, and despite her call to him earlier explaining why they were coming to see him, Mark still looked anxious. Jo couldn't blame him. Women were being horrifically killed; by someone who had intentionally tried to implicate him. He'd been repeatedly interviewed and held in a police cell, and driven to re-offend because of the stress. Clearly, the calming effect of setting fire to the farm outbuildings was wearing off.

Mark showed them into the living room, where he seemed to have made an attempt to clear up.

'Sorry we're a bit late Mark, I got caught up just as I was leaving,' Jo explained as she came into the living room.

'It's okay.' Despite Miller making for the sofa, Jo did not sit next to him. Experience had taught her to take the plastic picnic chair by the table, and not just because of the flora and fauna the sofa upholstery probably housed, but also because being too close to Miller tended to make it difficult to concentrate. She wondered how long it would be before she could work with him with total equanimity. Probably not until she was either in love with someone else or retired.

Miller cleared his throat once they were all seated comfortably.

'Right, as I was saying Mark, we know that these fires are not down to you, but they must be being started by someone you know.'

'But I keep saying, I don't know no one…'

'It's alright, Mark,' Jo said as soothingly as possible, 'we know you don't know who it is, but what Inspector Miller is trying to say is that he needs to ask you questions to try and help find out who it is, because I am sure you want them caught as much as we do, right?'

Mark stopped examining his fingernails long enough to look at Jo and nod. Once she was sure he was settled again, Jo nodded to Miller to continue.

'So, I know we've talked about the drinks cans found at the scene, but we really need to know how the killer got hold of those cans with your fingerprints on, okay?'

Mark nodded again, without looking up.

'Okay, so you buy them at the local shop right?'

'Yeah,' Mark agreed.

'And you take them with you when you go out?'

'Cheaper than buying drinks out.'

'Okay, so you take the cans out with you and when you have finished your drink, you throw them away. Where? On the ground?'

'In the bin,' Mark seemed insulted. 'I don't just chuck 'em on the floor.'

'Of course,' Miller agreed. 'So you take a can with you when you go to see Dr Hughes?' Miller indicated Jo.

'Sometimes, maybe.'

'Or to the hospital?'

Mark nodded.

'Or the job centre?'

'Don't go there,' Mark answered. 'I'm on the sick long-term.'

'Can you think of anywhere else you go to regularly that you've taken your drinks to?'

Mark thought for a few moments before shaking his head.

Miller sighed in frustration.

'Nowhere at all?' Jo asked him, but he shook his head again.

'Sorry.' He really did seem to want to help.

'How about when you meet up with your girlfriend?' Jo persevered.

'Nah. She gets them in for me.'

'Same brand?' Mark's reply interested Miller.

'Yeah, but she's not involved right? She wouldn't do this?'

'It's okay. It's just another way the person might get hold of them.'

'Yeah but lots of places have the same ones, they could've come from anywhere.'

'Not with your fingerprints on, Mark,' Miller persisted. 'The killer must be picking up your used cans from somewhere, and it has to be somewhere you go regularly. Do you see?'

Mark seemed to understand.

'You take the drinks with you to medical appointments and your girlfriend has them at her house. Is there anywhere else you drink them?'

Miller paused again while Mark gave it some more thought.

'Well, the centre, but I don't take them with me,' he finally said.

'What centre?'

'The youth support centre. Where I go and see Miss Austen. They have that brand there. They only charge 30p for a can so I buy them there, but they only have drinks and snacks on club nights, not all the time.'

'Club nights?' Miller queried.

'Yeah. Once a month they have nights when they put on talks and stuff, and you can play table tennis and that sort of thing. I have to go as part of my therapy and they're okay, but that fireman, you know the arson man, he's always there recently and it's…'

'Chris Butterworth? He goes to the centre?' Miller interrupted, unable to keep the excitement from his voice, making Mark more anxious again.

'Yeah. I don't have a problem with it, it's just…' His voice trailed off and he hunched over, looking at the floor.

'Difficult,' Jo finished for him. Miller was already on his feet, heading for the door and pulling out his mobile phone.

26

Surprisingly, Jo was on time for morning surgery despite warning Linda that she might be a bit late because of her early morning visit to Mark Caxton, and she was amazed when she was still only running slightly behind by the time she finished with her last patient. She would normally have gone upstairs to deal with any paperwork, referrals, and phone calls, but she decided not to give anyone the chance to delay her, and hurried out of her consulting room, pretending not to hear the receptionist calling to her as she raced through the waiting room and out of the surgery. She wanted to get to the police station and find out what was happening. The priority now was clearly to follow up on the news that Helen Austen and Chris Butterworth both had the knowledge about how Mark set fires and the means to collect his used drinks cans, and Miller had been abrupt to the point of rudeness when warning Jo not to call Helen before he'd had a chance to act on the information, hurrying away to arrange for them to be picked up without even saying goodbye. She couldn't blame him; they were clearly top of his suspect list now, particularly Butterworth, as it had been him who had pointed the finger at Mark in the first place. Jo couldn't imagine Helen was seriously a suspect. It was hard to see how she could be the murderer, but Butterworth was a different matter altogether.

By the time Jo had arrived at the police station and Jayne had collected her from reception she was pleased to hear that both Helen and Butterworth had been picked up, and that Helen had even had a preliminary interview.

'She really wanted to get things cleared up as quickly as possible,' Jayne explained.

'And did she?' Jo asked.

'Well, to be honest, that depends if you believe that it had never occurred to her that the cans might have come from the centre.'

'Do you?'

'I'm not sure, but no surprises for guessing which sergeant thinks it's a load of poppycock.'

'I'll bet he didn't use the word poppycock,' Jo answered with a grin.

'No. No he did not,' Jayne confirmed.

'What about the fireman, Chris Butterworth?'

'He was livid about being picked up at work and marched out in front of the duty fire crews. I think he would have refused to come if the boss hadn't made it clear that he would be arrested if he didn't. Anyway, he has refused to be interviewed without a lawyer present, so we're just waiting for one.'

'Is he divorced?' Jo asked as they reached the incident room door, and Jayne hesitated before going in.

'Well that's the strange thing; both he and Helen seem to be happily married, but one of the other social workers at the youth centre said it was assumed they were having an affair. Butterworth had come to the centre a while back to give a talk to the kids about fire safety, and nobody could see a reason why he kept hanging around, unless it was to spend time with Helen.'

'And it couldn't have been just that he was trying to help?'

'Give me a break,' Jayne rolled her eyes and opened the door. 'No one gives up their evenings to help kids like this without some sort of ulterior motive.'

Jo wasn't so sure as she followed Jayne into the room, but perhaps she wasn't as cynical as the average police officer.

As Jo entered the room Miller looked surprised to see her, but not unhappy, she thought with relief.

'Can't keep away from us, eh, Doc?' Jeffries said, and Jo looked a little abashed.

'I, um, well, I just wanted to see what had happened about the lead that the cans might have come from the centre.' Jo knew she had no real right to information about the ongoing investigation, but the fact that she had been so involved, and so had one of her patients, made her natural curiosity forgivable. At least she hoped it did.

Miller ushered her into his office and indicated for Jeffries to come with them, to Jo's surprise and disappointment. She couldn't help but notice that both of them seemed pumped up and that there was a palpable sense of excitement in the room. It had to mean that they felt they were getting somewhere with the case at last, and she felt an enormous relief to think that it might soon be over.

'Do you know anything about Helen Austen's personal life? Any rumours about her maybe having an affair?' Miller asked her once she had settled herself in the visitors' chair. He had perched on the edge of the desk rather than sitting in his chair, and Jeffries was leaning against a filing cabinet. This obviously wasn't going to be a long discussion.

'Helen?' Jo was not surprised by this question given Jayne's revelation that the staff at the centre had all assumed she was having an affair with Butterworth, and she gave it some thought. 'No. As far as I'm aware she has a really good marriage to a lovely guy called, oh, what is his name?' She wracked her brains. 'Clive! That's it. I think he's an accountant or something.'

'Children?'

'Not as far as I know. Look, are you telling me you think Helen is involved? That's ridiculous.'

'Why?' Miller retorted. 'Why is it ridiculous?'

'Mark's her client. She's a social worker. She helps people. She wouldn't set him up. Why are you so sure she is involved?' Jo couldn't believe it.

'If she isn't, why didn't she tell us that they served drinks and snacks at the youth centre? And not just any drinks, but the very brand that she knew we were trying to trace? And then when we questioned her about it earlier, and about anyone who might have had access to those cans, why did she not tell us that Chris Butterworth came to those sessions? The guy who implicated Mark in the first place?' Miller leant forward as he made final his point, and Jo flinched at his obvious anger and conviction that the social worker had to be guilty. She knew he wasn't really angry with her, but it certainly felt like it.

'I don't know,' she responded with as much dignity as she could muster after this onslaught, 'but I suspect you will find that she is as much a victim in this as Mark is. She would never do anything to harm one of her clients, and if she has omitted to tell you things, then it was probably for a good reason.'

'Like what?'

'Maybe because she was trying not to give anyone a reason to pull the centre's funding or maybe she was ashamed of something she'd done, like, like…' Jo scrabbled for a reason, 'not doing something by the book, fiddling the expenses or, or, cheating on her husband.'

Miller sat back and Jeffries looked interested.

'You think she might be nicking stuff?'

'I don't know!' Jo said in exasperation. 'I was just trying to think of a reason why she might not be candid with you under the circumstances, and that seemed like a good one, but honestly, I have no idea. Have you asked her?'

There was a knock on the door and Nigel put his head in.

'Duty solicitor's here, Guv,' he told Miller, before giving Jo a sympathetic look. It was clear he had heard every word of their exchange.

'It was just awful,' Jo groaned, as she curled up on Kate's comfortable sofa. 'He was just so angry.'

'I can understand why, though. I mean, if Helen had been less economical with the truth he might have caught up with the killer before he killed that last woman, if not before. Have they found out who she was, by the way?'

'I didn't even think to ask,' Jo admitted. 'That's terrible, isn't it? Imagine just being known as victim number four, and not even having the dignity of a name.'

'It doesn't bear thinking about.' Kate shivered. 'Poor woman. I do hope they manage to identify her and let her nearest and dearest know so that she can have a proper funeral.'

'That's if she has any nearest and dearest. I mean, just because she's on an adultery site doesn't necessarily mean she is actually in a relationship, she might just be there because promising sex without strings might be the only way she can get anyone.' They both thought about that sad idea for a moment.

'Like I said just now,' Kate finally said, 'it doesn't bear thinking about.'

Kate was seated diagonally opposite Jo in an armchair draped with a purple velvet throw, to hide the parts where the sun had faded the crimson upholstery to a pale orange.

'I don't know Helen well, but I can't see her turning a blind eye to her lover murdering women, let alone covering for him. And doesn't it rather undermine the motive if the killer is having an affair with a married woman anyway?' Kate mused, before taking another sip of her hot chocolate and then delicately wiping away a moustache of whipped cream and powdered cocoa.

'We don't know that they are having an affair,' Jo reminded her. 'That's what makes me so cross. Everyone is just jumping to conclusions. Even if they're attracted to one another, perhaps they are both behaving, and sacrificing their happiness in order to be faithful to their partners.'

'And maybe the fireman's wife is putting it about a bit and having loads of fun while he's being a good boy, and the frustration has turned him into a homicidal maniac.'

'Your imagination is even more lurid than mine, Kate Ward,' Jo admonished her. 'I'm sure Steve Miller is doing his best to get to the bottom of it and I, for one, will just be happy knowing the streets are safe again.'

'I'll drink to that,' Kate agreed as she took another slurp of hot chocolate.

27

It was all over the early morning news that someone had been arrested for the 'Death by Burning' murders. The news vans had moved from the picturesque scenes of the crimes and were now camped outside the utilitarian police station where they continued to speculate on very little real information. It would seem that the police had not, so far, named the suspect they had arrested. As Jo ate breakfast she sat glued to her television, watching an interview with an expert on arson who dropped the very large hint that people fascinated by fire often joined the fire service. Even her mother had joined her in the heinous crime of watching morning television as she sat in her dressing gown and sipped her Earl Grey tea.

'A fireman did this? A public servant?' She clearly couldn't believe that someone paid by the taxpayer could commit these crimes.

'No one's been charged, Ma.'

Her mother snorted. She clearly felt that being arrested was the same thing as being charged, but Jo knew there was a world of difference. Butterworth would have been arrested on suspicion of the murders, but the police had to meet the prosecution service criteria on evidence before they would allow him to be charged. Jo was interested that the press hadn't named the firefighter in question, but she wondered how long it would take before they did.

Throughout the morning Jo kept checking online for the latest news, but there were just endless rehashes of the same meagre facts. Despite Butterworth not having been charged, Jo could feel a palpable sense of relief in the air of the main office when she went up after morning surgery to collect her paperwork. Just knowing that the police had someone in custody had taken a weight off each and every one of them. She took her basket into the doctors' office, where Gauri was already working her way through her own pile of papers.

'Is it him, do you think?' Linda whispered, startling Jo, who had not noticed her following behind when she left the office. Linda had a batch of prescriptions in her hand and added them to the already overflowing pile in Jo's basket. Jo realised that Linda had probably kept them back deliberately so that she could come out and speak to her.

'I hope so,' Jo replied. 'They must have good reason to think so or they wouldn't have arrested him.'

'Yes, but you do hear of the police arresting the wrong people, like that landlord chap in Bristol,' Gauri said, having openly listened to the whispered conversation. 'It was only when someone else was convicted that people actually believed he was innocent.'

'You are so right, Gauri. And here was I hoping that now they had arrested that firefighter, Dr Hughes here might actually apologise for having accused me of being the murderer.'

Jo's heart sank as she realised Gerry Brown had also come into the office and heard their conversation, and that he had been closely followed by Dr Grantham.

'I didn't accuse you of anything, Gerry. I simply gave the police some information that you really should have given them yourself.' Despite her crisp tone, Jo could feel a flush rising up her neck and knew her cheeks would be burning in a moment. How she wished her body wouldn't betray her feelings of shame and embarrassment quite so readily.

Dr Grantham put a restraining hand on Gerry's arm and cleared his throat.

'Erm, unfortunately, Dr Brown has tendered his resignation and I have reluctantly agreed to accept it.' He looked around the room and allowed his eyes to rest on Jo. 'He will be leaving straightaway and has just come to collect his personal belongings and to say goodbye. I am sure we all wish him the best in his new role.' Wisely, Dr Grantham didn't mention what that role would be, but Jo could hazard a guess that it wouldn't be to do with medicine, as she speculated that his rapid departure was because the GMC had suspended him pending further enquiries regarding his antics at the sex addiction clinic. Or maybe Dr Grantham had decided he could no longer support a doctor who was not taking his rehabilitation seriously.

There was a short silence as Dr Grantham waited for someone to say something, and it was Linda who found her voice first.

'I'm sure I can speak on behalf of all the reception and office staff when I say we are all very sorry that you are going, Dr Brown.'

Jo knew that they wouldn't be sorry to see him go at all, just sorry about all the extra work it was going to cause, and Jo could sympathise with that.

'Yes,' she added to Linda's short speech, keeping it similarly general and vague, 'and I hope your new role is all you hope it will be.'

'Like you care,' Gerry wasn't going to keep things impersonal, it seemed. 'How do you think it feels to know that not only are you the subject of malicious gossip at work, but that one of your colleagues has actually gone and passed on that gossip to the police?'

'I think that's a little harsh, Gerry,' Dr Grantham cut in before Jo could respond. 'We all have a duty to be open with the police, and while I feel that Jo would have done better to bring the information to me as senior partner so that we could discuss it and ask you for an explanation before taking it to the police, her close working relationship with them probably influenced her decision.' He gave Jo a look redolent of disappointment rather than reproof and her flush deepened, because she knew he was right. 'However, I think that under the circumstances we should now close the subject. Have you got all your things, Dr Brown?' He was clearly keen to keep the goodbyes as short as possible.

Gerry nodded, and he turned to leave the room with a look that suggested to Jo he wasn't going to let matters rest there, and that she would be wise to watch her back.

'Good. Now, I suggest we get on with our work and remember that our patients must always come first,' Dr Grantham said firmly, as he showed Gerry out of the room, and, presumably, made sure he left the premises.

'At least his car won't be taking up space in the car park any more.' Gauri was as practical and unfazed as usual.

'Yes, but we will have to cover his surgeries,' Jo felt tired just thinking about it.

'We ended up seeing most of the patients he saw anyway, to actually give them the treatment they needed, so it won't be that much extra work.'

'It will increase the wait time,' Linda sighed. 'And we weren't meeting our target anyway.'

'We just need to be sure we see the truly sick quickly, and don't put the focus on arbitrary targets.' Gauri was refusing to be rattled, and Jo had to admit she was right. If all the worried well stopped cluttering up the surgery, they would have plenty of time to see the really sick.

'I'll get back onto the agency and see if they have anyone on their books,' Linda sighed, and hurried back to the main office.

'If they did we wouldn't have ended up with Dr Brown,' Gauri spoke to the closing door.

'I'm sorry,' Jo said.

'What have you got to be sorry about?' Gauri seemed genuinely not to know.

'Well, it's my fault he's left,' Jo explained, but Gauri waved her response away.

'It's not your fault, Jo. It's Dr Brown's. Perhaps he should have learnt to keep his trousers buttoned.'

Jo was relieved that her colleague did not seem to blame her. She sat down at the terminal next to Gauri's and started sorting her work into piles: one for repeat prescription requests, another for hospital letters, then further piles for test results and Post-it notes. She started with the pile of Post-it notes, which were mainly notes about patients who had phoned in during morning surgery. Most were asking for advice. One note, however, was more interesting.

Dr Simms, the GP who had agreed to take on the Hollingsworths as patients, had left a message asking her to give him a call. Jo began to reach for one of the phones when Hugh came back into the office, having seen Dr Brown out. She decided this call would probably be better done without an audience. Hugh would not be impressed that she was still involving herself with the Hollingsworths after their complaint of harassment, and she was already on the naughty step over Gerry, so it would be much better if he didn't know she was in touch with their new doctor. She packed all her paperwork back into her basket and left the room with a breezy, 'I have some phone calls to make and I don't want to disturb you all.' She hurried out, but not before Hugh had given her another look of disappointment. He didn't believe for one moment that she was anxious about disturbing her colleagues.

Once she was safely in the privacy of her own consulting room, Jo picked up the phone and called the mobile number that Dr Simms had asked her to use.

'Hello? Dr Simms?' she said, as he answered in his recognisable Scottish brogue. 'This is Jo Hughes returning your call.'

'Ah. Thank you, Dr Hughes. Let me just take this outside.' He didn't want this conversation overheard either, and she heard the sound of doors opening and closing before he continued. 'Yes, thank you for getting back to me so promptly. I received your email with the summary notes on both Mr and Mrs Hollingsworth, and having read them I realised I needed to see her as soon as possible to run those tests. I would have called the woman herself, but we only seemed to have a note of the husband's mobile phone number, with no landline or mobile number for the wife. So, I phoned the husband and left a message asking him to get his wife to make an appointment, and got no response. I called again a couple of days later without result, and so I got my practice manager to try. She left another message, saying that it was practice policy for all new patients to have a check with the practice nurse and please could he make appointments for them both.'

'Did you get a response to that?' Jo asked.

'Well, you could say that, yes. This morning my practice manager got a call to say they had changed their minds, as I was too far away, and they were going to find a GP in Hastings, which is what I suggested they do in the first place.'

'Did he say which practice they were going to?'

'No, he said he'd let us know when he found one.'

'And meanwhile they are in limbo, with no one looking after Mrs Hollingsworth and monitoring her thyroid, and with her having no way of getting her medication.'

'Exactly, which is why I thought I would let you know. I have real concerns about that poor woman.'

'Me too.'

'Not that I've ever met her, of course.'

'And it's a while since I've seen her,' Jo told him. 'A long while,' she added thoughtfully. Of course, Jo had many patients that she never saw from one year to the next, but that was usually because they were not sick or they were avoiding her because they didn't want to hear her advice about stopping smoking, cutting down on drinking or losing weight, but Jill Hollingsworth didn't fall into any of those categories. She had a chronic disease that needed medication in order for her to remain well. She had been delighted with how much better she had felt once her thyroid function levels improved. So why would she stop taking her drugs? And why was David Hollingsworth being so obstructive? What possible reason could he have for stopping his wife from being treated properly? All the while she was trying to push down the thought that had come to her when Dr Simms had said he hadn't met Jill. What if something had happened to her? It would certainly explain why she wasn't responding to letters or calls and, if something awful had happened and David was involved, it would explain why he was going to such great lengths to keep everyone from checking up on her. Jo continued with her paperwork, finishing it as fast as she could while still making sure it was done correctly. It was all too easy for a doctor to lose concentration and miss something important. Too easy to cause harm or even kill a patient because of a decimal point in the wrong place or a failure to spot drugs that interact.

When she had finished the last repeat prescription, a plan that had started as simply a possible course of action to allay her anxiety about Jill's wellbeing was still there, nagging away at her, and she hadn't thought of a better one. She was going to visit the Hollingsworth's farm in the hope that she would find Jill there on her own. It wasn't a great plan, not by a long way. She knew that if she bumped into David he would make another complaint and she wouldn't have a leg to stand on. After all, Jill wasn't even her patient any more.

Jo drove up the long track that led to the Hollingsworth's farm, carefully watching for signs that David was working in the surrounding fields in case he spotted her, but everywhere seemed deserted. She parked by the farmhouse and once again she was struck by how unloved and uncared for the place looked. It was a grey, damp day, although it wasn't actually raining, and somehow the weather seemed to suit these surroundings. There was no sign of David anywhere. She could hear no tractor engines or dogs barking, but that didn't mean he wasn't in the house having a late lunch.

Jo steeled herself to go and knock on the door. She couldn't stay in the car forever, apart from anything else she had to get back for evening surgery, so she got out, being careful to shut the driver's door quietly, and keeping the keys in her hand in case she needed to make a quick getaway. Looking and listening as she walked, she approached the silent house and knocked on the door. Her heart was hammering and her hands felt damp with sweat. She had no idea what she would do if he answered rather than Jill. Run for it probably.

There was no answer, so Jo knocked again, a little louder, and still hearing nothing, gently tried the door. It was unlocked, so she opened it wide enough to go in and stand just inside the doorway. The door opened straight into the large farmhouse kitchen. When Jo had visited here before, she had always been struck by how warm and welcoming it was, with the big range cooker pumping out heat and wonderful smells of baking, the well-used, solid wood kitchen table, pretty chintz curtains and a large, saggy armchair draped with a hand-crocheted blanket. Now, the room seemed cold and untidy. The range was unlit, and the washing up was piled high in the sink. The armchair was still there though, and Jill was fast asleep in it, with the familiar blanket wrapped around her.

'Hello?' Jo said quietly, relieved to find out that her worst fear, that Jill was dead, was unfounded. There was no response other than a little snort from Jill, so Jo went up to the chair and gave her a little shake.

'Jill? Jill? It's me, Dr Hughes.' Jill woke with a start and stared at Jo without recognition for a moment before realising who she was.

'Dr Hughes, of course, yes.' She struggled out of the chair. 'I must have fallen asleep,' she said with a little laugh. 'I'll put the kettle on. I must have forgotten you were coming.'

'I was just passing and thought I'd drop in. Is that okay?'

'Oh, of course. My memory's so bad these days, I just assumed...' Jill turned back to the sink and slowly filled the kettle. Jo was disappointed to see that Jill had put all the weight back on that she had lost once her thyroid function had been stabilised.

'How are you feeling, Jill?' She asked gently.

'Oh I'm fine, just a bit tired, that's all,' Jill explained as she put the kettle on the range before realising that it was cold. 'Damn! I must have let it go out. Not to worry, I'll just stick the electric one on.'

'Jill, stop a moment.' Jill turned to look at Jo, surprised at her stern voice. 'I don't need a cup of tea. I know you are no longer my patient, but I'm concerned…'

'What do you mean?' Jill was genuinely surprised. 'No longer your patient? Have you taken us off your list?'

'No,' Jo was equally taken aback. 'You changed doctors. Moved to a practice the other side of Winchelsea. Did you not know?'

Jill sat back down in the chair.

'Why would I change doctors?'

'I don't really know,' Jo admitted. 'Except that you haven't been to see me in ages, despite repeated requests to do so. Look, I'm concerned, Jill. Are you taking your tablets?'

'Of course. Every day, just as you said I had to, although I don't think these new ones are as good as the old ones.'

'What new ones?'

'The new make of thyroxine you've started me on.' Jill levered herself out of her chair again, went over to a cupboard, took out a small brown bottle containing white pills and gave it to Jo. Jo looked at the label. It had a pharmacy label on it, slightly askew, claiming this bottle contained Levothyroxine 125 mcg and one tablet was to be taken each day before breakfast. The label seemed to be in order, but the tablets inside were white and round, not lozenge-shaped as she expected. She turned the tablet over and couldn't see any writing etched on it, and she was fairly sure there should be some kind of identifier. Also, it was no longer accepted practice to dispense tablets in bottles. The pharmacy named on the bottle was in Hastings and Jo couldn't believe they would have done this.

'Pharmacies have to dispense medicines in calendar packs these days, Jill.' Jo explained. 'You know, those foil strips with fourteen tablets in? So that patients can see if they've missed a dose.'

'I did wonder why they seemed to have changed,' Jill agreed, but it looked as though she had long since given up trying to work out what was going on.

Jo opened the bottle and tipped a few of the tablets out into the palm of her hand. They looked like sweeteners rather than thyroxine tablets, and Jo rubbed one of the tablets between her finger and thumb before tentatively licking the residue off her thumb, just as the farm-house door was flung open by a furious-looking David Hollingsworth.

'I don't know what this is, but I'm pretty sure it's not your thyroid tablet,' she said with conviction as she looked him in the eye.

28

They sat around the wooden table in the kitchen drinking cups of tea that Jo had made once she had calmed the situation down. There was still a lingering atmosphere, but at least David had stopped shouting at her once he realised that it was too late and Jill finally knew what had been going on. He had confessed to giving her vitamin D tablets he bought from a health food shop, convincing himself that at least they wouldn't hurt her and might even do her some good.

'I still don't understand why you did it, David,' Jill said. The anger that she had felt once she realised her husband had been substituting her medicine with vitamins had subsided, and she had reverted to her previous lethargic state.

'Because of who you became when you took 'em,' David rubbed his face and tried to explain.

'When we met, you was lovely, a bit quiet mebbe, but we had a good life here and you never complained. Then the doc here,' he gestured at Jo, 'said you needed tablets 'cos your thyroid wasn't working proper, and you changed.'

'How do you mean?'

'Suddenly you was rushing round and arguing with me all the time.'

'No I wasn't!' But Jo could see that Jill wasn't sure, and was wondering if perhaps she had been more argumentative.

'Telling me to do this, do that, fix the windows, paint the kitchen. Nag, nag, nag. That's all you did. You weren't the same woman I married.'

Jill looked at her husband in shocked silence, but he couldn't hold her gaze.

'All I wanted was a bit of peace and quiet.' He stood up and turned towards the door. 'I've got things to do.'

'Just you wait one minute, David Hollingsworth.' Jill stood up so suddenly her chair tipped over, and David turned back to her in surprise. 'Are you telling me that you like me tired, overweight and depressed because it means you get a quiet life, to the point that when the doctor here made me better with the thyroid pills you switched them to make me ill again?'

'Well,' David looked ashamed of himself and he struggled to find a better way of expressing it, 'yes, I did. I didn't want you to be ill, though, but, I suppose, I mean, I'd have been happy if you were a bit better, more cheerful like, but I just couldn't take your constant...'

'Nagging, yes, I've got the picture.'

Jill sat down again.

'Why didn't you say?'

David came back to the table and sat down again as well.

'It weren't easy, like. You was so busy doing stuff all the time. Rushing here, rushing there.'

'For the first time in years, I had energy. I wanted to get things done.'

'I know.'

Jill gave a little laugh.

'Now you mention it, I must have been hell to live with. I never stopped, hardly slept.'

David nodded.

'It weren't easy.'

'But I can't live like this.'

'No. I know that,' David sighed.

'What do you say we give it another try?'

He nodded his agreement, but looked miserable.

Jo cleared her throat and they both turned to her.

'It might just be that the dose was too high and made you a little hyperthyroid,' she suggested. 'Perhaps we could start with a lower dose? Monitor it carefully and see how things go. Make sure you don't get so hyperactive?'

Jill nodded, 'That sounds like a good idea.' She turned to her husband, 'What do you think, David?'

'Alright.' He mumbled, sounding very unsure.

'You'll need to re-register with me though, Jill.'

'Of course.'

Jo looked directly at David. 'Where you register is entirely up to you, but you need to know that if Jill stops coming in for her regular reviews, I'll be up here in a flash. And if I suspect you have started messing with her tablets again, I'll have no option but to involve the police.' Jo wasn't quite sure what crime he could be charged with, but she was sure there would be something.

'I won't do that, I promise.' David looked honestly ashamed of what he had been doing, and Jo believed him.

'Don't you worry, Dr Hughes, now I know what he's been up to, I'll be keeping a close eye and making sure I see you regularly.' Jo was pretty sure Jill would do exactly that, now she knew what had been going on.

'Right, I'll just go and get my bag so that I can do a prescription for you, and I'll leave a blood test form. You need to get that done in a couple of weeks, so we can see how you're responding. Okay?'

As Jo went to her car, she wondered how they were going to get on. While she had some sympathy with David if Jill had been as bad as he was making out, had Jo found out her own husband had been deliberately keeping her in a state of hypothyroidism, she would have left him without hesitation. Provided she had the energy to leave, once she was better. Perhaps Jill would do that, or maybe she had other plans to exact her revenge. Either way, Jo had a sneaky suspicion that Jill was never going to let David forget what he had done.

Jo got into her car and had to stop herself from giving a triumphant shout and doing a fist pump, an action she abhorred, but it was amazing how invigorating it felt to actually solve one of her many problems, or at least to move it forward. She had no illusions about the difficulties that lay ahead. Still, it inspired her to go through her problem list and see if there were any others that she could solve and, as she drove away from the farm, her thoughts turned once more to her parents. There had been no suitable flats for her mother in the local paper, but as she parked outside her home and hurried down the steps towards the surgery, she had an idea. She looked at her watch and saw that she had just enough time to pick up a local paper.

Jo's hair was still damp from the shower, and her face had a rosy glow brought on by exercise and self-righteousness as she sipped her green tea and watched Kate tuck into a slice of Bakewell Tart, slathered in cream. They were in the small café area of the gym. Kate's hair was dry, not just because she hadn't showered, but also because she hadn't exercised either.

'Yum,' Kate murmured her appreciation of the tart. 'Are you sure you don't want to try some?'

'No thanks, not after working out for an hour.'

'Go on. Loosen your stays and live a little.'

'It's not because I'm treating my body as a temple, I can assure you, it's just that I'm too tired to eat.'

Kate smiled.

'I trust your appetite will have recovered later. If not, your mother will have a field day.'

'She'll have a field day whether I eat anything or not.'

Kate looked at her friend, concern written all over her face.

'Are you sure tricking your parents into having dinner with you is a good idea?'

'Well, either it will get them back together or neither of them will ever speak to me again.'

'So it's a win/win situation.'

'Exactly.' Jo took another sip of tea and tried not to wrinkle her nose. One day she'd develop a liking for it, she was sure, but in the meantime it tasted pretty awful. 'I just need to get them to see that it would be such a waste to divorce after all this time, particularly over something so trivial.' She sighed. 'It's not like Dad's been unfaithful or tried to poison her.'

'Or drugged her and tried to kill her in a burning car.'

'Exactly.'

'Perhaps you could put that to them?' Kate seemed to be enjoying herself. 'You know, "Marriage guidance counselling using a serial killer as an example of how bad things could be." You should market it straight away.'

'You can laugh, but it might just work, and anyway, I'm fast coming to the conclusion that marriage is decidedly over-rated.' Kate looked sharply at her friend. This was very unlike her. Jo straightened her back and groaned slightly. 'I should do this more often and then it wouldn't hurt so much.'

'Nonsense. It would just hurt more often. Exercise isn't good for you.'

'I don't understand why you keep paying for gym membership when you never use it.'

'What do you mean, never use it? I'm here aren't I?'

'Yes, but…'

'And I'm enjoying myself, eating cake and watching all these fit young men in shorts getting hot and sweaty.'

'You are awful.'

'But you like me.' Kate finished the catchphrase for her and ate more cake. 'So have they charged the fireman yet?'

'Not as far as I know. I heard they had found a matchbook similar to the ones used in the crimes, in a drawer in his desk I think, but they haven't linked him to the website yet or identified the last victim either, if my informant is right, which I think she is.'

Kate clocked the fact that Jo's information was not coming directly from Miller.

'They probably won't charge him until at least tomorrow lunchtime, if they have any sense. They'll want to do as much as they can before having to commit themselves.'

'That's always supposing they have enough evidence by then.' Jo wasn't sure what they could have found in the time. 'Are you still in touch with anyone from the website?'

'Absolutely,' Kate confirmed. 'I'm meeting one tomorrow night.'

Jo looked worried.

'What?' Kate asked her. 'Even if they have to let him go, it can't be the fireman that I'm meeting because we've been texting while he's been at the nick, and I can't believe they would allow him to continue to contact potential victims in between interrogations.'

Jo knew she was right, but she couldn't help feeling anxious for her friend.

'At least let me be wherever you have arranged to meet. Just in case.'

'I'm not a child. I've done this before and I do know how to look after myself.'

'I won't interfere, I'll sit quietly in a corner and just be there if you need me. At least if I see you suddenly acting like you've been drugged I can come to the rescue.'

'What are you like? Do you not think I know how to protect my own drink from someone wanting to add a date rape drug? I have done this before, you know.'

'I know, I know, but humour me, will you?'

Kate sighed. She knew that Jo would indeed worry if she didn't let her be there. Jo's level of anxiety about those she cared for was part of what Kate loved about her friend.

'Oh alright.'

'Thank you.'

'But if I decide to take him home, you're not coming with me.'

'You wouldn't, would you? Not on a first date!' Jo was horrified.

'Depends how fit he is,' Kate said with a wicked smile, before turning her attention back to the last of her cake.

Jo checked her watch again.

'Right, I've got to go.'

'Good luck!' Kate called as Jo picked up her bag and hurried out, anxiety building like a knot in her stomach despite the stress-relieving workout she had just completed.

If Jo was honest, she wasn't so sure her plan was such a good idea. Pumped up by her success with the Hollingsworths, she had rung each of her parents individually and asked them to dinner. She had picked the poshest restaurant she knew in the hope that they wouldn't create a scene in a place where it was considered unseemly to speak above a whisper, but that wouldn't stop one or both walking out, and now that she was sitting in the bar area just off the dining room, waiting for them to arrive, her nerves were beginning to get the better of her.

She had arranged for her mother to arrive first, and had a gin and tonic ready and waiting. Her father was due in ten minutes, but there was no sign of her mother. It would be just like her to upset the plan by arriving late, Jo thought, as she fiddled with her glass of wine. She would have to be careful. The temptation was to gulp it down, but there was no way was she going to get drunk. That certainly wouldn't help matters.

'Jocasta, darling,' her mother wafted in to the bar in a haze of Rive Gauche and saw the glass of gin and tonic waiting for her. 'How lovely.'

They made small talk for a few minutes, the terrible weather, Jo's work, the bridge club; carefully avoiding any discussion of either the murders or the marital difficulties. Jo fiddled nervously with her glass.

'Is our table ready?' Diana Hughes asked a passing waiter, who looked faintly bemused.

'Are you all here, Madam?' the waiter replied, to Jo's dismay. 'The booking is for three persons.'

'That's fine,' Jo told him, before her mother could say anything. 'Perhaps we could look at the menu?'

The waiter hurried to fetch the menus as Diana fixed her daughter with a beady eye. It was clear the penny had dropped and she knew exactly what Jo was up to, and was not happy about it at all.

'You have no right to interfere,' she hissed, standing up. Jo stood as well, as the waiter hovered, waving the two menus in his hand ineffectually and looking round anxiously as he realised there was about to be a scene.

'I have every right. After all, you are living in my home.'

'It's only temporary.' Diana turned to leave, but Jo's father was standing in the doorway, a look of irritation on his face.

'Jocasta, I am disappointed in you,' he said, as he turned to leave.

'No! Sit down, both of you,' Jo ordered them in a loud voice that silenced them and surprised herself. What was even more surprising was the fact that they both did as they were told. Thankfully, the waiter seemed to have disappeared after bringing the menus, although, more embarrassingly, most of the occupants of the dining room were watching the scene unfold with great interest.

'Now,' she continued in a quieter voice, once they were both settled and the barman had brought a large whisky over for Charles, 'I know neither of you want me to interfere, but I'm going to anyway.' She rummaged in her rather large bag and pulled out a local paper and opened the property pages.

'I am quite capable of finding my own flat,' Diana said icily, before seeing that Jo was looking at the commercial property pages.

'Here, in Crowhurst.' She pointed at an advertisement and handed the paper to her father. 'Workshop to rent.'

He took the paper and looked at it closely.

'It's got plenty of space and electricity points, a kitchenette and a shower room, so you can clean up after working on the bike. There's even space for a washing machine if you wanted, so you wouldn't have to bring your overalls home to wash.'

Charles was clearly interested.

'Hmm, yes, it's certainly a possibility. I'll go and look at it tomorrow.'

'No, you'll start moving into it tomorrow. I got your friend Roy to take a look. He said it was perfect and I've already signed the contract. It's a six-month lease. After that, it's up to you to continue it.'

Jo was pretty certain her father would agree. He was already busy planning all the things he would need to do, but her mother was an entirely different matter and she looked as if she was about to throw a spanner in the works.

'But that's…'

'You told me that the only reason you left was the dirt and the bike parts in the house, well now you won't have that, so you will be moving back home, tomorrow.' Jo wasn't going to give her mother the chance to upset the plan. 'Now, shall we take a look at the menu?'

Charles was grinning, and Diana didn't look as if she quite knew what to say, so she picked up the menu and began looking at the choices. Jo sat back knowing that she'd won, and she would have her home to herself again. Tomorrow.

29

Jo had a busy surgery, full of people who really didn't need to be seen on a Saturday morning. It always amazed her that the government made such a fuss about surgeries being open seven days a week to stop people having to go to hospital for minor problems, but if any of them actually sat in on one of her Saturday surgeries, they would soon realise that she only ever saw things that could easily have waited until the following week. She might have understood if they were people who couldn't take time off work from Monday to Friday, but the majority of her list comprised pensioners and the unemployed, so they really had no excuse at all. Perhaps, to them, one day seemed much the same as the other and they didn't realise how precious weekends off were for those who had children at school during the week, both doctors and patients alike.

Her only truly urgent patient that morning was a young mum with a sick baby, and Jo ended up sending her straight to A&E. Once she had finished her list, and happy in the knowledge that she had prevented all these people from cluttering up the local emergency department, Jo made herself a cup of strong coffee and sat down to tackle the unending paperwork. At least if she cleared her basket now there wouldn't seem quite so much to do on Monday, and a glance at her watch told her she had time before helping her mother move back to her own home. Quite why her mother needed help to move back in when she hadn't need any help moving out was anybody's guess.

The papers that morning were full of the story that the fourth victim had been identified as an unmarried bakery worker. It could mean that Jo was wrong with her theory about the deaths being punishment for adultery, or it could simply be that the killer had made a mistake and murdered someone who didn't fit his criteria. Jo knew that the police would be using that fact in their continued questioning of Chris Butterworth, telling him he had killed an innocent woman, and she hoped that the tactic worked. No one in their right mind would think it reasonable to sentence a woman to death for adultery, but the sort of man who did think it was justified might be shamed into an admission of guilt if he knew he had chosen his victim wrongly. She was desperate for this to be over, for Miller to have got his man, and for the murderer to be safely off the streets, but she knew that without any concrete evidence it was unlikely that Miller would be able to hold Butterworth and that he would be bailed later in the day. Even with Kate's breezy assurance that her date couldn't be the killer, Jo couldn't help but worry about Kate's plan for the evening. Until she was quite sure the murderer had been caught, charged and was languishing in jail somewhere, she didn't think her friend should be internet dating at all, and certainly not using the SSE website. If she was honest, she had misgivings about the safety of internet dating anyway, without the added danger of a serial killer using it to find his victims.

Her hand hesitated over the phone. With Chris Butterworth in custody, it seemed likely that Miller would be frantically trying to make his case and really wouldn't have time to speak to her. On the other hand, her friend's safety was at stake.

She took a deep breath, picked up the receiver, and dialled. She needed the reassurance that Miller had the right man, and she just hoped he would be able to give it to her.

As Jo lifted the last suitcase into the boot of her mother's car she wondered how it was that the few possessions she'd had with her the night she arrived had grown to such an extent. Jo closed the lid of the boot with a sigh and checked her phone again, knowing that she hadn't missed a call or text from Miller, but disappointed to have it confirmed all the same. She had been unable to get hold of him when she called after surgery, so she'd had to make do with the information she prised out of Nigel. He told her that Chris Butterworth was in the process of being interviewed and that therefore she couldn't speak to Miller or Jeffries, but he hadn't been able to put her mind at rest. He wouldn't give her any further details and certainly would not hazard an opinion about the likelihood of Butterworth being the murderer. She had, at least, persuaded Nigel to leave a note on Miller's desk asking him to ring her as soon as he was free. She had then tried Jayne, but she was busy overseeing the search of Butterworth's home and office and so had little time to update Jo. The search had so far revealed a matchbook similar to those used in the fires, which was useful but not conclusive, Jayne confided. She had little doubt that Butterworth would be able to explain it away, particularly as it was from California, and neither those in Mark's collection nor the ones used in the murders had been from anywhere other than England. Jo felt no further forward, and she would just have to hope that either Butterworth was charged or that Miller would be able to call her back before Kate's date that evening. She wanted to hear from him that he was sure Butterworth was their man, or she would be tempted to disrupt the date to make sure Kate was safe, even if it made her friend cross. There was no way she could let Kate put herself in danger and do nothing to stop it. What if Kate became victim number five? She would never forgive herself. If she thought there was any risk, Jo would stop the date even if it made Kate so angry that she never spoke to her again.

Her dad had been thrilled with the workshop and had spent the morning moving all his tools and pieces of bike into it, so the coast should be clear. Now she just had to follow her mother home in her own car, to make sure she actually got there, get her settled in, and make sure there were no residual problems between her parents, before dashing back so she could get ready to go out with Kate.

As she dried her hair, Jo watched the press conference on TV, hoping to hear that Butterworth had been charged, so she was very disappointed to find that he had been released. Miller looked tired as questions and criticisms were fired at him, his normal bullish attitude barely noticeable. She worried that this investigation was taking more of a toll on him than expected. Perhaps his home life was adding to his problems. She knew he loved his wife, but Miller would be the first to admit their marriage had many problems, and it wouldn't be that much of a surprise if they split up, given that even her parents seemingly solid marriage had been close to ending. And then what? Would Jo consider him a free agent? Or would she need the split to be final, undisputed, with a decree absolute as evidence before she would give in to her feelings? How strong was her commitment to not dating married men? Jo didn't know. She looked at her watch. It was another hour before she was due to meet Kate. She reached for the phone.

Time to try Miller one last time, to see if she could get the reassurance she needed that he had the right man.

So that stupid girl had been single? Having spent an evening with her, he could understand why. The bitch! It made him angry to think that he had wasted his time with her. Her constant chatter about trivial things, soap operas and so-called celebrities, in which he had no interest whatsoever, had been tedious and irritating. If he hadn't been thinking about what he had planned for her he would have been unable to keep the boredom from his face. Not that she would have noticed, she was so caught up in the intimate details of her fake plastic world. But that didn't change the fact that she had deliberately used a website for cheats and whores. Why would she do that if she wasn't married? Did she hate married people? Had envy turned to hate when she couldn't find a man desperate enough to marry her? Why would she choose to tempt and ensnare married men if not to destroy their marriages? To destroy other people's happy lives? She was as guilty as the whores who cheated on their husbands, and so her punishment had been just. She had deserved it and he was right to have done it. There couldn't be many like her using the website. The first three had all been married, and he was sure the one he had lined up for tonight was married, from what she had told him, but he could always check once he met her. It would be hard to walk away when he was all prepped and ready to go, but he could do, if he needed to. He just hoped he wouldn't need to. He was ready to kill again. He was ready for the thrill. He was ready to glory in the achievement of punishing another vicious, conniving, adulterous bitch. Killing tonight would be the only way he could wipe away the sickness he felt at having been cheated by that deceitful little whore.

30

Jo looked round the packed bar and tried to find somewhere to sit where she could keep an eye on Kate without being too obvious. The Mojo was a well-known meeting place on the singles scene, unless there was some televised sporting event, when it was filled with drunken fans. It being a Saturday night the singles had taken precedence over sport, the multiple televisions were muted, and music was thumping out from the sound system. The current clientele were busy eating the gourmet burgers off what looked like lengths of plank, and knocking back the cocktail of the week; a vivid pink affair served in a jam jar. According to the posters stuck up around the room there would be a DJ later, to enhance their entertainment. Or not. Jo hoped she wasn't still there by the time the women were drunk enough to make use of the pole set up on the stage, so that they could show off their dance moves and their underwear.

Searching round for somewhere to sit she spotted a small table in the corner, but much as she would have liked to tuck herself away from the main throng she rejected it, because there was no way she could keep Kate in view from there. Kate was seated at the bar, sipping an incredibly expensive Mojito. Jo had decided she wouldn't drink alcohol, partly so that she would stay alert and partly because she wanted to be able to drive herself home.

Having finally found a stool to sit on at the corner of a table, Jo sipped her lime and soda. It was far too heavy on the lime, a common mistake of bartenders in her experience, but she had no intention of fighting her way back to the bar for a replacement. She checked her phone again, hoping for a message from Miller. There was none, and there was no point trying to call him from the bar as the noise level would mean she couldn't possibly hear anything he said. Instead, she sent him a text message, asking if he was sure the killer was Butterworth and explaining that Kate was meeting a date from SSE at the Mojo, and that she was going to be there just to make sure she was okay. She had been reassured to hear from Jayne Hales that Miller had ordered round the clock surveillance on Butterworth. Jayne had really stuck her neck out telling her that, and had taken her mobile into the corridor outside the incident room so that she wouldn't be overheard. It was one thing for the boss to okay her giving more general information to Jo, but this was far more sensitive, and she knew it could backfire on her if anyone found out. Jo was very grateful for the information, otherwise she would have had no choice but to march Kate home and lock her in to prevent her meeting anyone. Miller clearly still thought Butterworth was their man or he wouldn't have authorised the watch, she reasoned. He didn't have enough men on the squad to waste their time like that, and even if Butterworth managed to somehow slip past the surveillance team, she would recognise him as soon as he walked in the pub.

Jo looked up sharply and held her breath as she saw Kate being approached by a man, but it clearly wasn't her date as she said something and he moved away. It was hardly surprising that Kate was attracting men in a bar like this, particularly as she was dressed in a red chiffon blouse that left little to the imagination. Jo hoped she wasn't knocking back the Mojito at the same pace she normally drank beer, or she would be on the floor before her date showed up.

Jo checked her watch again. Kate's date should have been here by now. Perhaps he would stand her up and they could spend the rest of the evening in The Stag or go for a meal somewhere nice. It would certainly be a relief after the noise in the bar, not to mention the men who kept trying to engage her in conversation, only to be given her best 'leave me alone' stare. Jo had found, to her cost on a number of occasions, that you had to be blunt in these sorts of situations, as being polite or pleasant when saying no to a drink or to a chat was taken as acquiescence. It seemed that a couple of drinks made most men convinced that they were irresistible. And funny.

Jo looked round the room, wondering if there was CCTV anywhere in the bar, but the only camera she could see was at the end of the bar by the till, presumably to keep an eye on the staff rather than the clientele. This close to the town centre there would almost certainly be cameras in the streets outside, which made her feel safer, as she knew that the killer liked to meet in places where there was no CCTV around, although there must be precious few venues left without some kind of surveillance. She panicked slightly when her view of Kate was blocked by a bunch of rowdy young men trying to get served at the bar. She shifted her position, ignoring the looks from the people whose space she was now invading, and caught Kate's eye. Kate shrugged and held up her hand palm out, indicating that she would give him another five minutes. Jo nodded that she understood.

At last, a man came up to Kate and they started talking. He was well-dressed and incredibly good-looking. Jo wondered why he had to resort to a dating website, but then kicked herself as she remembered that it was because he was already married. Kate was smiling and flirting with him, and when he turned to the bar to get them both a drink, she gave Jo a theatrical wink and a thumbs up. She was clearly taken with him.

Jo was so busy concentrating on watching Kate that when she turned back to take a sip of her drink it took her a moment or two to realise that Adrian Lambourne had just come in to the bar and appeared to be looking for someone. What on earth was he doing here? She stood up and started to walk towards him just as he looked round and saw her. A look of surprise and mild panic swept across his face, and Jo wondered if it was because he wasn't sure if she was still angry with him about Mark.

'Hi, Adrian, I didn't expect to see you in a place like this.'

'Dr Hughes. How lovely.' He had recovered quickly and managed to smile at her.

'I'm sorry, you were probably meeting someone here. Don't think you have to stay and talk to me.' Jo saw that her seat had already been taken by someone else and she started looking around to see if there were any other spaces.

'I can't seem to see her. I think I may have been stood up. I may as well go,' he indicated towards the door. He seemed eager to leave and his embarrassment was really quite endearing. Jo felt sorry him.

'Oh well, we're both in the same boat then,' Jo nodded towards Kate who was still engrossed in her date. 'My friend seems to have pulled.'

'Oh, right.' Adrian looked at Kate and gave a little smile of understanding. Jo realised that she had put him in an awkward situation, as he now couldn't leave without seeming ungallant for abandoning her, but it would be easier from her point of view to have someone to talk to, even if it was only for a few minutes, until she was sure Kate was okay.

'Let me get you a drink by way of an apology for being so sharp with you over my patient. I really do understand how hard it must be to find beds at short notice. What will you have?'

'No, no, there's no need…'

'I insist, Adrian, or else I will never believe you have forgiven me.' Jo turned to the bar to try and get the bartender's attention, which wasn't going to be easy given how crowded the place was. 'Who were you meeting?' She asked casually.

'Oh, just a friend of a friend. Look I really…'

'Friends always try to set you up with the most unsuitable people, don't they?' Jo could think of several tortured evenings. 'I've often wondered about using dating websites, but wrote them off as full of weirdos, not to mention murderers, but my friend seems to have found someone reasonable,' she nodded towards Kate. 'In fact, he doesn't look bad at all. Have you ever given them a go?' Jo had finally managed to catch the bartender's eye, so she missed the look of fear that briefly crossed Adrian's face and he had regained his anxious but unassuming look before she turned and asked, 'What was it you said you wanted?'

'Um, slimline tonic, but really…'

'Slimline tonic and a lime and soda, please,' she ordered.

As they waited for their drinks, Jo went back to the topic of dating websites.

'So have you ever used internet dating?' she asked again.

'No,' he responded. 'Like you, it never appealed to me.'

Something about the way he said it made her think that he was lying. Perhaps he was embarrassed about it. She realised that he had spotted her disbelief and was relieved when the barman brought the drinks over.

Adrian poured all his tonic into the glass while Jo paid the bartender. She looked over at Kate who was laughing at something her date had said. She seemed happy, and the man didn't look like a serial killer, but Jo didn't intend leaving the bar just yet. She'd keep an eye on her friend for a while longer. When she turned back to Adrian he had picked up both their drinks.

258

'Can you see anywhere to sit?' she looked around, but she couldn't see anywhere free.

'It's quieter outside,' Adrian said. 'It's a nice evening. Quite warm for the time of year.'

Jo hesitated. He was right, it was a warm evening and it would be much nicer outside, but she was unsure that she wanted to let Kate out of her sight yet.

'You'll be able to see if your friend leaves,' Adrian seemed to understand her concerns, and Jo realised that he was right. There was only the one way in and Kate would have to walk past them if she left.

'Okay,' Jo followed him outside to where a few tables had been placed on the wide pavement, mainly to allow smokers a chance to get their fix in relative comfort. There were a few people puffing at their cigarettes or vaping, but several of the tables were empty. Adrian led the way to one that was a little apart from the others, but didn't sit down. Jo looked at the seats and saw they were a little damp and also stayed standing.

'So we don't have to breathe in any second-hand smoke,' he explained.

Jo was pleased by his thoughtfulness.

'I won't stay much longer, anyway. My friend seems to be getting on just fine.'

Jo sipped her drink, wondering if she should have had it topped up with soda because, once again, there was far too much lime in it. She shivered slightly in the cooler air.

'I'm sorry. Are you cold?' Adrian asked. 'It's just a relief to get away from that terrible music.'

'I'm fine,' Jo insisted. 'And it is a relief. Why they have to have it up so loud, I don't know. Oh dear,' Jo laughed as she took another drink, 'I sound like my mother.'

Adrian smiled.

'Would you like to sit down?' he asked, and she decided that yes she did want to sit down, because she was feeling a bit strange. He hastily wiped the seat with his handkerchief as she sat with a bump and wondered if she was going to faint. Everything seemed very distant. She thought she could hear her phone ringing, and she pulled it out of her pocket to answer, but it was beyond her. She was aware of someone nearby speaking to her.

'How are you feeling, Jo?'

She wanted to answer, but couldn't get the words out.

'Here, let me help you over to my car. I'll take you home.'

It was a kind voice, a voice she recognised but couldn't quite place, and she allowed herself to be led away from the noise and the lights. She wanted to sleep, and this kind person with his reassuring voice was offering to take her home.

'It's not far, just over here,' the voice encouraged her when she stumbled, and she walked on, leaning heavily on his arm, grateful for his help.

31

As she drifted in and out of consciousness, Jo realised that she was in the front passenger seat of a car she didn't recognise. She felt ill and her mind was fuzzy, spaced out, in fact. She vaguely registered that the car was small and that she was feeling sick partly because of whatever was making her feel spaced out, but also because she was being thrown around as the car travelled at speed through the streets, using minor roads that twisted and turned nauseatingly. She turned to get a look at who was driving, but that made her nausea worse and she closed her eyes again.

'Please slow down,' she thought she said, but she wasn't sure it came out clearly.

'Shush now, it will all be fine,' the voice responded, and she thought she recognised it. Who was it? She couldn't quite put her finger on it, but the voice was reassuring, and she allowed herself to drift away for a moment. She came to with a start as they made a violent right turn that flung her against the door. Through the fog that was enveloping her mind she managed to place the voice as belonging to the psychologist, Adrian something. She really couldn't think clearly, but she knew she was with a friend and only half listened to what he continued to tell her in his soothing voice.

'I never would have taken you, but you were bound to put two and two together eventually. Tomorrow or the next day you would have realised your friend was meeting me, and then realised that I had connections to Mark Caxton. You'd begin to be suspicious of me then and, given your work with the police, you'd tell them. I couldn't let you do that. You must understand.'

His words made no sense at all. What on earth was he talking about? She was so tired, maybe she should have a little sleep and then she would feel better and be able to understand what was going on. She closed her eyes again and let his words wash over her. But instead of being able to sleep, she had a flash of clarity. Kate's date. Mark Caxton. Police. Suddenly she was wide awake.

'Stop!' she cried out, and started opening her door. There was something stopping her from moving and she realise that her seat belt was fastened. The car veered across the road as Adrian reached across her and the door swung wide, hitting something, a car, a road sign, Jo wasn't sure, but there was a bang and she heard a shout before the car lurched again, the door swung back and Adrian grabbed it, slamming it shut. She was still struggling to free the seat belt clasp when he hit her in the face, and everything went black.

When she came to, Jo's head hurt and she couldn't think straight. She had no idea how long she had been unconscious. She lay back in her seat trying to brace herself against the lurches of the car. They were driving at great speed. She tentatively opened one eye and saw they were on a minor road with cars parked on both sides. If anyone came the other way they would have no time to stop. She tried to think. She was in a car with Adrian Lambourne. He had hit her and that was why her head hurt. Why had he hit her? Her stomach lurched as she remembered. Adrian was the serial killer. She still felt woozy. What was it he had used to drug the other women? GHB, that was it. Unlike the others, she hadn't been drinking, so she'd come round much more quickly, which had given her the chance to try and escape. That's why he'd knocked her out. She tensed as the car swerved round a corner and she was thrown against the door. She couldn't help a small grunt of pain escaping as her head hit the glass.

'Don't even think about trying anything at this speed, we'll both be killed.' Lambourne had heard the grunt and was aware she was conscious again.

Jo knew he was right, but she would rather take her chances in a car crash than wait for him to set the car, and her, on fire.

She wondered if Kate had noticed she was missing, or if anyone at the bar had seen her being taken. Then she wondered why he was driving so fast. Surely he wouldn't want to draw attention to himself? He kept looking in the mirror and, as she realised why, her heart soared. They were being followed. That's why he didn't care about attracting attention for speeding; he was trying to get away. She listened very carefully and thought she could hear a siren in the distance, so they couldn't be far behind. She took a closer look at where they were, the regular rows of houses and parked cars had given way to hedgerows. They were out in the countryside, but she wasn't quite sure where. She could see he was watching closely, occasionally slowing to look at potential lanes and tracks where he could hide with the car, and she knew she couldn't let him. He saw a turning up ahead, and turned off his lights as he approached it. Jo knew that the moment he stopped driving he would be able to turn his full attention to stopping her from escaping or making a noise. He would be able to knock her out or even kill her. She had no illusions about her ability to defend herself. Perhaps she would have been wise to take up martial arts or self-defence classes, but it was too late now. She had to take her chance while he was still preoccupied.

They had turned off the road onto what was little more than a rutted dirt track, so he'd been forced to slow down. Jo slid one hand onto the seat belt release, and as Lambourne turned again onto a muddy farmyard track, she simultaneously undid her seat belt and pulled the door handle. Rolling out of the car before the door had really opened, her arm got caught in the seat belt, stopping her from fully falling from the car.

Lambourne slammed on the brakes and made a grab for her, but the sudden jerk of the car coming to a halt had released her arm from the seat belt, and he was only able to grasp the sleeve of her jacket.

She pulled against Lambourne's grip, but he had hold of her too tightly, so she cried out in anger, twisted and kicked at the car and in one desperate, ferocious move that tore her jacket, she managed to free herself from his grasp. The sudden release sent her sprawling and winded her. For precious seconds, she couldn't move. She heard him come after her and she hardly knew where she got the strength, but she was up and running out into the lane, Lambourne close on her heels.

With a final burst of speed she flew out into the lane. She was dazzled by headlights, and there was a screech of brakes.

'Fuuuuck!' she heard someone shout as the car skidded to a stop, inches short of hitting her.

Miller was out of the car and running towards her as Lambourne careered onto the lane, then seeing Miller and Jeffries, he turned and ran.

'Go!' Jeffries shouted at his boss. 'I've got her.' Jeffries ran to Jo, who had slumped down in the middle of the road, overwhelmed with relief.

32

They had the heaters on full blast in the back of the ambulance where Jo sat with a blanket round her shoulders. It was very warm, but she couldn't seem to stop shivering. The after-effects of the drug, she told herself, and shock, but knowing the cause made no difference, she still shook like a leaf. Jayne Hales sat next to her with her notebook open, ostensibly to take a statement, but she was doing most of the talking.

'Good thing you left those messages on the Guv's phone or we wouldn't have known where to start looking for you.' She had already explained that Miller had switched his phone off while interviewing Butterworth, and it wasn't until after the evening briefing that he had remembered to turn it back on.

'But how did you know it was Lambourne?' Jo asked between spasms of shaking.

'We didn't,' Jayne admitted, giving her a worried look, probably wondering if she ought to get the paramedic back in, but Jo smiled encouragement and clenched her teeth more firmly together to stop them chattering. Slightly reassured, Jayne continued, 'The techies had analysed the wording in all the posts on the website connected to our victims and spotted a pattern. The killer was changing names and burner phones for every target, but recycled bits of his profile and messages, using the same words and phrases.'

'Clever techies.'

'Nigel helped them with that. Of course, he would have got onto the pattern much earlier if we'd been able to access the instant messaging app Lambourne used once he'd made contact with the victims, but they were encrypted and it wasn't a matter of national security, apparently.'

Jo, normally a staunch supporter of civil liberties and the right to privacy, had to concede that the police would have caught the killer earlier if they'd had access to those messages, and it gave her pause for thought.

'But how did all that lead you to me?'

'The tech department called urgently this evening to say that they were pretty sure the same person was in contact with someone else and sent us the details. We recognised the photo as your friend Kate, which was just as well, as that wasn't the name she was using.' Jayne looked amused, but Jo just nodded her understanding, she was absolutely not going to ask what name Kate had used.

'So we phoned her,' Jayne continued, 'and she said she was supposed to be meeting him tonight but he had been a no-show and someone better had come along.'

That explained it, Jo thought. The man with Kate was not the date from the website. That date was Adrian. He'd arrived a little late, by which time Kate had found someone else. Jo shuddered at how close they had both come to being the next victim.

'We were relieved,' Jayne went on, once she was sure Jo was okay, 'but then she realised you had gone AWOL and weren't answering your phone. She went outside and rang you again, heard the ring tone, found your phone in the gutter and called us back immediately. The boss charged over there and some witnesses remembered seeing a women who fitted your description, and whom they took to be drunk, being helped into a car. Fortunately one of them was able to give us a good description. Caused a bit of a panic, I can tell you.'

Jo shuddered. She hated to think what could so easily have happened, if Kate had just assumed she'd gone home.

'I'm just so glad they managed to track down the route he was taking.'

'Well, that was down to you, I reckon. You tried to get out of the moving car, didn't you?'

Jo nodded.

'When you opened the door it took the wing mirror off a cab as the driver was dropping off a passenger. He was absolutely livid. He gave chase and radioed all his mates to help. We just had to follow the taxis.'

Jo smiled again, but this time it was for real. The thought of the police cars, chasing the taxis, chasing the car she was in, was like something out of a cartoon, although she knew it hadn't really been that comical.

'Well, I'm very grateful to them,' she sighed and shook her head. 'It never occurred to me that Adrian was the killer. I mean, I even knew he been through a terrible divorce. But he just seemed boring, petty and ordinary. How can I have been so stupid?'

She looked over at the police car where she could see Lambourne sitting in the back, hunched and defeated, with his hands cuffed and with a grim-looking police officer sitting beside him. Lambourne had a small cut above the eye and some incipient bruising to his jaw. She hoped it hurt. As she watched, the car pulled away, taking him to the police station.

Jayne made herself scarce as Miller hurried over to the ambulance, limping slightly.

'How're you doing?' he asked, concern and exhaustion etched across his face.

'I'm fine,' she lied. 'What about you?'

'Just a knock,' he shook his head impatiently. 'It's you I'm worried about.'

'Why?'

'You, I, well…' he gave up trying to express himself and wrapped her in a hug instead, which surprised her. She would normally have felt uncomfortable about such a display of affection in front of everybody, but tonight it felt good. It was what she needed, and she couldn't help but close her eyes and sink into the warm embrace, hugging him back as tightly as he held her.

'Boss?' Miller tensed as Jeffries called to him, and Jo reluctantly released him. With a slight groan, he turned and waved Jeffries away impatiently before turning back to Jo and looked into her eyes with a fierce intensity that left her feeling both uncomfortable and breathless.

She could see Jeffries behind Miller's back, gesturing impatiently as he muttered, 'For fuck's sake,' which rather broke the mood, for Jo at least, and she pushed Miller away.

'Go,' she told him. 'You're needed at the station.'

'But…' she could see he was torn between wanting to stay with her, and knowing that he had work to do.

'Go,' she repeated firmly. 'I'm fine. I need to go to the hospital and get checked over and have my blood taken to check for GHB before it's out of my system. Now you go and do the interview and make sure you build a rock solid case against him.'

He nodded, and with a last look at her, turned to where Jeffries was waiting to drive him back to the station.

Jayne was under orders to go with Jo in the ambulance. Much as she liked the policewoman, and even counted her as a friend after the events of the past few weeks, Jo was pleased to find Kate already at the hospital waiting for her. She must have been frantic with worry, not knowing what was happening, and Jo was glad someone had found the time to ring her to let her know she was safe.

'I would never have forgiven myself if you weren't all right,' Kate later confessed. 'After all, it was my fault you were there in the first place.'

But Jo didn't blame her friend one bit. She was okay, and the killer was in custody. She just wanted to make sure he stayed there. There was no doubting that he had drugged and abducted her. She'd had the blood tests done and was sure that they would prove it. Lambourne would go down for her abduction, if nothing else. She just hoped that the interview or the search of his home and office would provide further evidence of his guilt as far as the other victims were concerned, because a good lawyer might get him off the murders and she needed to know that he was going away for a long time. A very long time.

The following morning, after a fitful night's sleep, Jo insisted that she was feeling fine and persuaded a reluctant Kate, who had slept on the couch in case her friend needed anything in the night, to leave. She wanted some time to herself, she said, to think about the previous night, but in reality, it was more because she didn't want to think about it that she wanted to be alone. Kate meant well, but she was so wracked with guilt and the fright of what could have happened to Jo that she couldn't stop talking about it. Jo appreciated that different people have different ways of dealing with trauma, but while Kate needed to discuss it, Jo very much needed to put the fear and the horror of her abduction into a little box somewhere deep in her brain, to be taken out and examined at a later date when she felt stronger. For now, she needed to do something physical and banal, like cleaning. So once she was alone, she donned rubber gloves, armed herself with a cleaning spray and sponge, and tackled the bathroom.

Between the cleaning and making sure her mother didn't come over to look after her, because the last thing she needed was another lecture on the sort of men she attracted, the morning flew by and it was almost lunchtime when the intercom buzzed to let her know that she had a visitor.

As she pressed the intercom button, crossing her fingers that her mother hadn't ignored her request to be left alone, a slightly hesitant voice announced, 'It's me, Steve.' What she didn't know as she buzzed him in and opened her front door was whether or not he was on his own. It occurred to her that a video entry system would be a good idea, and added it to her mental shopping list. She was relieved when she saw just Miller coming up the stairs, looking uncertain as to what sort of reception he would get.

'Come in,' Jo was a little uncertain herself, and carefully checked the stairs behind him in case Jeffries was lurking in the stairwell, but the absence of either heavy breathing or swearing indicated that Miller truly was alone. She looked down and realised with horror that she was still wearing her yellow rubber gloves.

He stood just inside the door and made no move to come further into the flat. His coat was wet and she realised she hadn't even noticed that it was raining outside, she had been so intent on her cleaning.

'May I?' she indicated his coat and moved towards him, hoping that another hug might be on offer.

'I can't stay,' he said, a little too quickly, and it shocked her to see him move slightly away from her.

'That's fine. You must be really busy. So much going on,' she was gabbling, she realised, in an attempt to hide her disappointment.

'I just wanted to let you know what was happening, and see how you were.' It seemed to take a real physical effort on his part not to look at her as he said this.

'That's good of you,' she said, a little too brightly, and turned her back on him, walking into the kitchen area, hurriedly pulling off her rubber gloves and straightening some items that were already in line. 'So, what's going on? Has he confessed?'

He cleared his throat, and a quick glance showed her that he was relieved she wasn't going to throw herself at him. As if she would, she thought, her mouth hardening. He clearly regretted holding her last night, and her conjecture about the state of his marriage must have been wrong.

'No, not yet. He's not saying anything, but I've no doubt he will if you're right.'

She looked at him enquiringly.

'If he did this to punish women for adultery, he'll want to tell the world about it. Make sure everyone knows why they deserved it, in his mind.'

'You're right. He'll want to justify his actions.' She briefly wondered if it was this that had made him suddenly draw away from her; the thought that it could lead to adultery.

'I'm hoping he doesn't save it for the trial, though. It would be good to have a confession before we get there.'

'Do you have enough evidence if he does make you wait?'

He nodded, and she let her breath out in relief, not having been aware that she was holding it as she waited for his answer.

'The car had a foldaway bike in the boot for his getaway, as well as a container of petrol,' he said, and Jo couldn't stop a slight shiver at the thought of what might have been, 'and we found fake number plates in his garage. His laptop has gone for analysis, but they have already confirmed that he used the SusSEXtra website and was in touch with each of the victims under a variety of aliases. We also found a bottle of...' he hesitated, 'I'm not sure how to pronounce it, but sodium oxybate?' He looked at her questioningly.

'Medical GHB. Used for narcolepsy, I think.' She was glad to have something practical to think about. 'But I've never had a patient on it. It's very rarely used.'

He nodded.

'We're going through the hospital controlled drug records, but it seems that he used to help out in a sleep clinic.' Jo mentally kicked herself. She had known that, why didn't she make the connection earlier?

'But surely someone would have noticed it missing? It's a controlled drug.'

'You would have thought so, but apparently they recently had a bottle that was out of date and listed as destroyed. The two signatures on the statement of destruction are pretty unreadable, so no prizes for guessing that they could both be him.'

'But you'll need to prove that. I could help. I could check the previous drug registers…'

'You're too involved,' he cut her off sharply, then softened. 'We have people checking the registers and doing handwriting analyses. We'll prove he took it, don't you worry.'

Jo nodded.

'Well, it looks like you've got it all sewn up. Thank you for coming to tell me. If there's anything I can do, please let me know.' Her tone was deliberately dismissive as she walked towards the door. She really couldn't bear him being so close and yet so far and, just as with the trauma of the previous night, she wanted to put her feelings for him in a box and do something physical like clean the oven or go for a long cliff-top walk.

As she opened the door, she looked up at him, and for the first time he looked back at her. She could see that he was feeling the pain, too. He hesitated again, but then he looked away. His voice cracked slightly as he spoke.

'Lizzie's pregnant. Fifteen weeks.' For the first time she fully understood why he had been so distant recently.

'That's wonderful news,' she said in a very carefully controlled voice. 'I'm very happy for you both, you must be thrilled.' He nodded, but neither of them looked very happy.

'Goodbye, Detective Inspector Miller,' she said, holding her hand out. 'And thank you.'

His warm grasp felt more fragile than usual as he briefly enclosed her hand in his, before quickly turning and hurrying down the stairs. She closed the door firmly behind him, his footsteps growing more and more distant until she could no longer hear him at all, then she sank to the floor and, finally, allowed herself to cry.

About the Author

Candy Denman trained as a nurse, and worked in the NHS almost all her life, until recently managing to disengage herself in order to become a full-time crime writer.

She has also written a number of scripts for such highly-acclaimed TV series as *The Bill* and *Heartbeat*.

Other books in the Jocasta Hughes Mysteries:

Dead Pretty (Book 1)

Dear Reader,

I would like to say a big thank you for choosing to read *Body Heat*. This is the second instalment of the Dr Jocasta Hughes story, *Dead Pretty* being the first. She is a strong and intelligent woman, stubborn and loyal, a good friend and someone prepared to go the extra mile for her patients. Unfortunately, she is also prone to putting herself in danger and being downright reckless at times!

I hope you enjoyed reading the book as much as I enjoyed writing it and I would be very grateful if you would write a review. I would also love to hear what you think about the stories and the characters. Will Miller and Jo ever get together? Should they? Who do you think could play them on television? Would you recommend this book to friends and family? If not, why not?

I hope you will continue to follow Jo's story with me, wherever it goes. Do please get in touch, through my Facebook page, Goodreads, Twitter or my website.

www.candydenman.co.uk
www.twitter.com/@CrimeCandy
www.facebook.com/CrimeCandy